The doctor h
doing physic
but Gary wa
out what he
out on his own.

He did most things on his own. He didn't feel any need for a cheerleader.

Besides, he'd been considering a trip. What better time? While convalescing, he'd discovered he was curious about these sisters it seemed he had. One who was apparently heartbroken because he hadn't been excited about some kind of reunion, and the other who'd wanted to chew a strip off him because he wanted to be left alone.

Funny thing, since he'd got first the call from the PI and then the one from the sister, he'd found he did remember them. Or at least he thought he did. His memories from before he went to live with the Lindstroms in Bakersfield had a hazy, dreamlike quality.

He wasn't one hundred per cent sure which people were the family he'd lost and which were foster families. But chasing memories that refused to be caught was getting old.

So he figured he'd take a ride across country to Washington state, maybe stay a couple of weeks, talk to this Carrie and Suzanne a few times, hear the real story.

Then decide what he wanted to do with the rest of his life…

Lost Cause

JANICE KAY JOHNSON

MILLS & BOON

Pure reading pleasure

First published in Great Britain 2007
by Harlequin Mills & Boon Limited,
Eton House, 18-24 Paradise Road, Richmond, Surrey TW9 1SR

ISBN: 978 0 263 85807 5

38-1107

Harlequin Mills & Boon policy is to use papers that are natural, renewable and recyclable products and made from wood grown in sustainable forests. The logging and manufacturing processes conform to the legal environmental regulations of the country of origin.

Printed and bound in Spain
by Litografia Rosés S.A., Barcelona

Dear Reader,

Once in a while, a character just takes over a story. We writers like to think we're in control, so it's a little disconcerting to have a hero or heroine become someone we *didn't* plan for at all. This is one of those books.

I knew Gary Lindstrom had had a terrible childhood. (After all, I planned it that way!) What I'd forgotten was that he'd had three happy years in a loving family before his parents died. That part of him reawakens when he falls in love as an adult and does battle with the cynicism and deep distrust of fellow humans he thinks is his basic nature.

This wasn't an easy book to write. I kept complaining to everyone who would listen that I had no plot. I began to wish for a car chase or a gun battle! The more subtle, internal change is always a greater challenge. But by the time I finished *Lost Cause*, I realised it had become a favourite of my own books. Gary came to life for me in a way fictional characters rarely do. In many ways, he told his own story, and I found myself hurting for his loneliness and touched by the man he proved to be.

I'm eager to hear from readers and to talk to some of you at book signings.

Janice Kay Johnson

CHAPTER ONE

A SINGLE MOMENT, an unbidden thought, is all it takes to change a man's life. Or at least motivate him to change it.

Gary Lindstrom became conscious and, without even opening his eyes, knew he was in the hospital. The smell, the quality of the air, the beep beep of a monitor were familiar.

His leg hurt like hell, he had the mother of all headaches, and when he flexed experimentally, every muscle in his body screamed.

He opened his eyes a slit, confirmed by the sight of the white bedding, a larger than expected mound over his legs and the curtain pulled around the bed that, yep, he was indeed in the hospital, and closed them again.

Damn it. The last thing he remembered was... Oh, crap, yeah. He'd been riding the winding canyon road, nothing but the night around him, occasional cars passing in the other direction. He'd taken each curve faster than the one before, until oncoming head-lights had momentarily blinded him and he'd gone wide enough to catch some gravel under the tires. He'd felt the bike skidding, the spurt of fear and adrenaline as the guardrail rushed toward him. He recalled knowing he'd lost it, his leg scraping pavement. Then…nothing.

Footsteps, then the rattle of the curtain rings, coaxed his eyes open again. A young Hispanic nurse smiled at him.

"Mr. Lindstrom. You're awake. How are you feeling?" She checked the bag hanging on the IV pole beside the bed.

"Hurt." His voice came out rusty. "Accident?"

"Yes. Don't you remember? You were very fortunate that you wore a helmet."

"Leg?" he croaked.

"You had a nasty fracture." She patted him. "No more questions. I'll have the doctor come in and talk to you."

Five minutes later, the doctor, an older man, arrived to recite a laundry list of bruises and contusions as well as cracked ribs, a leg fractured in three places, and a concussion.

"My bike?"

"From what I hear, a mangled mess."

Regret speared Gary. Damn it, he'd

worked hard to restore the 1950 FLE model Panhead. He'd intended to sell it when something else came along that interested him. He supposed insurance would cover the more than $20,000 he was out, but the accident wouldn't be good for his rates.

"You're not a pretty sight," the doctor added, scanning Gary's face with interest. "But you'd be a dead man if you hadn't worn a helmet."

Funny thing. He almost hadn't. He'd slung his leg over his Harley, picked up the helmet, hesitated, then shrugged and put it on. He wore it most of the time, but he'd been in the mood to toss it aside.

Lucky I didn't, Gary thought, as the doctor left the room. *Or maybe not.*

Shock punched through the pain.

Goddamn. Had he been *trying* to kill himself?

He closed his eyes and saw again the road, unwinding before the narrow beam of his headlight. As always, he'd exulted in the power of the Harley between his legs, but it alone hadn't been enough. He'd sought out this road, perhaps because it was carved from the face of a cliff. Sometimes, he just plain needed to be reckless, to toy with oblivion. Tonight had been one of those times.

Or had it been last night? He realized he had no idea how long he'd been unconscious. Hours? Days? With indifference, he dismissed his speculation and returned to his main preoccupation.

Speeding down the canyon road, he'd felt the pull of the darkness beyond the white strip of guardrail. He'd known it before; who didn't have those fleeting thoughts: *What would it feel like if I sailed off the road?* Maybe fantasies like that were a brief surfacing of the subconscious awareness of danger.

But tonight… Tonight, it had been stronger than that. He'd *wanted* danger. Maybe he'd wanted to die.

Bleakly, he examined the possibility. Could you be suicidal without realizing it?

Yeah, he decided; you could. But he didn't think he'd gone that far. Flirting with death was one thing, marrying her another. He didn't feel ready to cash it in. But he also had a little trouble pinpointing what appeal living held.

Maybe his attitude wasn't so good. He'd been calling his despair cynicism. Loneliness was his choice.

A choice that meant darkness, the seductress, called to him. Or was it ignoring him, and he was the one sidling closer?

Either way, lying in that hospital bed, he saw he did have a choice now. Let himself keep sidling, or figure out how other people made themselves happy and try some of it on for size.

He shifted in bed and had to go still until the pain eased back on the throttle. One leg hadn't shifted at all, weighted down as it was with plaster.

Okay, he thought, with a flicker of humor: he wouldn't be trying anything on for size for a while.

But once the cast was cut off and he could throw away the crutches he predicted in his future, he had to find a way to give his life some meaning, or another time he *would* toss aside that helmet.

The nurse came in and showed him how to give himself minishots of morphine, then went. Gary punched the button and felt a wave of relief that clouded his mind and made his eyes heavy.

As he drifted, he heard himself saying, *Was that my name? Chauvin?*

That's right, someone said. *Lucien Chauvin.*

He'd always known that he'd once been Lucien, not Gary. When he was younger, he hadn't understood how that could be or who the people he remembered were, but later he was told about the adoption.

Your sister, Suzanne Chauvin, hired me to find you, the other man said.

He heard himself again. *This sister looking for me? Too little, too late. Don't need her, don't want a sister.*

As the comfort of sleep rolled over him, Gary's last sensation was surprise.

He'd lied.

THE VOICE ON THE PHONE was light and pleasant. "Ms. Chauvin, I'm calling from The Complete Family Adoption Agency. My name is Rebecca Wilson, and I've been given your file. I'd like to set up a home visit."

Suzanne's heartbeat did a hop, skip and jump. "Wow, that was fast!"

"Having second thoughts?"

"Not a one! I was just afraid months would go by. I'd love to have you come over." But she'd need time to clean house first.

They settled on a day almost three weeks away. Plenty of time to organize every closet and cupboard the social worker wouldn't look into anyway. Suzanne wasn't that bad a house-keeper, but she wanted the house to shine when Rebecca Wilson came. If she didn't impress her, the agency wouldn't give her a child. She had to impress her! She just had to.

She'd start today. The sun had peeped out after a rainy week, so she would rake up the soggy, fallen leaves and then consider loading her temperamental lawn mower into the trunk of her car and taking it to the shop. Once again it had refused to start Sunday when she'd tried. Maybe, if she were really lucky, she'd get it back soon enough to mow one more time before the ground got too wet—and before the home visit.

Bursting with energy and ambition, she changed into scroungy gardening clothes and pulled up the garage door. She'd get the automatic opener replaced this week, just in case she had reason to open the door when Rebecca Wilson was here. She wouldn't want to look as if she couldn't afford to maintain her house, let alone take care of a child.

She stole a glance toward her neighbor's before stepping outside with her rake and a box of plastic garbage sacks. She tried to work outdoors when Tom Stefanic wasn't in his yard. Not that he wasn't perfectly pleasant when they exchanged their occasional neighborly greetings, but, darn it, his lawn was smooth enough to be the 18th hole of the

U.S. Open, his flower beds were edged with military precision, his driveway power-sprayed weekly. No moss grew on *his* roof, the leaves barely dared drop from his trees. In fact... She studied the two flowering cherries along the street in front of his house with suspicion. Neither bore a single leaf, even though *her* trees were still festooned with slimy dead leaves hanging like dirty, wet socks. She knew he had a blower. Did it vacuum, too? Would he have *vacuumed* his trees? she wondered incredulously.

But his garage door was shut, and she heard no sound from the backyard. Maybe he was gone today. Determined to put him out of her mind and pretend the contrast between their respective properties wasn't painful, Suzanne breathed in a lungful of damp, earthy-smelling air.

She loved autumn almost as much as spring. The leaves had been spectacular, until the heavy rains the last couple of weeks had finished them off. There was something satisfying about tucking in flower beds, so to speak—trimming the dead stems of the perennials, pulling out last weeds, mulching. Partly she looked forward to a break from outside work, and partly she enjoyed anticipating the new growth that would poke from the dark earth in just a few months.

Would she have a child by then? A little boy or girl to crouch beside her as she worked? Or one old enough to actually help, even to mow?

She still wasn't all that fixed on how old a child she preferred. Suzanne thought she'd like to adopt a girl, just because it might be easier as a single mom, but she hadn't ruled out a boy if the agency had one who needed a home. Her sister, Carrie, had just married a man who had a six-year-old, and Suzanne would adopt Michael's clone in a second if she could.

She worried that the agency would look with more favor on her if she'd made up her mind about what she wanted, but then sometimes she convinced herself she was more likely to be given a child sooner if she wasn't too demanding about specifics. After all, if she were having a child the normal way, she couldn't be, could she? When you got pregnant, you didn't know if you would have a boy or girl, a towhead or a brunette, a child with a placid nature or one who couldn't sit still. And you didn't care; you just wanted a baby to love.

She'd turned thirty-two this summer, and she

was beginning to think she would never have children. Of course she could have gone the route of finding donor sperm, but she didn't feel that compelling a need to actually be pregnant. In fact, she liked the idea of adopting.

Carrie was right. Adopting a child who needed her would be Suzanne's way of atoning for not being able to hold on to her baby sister and little brother when they were taken away after their parents' deaths. What she couldn't do for them, she could do for someone else.

Raking wet leaves, she smiled thinking about Carrie. She was so lucky to have found her. Okay, to have been able to afford to hire a P.I. to find her. And to have discovered that Carrie was living so near, right in Seattle! Not twenty miles from Suzanne's home in Edmonds. They might have met by accident.

Wouldn't that have been amazing, she marveled, not for the first time. They looked enough alike to have recognized each other if they'd come face to face.

Well, *she* would have known who Carrie was in a heartbeat. Carrie, who hadn't been told by her adoptive parents that she was adopted, might have been more confused.

But they hadn't met that way. Suzanne had

gone seeking her, and found her just this past spring. With very few glitches, it seemed as if they'd known each other all their lives. Carrie had planned to live with Suzanne this year, while she went back to the University of Washington to get her teaching certificate. But in the end, she and Mark Kincaid, the P.I. who'd found her, had decided to marry in August, so she never had moved in.

Suzanne was rather sorry. She'd imagined them having the year together to make up for all the ones they'd missed, with her growing up with Uncle Miles and Aunt Marie and Carrie with her adoptive parents. But at least they weren't far apart. They talked almost every day, and did the kind of things together that sisters did, like shopping and visiting art fairs. And Suzanne *was* glad that Carrie was marrying Mark.

As she did almost every day, Suzanne spared a thought for her little brother, although of course he wouldn't be so little anymore. He was twenty-nine now. She hadn't seen him since he was three years old. After Aunt Marie and Uncle Miles decided they could keep only one of the three orphaned children, a social worker had come to the house and taken Carrie—then

Linette—and Lucien away. Carrie had been asleep, but Lucien… Standing in the middle of her front yard, Suzanne shuddered at the memory. Lucien had sobbed. Every time she thought of him, she saw his tear-wet face, framed in the car window as it pulled away from the curb.

And she remembered with guilt her own gratitude that *she* wasn't being taken away.

When she hired him, Mark had found Lucien, too, but her brother didn't want any contact with his sisters. Carrie had tried calling him, but he'd told her rather rudely that their overture was too little, too late.

Suzanne was trying to resign herself to the fact that she would never see him again, never be able to give him the photo album she'd prepared with pictures of their parents and of them growing up, never be able to explain how sorry she was that she couldn't, somehow, have kept them all together, even though she'd been only six herself when their parents had died.

Suzanne knew that guilt was illogical; even if her mother had always said that, as the big sister, Suzanne should take care of her little sister and brother, she'd been far, far too young to influence even her own fate. But she couldn't quite quell the nagging guilt anyway.

Shaking off the familiar depression, she began raking, working steadily until she'd bundled the soggy heaps into plastic bags and set them at the curb for pickup. Then she settled on a knee pad to pull weeds and toss them into a bucket she moved along with her. Finally, wishing she hadn't put off the most hateful task till last, she dumped the weeds into her garbage can and set the bucket in her garage. Oh, boy. Time to tackle the problem of heaving the blasted mower into her trunk.

No, she could procrastinate for a second more—she'd left her trowel behind.

She was just crossing the lawn, tool in hand, when she heard the familiar sound of her neighbor's pickup coming down the street and a hum that presaged the rising of his garage door. She turned her head to see his huge black pickup pulling into his driveway. Maybe, if she hurried, he wouldn't notice her out here.

But she didn't reach the cover of the garage in time.

The pickup door slammed and a moment later Tom approached across the narrow strip of lawn between their houses. Maybe a few years older than her, he was powerfully built but had a face that most would call homely. All she saw was the buzz-cut hair to match his lawn, the neat polo shirt and crisply creased slacks. Suzanne never, ever, met his eyes. Not quite. She'd discovered you could talk to someone and avoid their gaze without being obvious.

"Hi," he said. "Putting in a day of work out here, I see."

"I finally got the leaves raked up."

"And you're lucky. Today's dry enough to mow."

Suzanne sighed. He was the last person to whom she wanted to admit defeat. "No such luck. My nemesis won't start. I was just going to load it up to take into the shop. For the third time this year."

He was nice enough not to acknowledge the grimness in her tone. He rubbed his jaw. "One more mow should do it. Maybe two."

"Yes." Although *he* would probably manicure his all winter long, whenever the weather permitted.

"Tell you what," he said. "If you can wait until Saturday, I'll do it. That way you won't have to worry about fixing your machine or replacing it until spring."

She gaped at him. He was offering to mow

her lawn? In the silence that stretched just a little too long, pride and desperation arm wrestled. Pride thumped to the table.

"I can't let you… If you'd let me borrow your mower…"

He cleared his throat. "You seem to have trouble keeping engines running."

In other words, he didn't trust her with his gleaming, buff machine. She didn't even blame him.

"Are you sure?"

"Nothing better to do." When she bit her lip, he added, "Really. Happy to."

Her shoulders slumped. "Thank you. I really want the yard to look nice."

"Something special coming up?"

This was far and away the most personal conversation they'd had in five years of being next-door neighbors. She hesitated, but wasn't sure why. He'd notice sooner or later if a little girl or boy was riding a bike down the sidewalk and going in and out of her house holding her hand.

"I'm trying to adopt."

She felt him stare at her.

"A child," she elaborated. "Not a baby. Maybe a six- or eight-year-old. The social worker from the agency is coming to do a home study. That's why I need the house to look its best."

"You don't expect to remarry?"

Too personal. She took a step back. Way, wa-ay, too personal, given what he knew about her.

"Oh, I don't know." She inched back some more. "I can't predict the future. But I hope you won't mind having a child next door."

She half expected him to say, *Not if you keep the kid on your side of the property line.*

Instead he shook his head. "Of course not." He started to turn away, pausing. "I'll be over Saturday to mow. The backyard, too?"

"If you don't mind," Suzanne said meekly.

"Not at all. Let me know if there's anything else I can do." He nodded and walked away, disappearing into his garage. A moment later, the door rolled down.

Bemused and grateful—and she did hate the grateful part—Suzanne put away her trowel and closed her own garage door.

GARY WATCHED the saw buzz through the dirty plaster of his cast. The leg that emerged was fish-belly white except for the angry red rash that had caused godawful itching. He leaned over and ran a hand down his shin.

"Well, it's still there."

The nurse or technician or whatever he was glanced up with a grin. "Seeing your toes didn't convince you? What about the itch?"

"Could have been a phantom itch." Gary flexed his foot and grimaced at the weakness in muscles he'd taken for granted. "Damn, I'm glad to get rid of that."

"I haven't seen a patient yet mourn the loss of a cast. Except for the teenagers who want to take it home because all their friends wrote on it."

They both looked at Gary's cast. Nobody had written on it.

"You're welcome to chuck mine in the Dumpster." He bent to put on the sock and boot he'd brought and then stood up, the slit leg of his jeans flapping. "Thanks," he said with a nod, and walked out, trying not to limp.

Well, that had been a long three months. He'd been able to ride his bike, but he'd felt clumsy with the crutches, and the walking cast hadn't been much better. At least the bruises that had decorated his body and face had finished blooming as colorfully as the desert after a rare cloudburst and finally faded from puce to yellow to skin color. His leather pants and jacket had protected him from being skinned alive, although they'd had to cut those off him and throw them away, another loss. Heck, he could even take a deep breath now without wanting to puke.

The doctor had talked about him going to physical therapy for several months, but Gary was thinking he'd find out what he had to do and carry it out on his own. He did most things on his own. He didn't feel any need for a cheerleader.

Besides, he'd been considering a trip. What better time? While convalescing, he'd discovered he was curious about these sisters it seemed he had. One who was apparently going to be heartbroken because he hadn't been real excited about some kind of reunion, and the other who'd wanted to chew a strip off him because he was being selfish enough to tell them to leave him alone.

Funny thing, since he'd gotten first the call from the P.I. and then the one from the sister—Carrie, he thought her name was—he'd found he did remember them. Or at least he thought he did. His memories from before he went to live with the Lindstroms in Bakersfield had a hazy, dreamlike quality.

He supposed he'd lived in a foster home, too; maybe a couple, for all he knew. He wasn't a hundred percent sure which people were the family he'd lost and which were foster families. But sometimes he saw this woman, pretty and dark-haired, smiling as she bent to swoop him up. There'd been a girl, too, dark-haired and skinny. And a baby. He had this memory of crying in terror when someone tried to get him to go to bed in a room by himself. He wanted to stay with… He didn't know. The baby sister? Well, that made sense. From what the P.I. and this Carrie had said, the two of them had been taken away and then adopted out, and the big sister got to stay with family.

And he was supposed to worry about hurting her. Gary grunted and shook his head.

But he guessed the fact that she'd gotten the breaks wasn't her fault. And chasing memories that refused to be caught was getting old.

So he figured he'd take a ride cross-country to Washington state, maybe stay a couple of weeks, talk to this Carrie and…Suzanne? yeah, Suzanne, a few times, hear the real story.

Then figure out what he wanted to do with the rest of his life that would keep him from flying over the guardrail the next time, into the welcoming darkness.

CHAPTER TWO

REBECCA WILSON LOOKED forward to this home visit. She'd scheduled it almost three weeks ago, so she had reread the file this morning. Once again, she liked what it said about Suzanne Chauvin, especially her open attitude about what age or gender or race of child she'd take. So many people acted as if they were shopping for a garment of a particular color and style.

"We'd consider a girl up to two and a half," they'd say. Two and three-quarters would apparently be too old. "We'd like fair skin. Nobody in our family can even tan! Blond would be great. And blue eyes."

She could tell that they were really envisioning a baby. Their ideal. Which left her wondering: Would they be disappointed by a healthy, happy two-year-old with brown hair, hazel eyes and a golden tint to her skin?

Oh, well. Rebecca understood the desire to

adopt a child who looked as if she could be yours. Nonetheless, she was grateful for the occasional parents-to-be who just wanted a kid to love and didn't care if people could tell their children were adopted.

She glanced again at the map of Edmonds in the Thomas Guide that lay open on the seat beside her. If she turned up ahead…

Edmonds was so pretty. Climbing a hillside rising from Puget Sound were neighborhoods of a mix of older and new homes, many on lots terraced by stone or cement retaining walls. Even several of the more modest houses had peekaboo views of the Sound, blue and choppy today, the green-and-white Washington State ferries that arrived and departed every forty-five minutes, and the Olympic Mountains on the other side, already white-capped in mid-October. Rebecca wished she could afford to live here, rather than in her small condo in Lynnwood within earshot of I-5 and night-and-day traffic.

But social work of any kind didn't pay that well, even though she had a master's degree. It would help if she'd stayed put rather than changing jobs, but after three years of dealing with an overwhelming caseload of abused and neglected children and their horrifically dysfunctional families, she hadn't been able to handle the stress anymore. What she'd done there had been so important, she felt guilty for quitting.

She kept telling herself this job was a break. A vacation. She'd be ready again someday to rescue children from the parents they loved desperately despite the blows and the filthy homes and the nights huddled alone because Mommy hadn't come home. But not yet.

She turned onto the street and looked eagerly ahead. Halfway down the block...yes, it was the gray rambler with white trim, dwarfed by the two-story next door. The house was friendly-looking, Rebecca decided immediately, before laughing at herself. Way to jump to conclusions!

As she approached from one direction, she noticed a gleaming black-and-chrome motorcycle coming from the other way, the powerful roar out of place on this quiet street. The rider was going slowly, just as she'd been, as if also scanning house numbers. When she pulled to the curb, he did the same, swerving onto her side of the street and stopping with the front tire of his bike only a few feet from her front bumper.

She turned off the engine and checked in the rearview mirror to be sure her makeup was intact and her shoulder-length, copper-red hair was smooth. As she reached for her briefcase, she saw him set the kickstand and swing his leg over the back of the bike. He pulled the helmet from his head and hung it over the handle bar. Although he wasn't obvious about it, she had the feeling he was watching her, which made her nervous. Without standing next to him, she couldn't be sure, but she didn't think he was a huge man. Still, there was something...*tough* about him. His dark, straight hair was shaggy, his blue jeans and black leather jacket well worn, his gaze narrow-eyed and...well, she couldn't tell whether he was wary, hostile or just naturally unfriendly looking.

Was he Suzanne Chauvin's boyfriend? She'd denied having a serious relationship in the questionnaires she'd filled out.

Rebecca hesitated, then got out. For Pete's sake, it was broad daylight! And just because a man rode a Harley-Davidson—at least, she thought that's what it was—didn't mean he was a Bandido or Hells Angel.

Nonetheless, she circled the back of her car

so that she wasn't too near him on the sidewalk. She gave a vague, pleasant nod in his direction, then started toward the driveway.

His voice followed her. "Are you Suzanne?" He sounded doubtful.

"Me?" She turned, startled. "No. Is that who you're looking for?"

"Yeah." He nodded toward the house. "This is the address I have for her."

"It is her address." Should she have told him that? "If you don't know what she looks like, I guess you're not an old friend."

A nerve jumped in his cheek. "She's my sister."

She gaped. "Your…what? But…"

"I don't know what she looks like. Yeah." His mouth twisted. "Long story. Do you know her?"

"Not yet. I'm here to interview her." None of his business, she reminded herself. He didn't know what his own sister looked like. Sure. "Well." Out of her element, she said, "Shall we go to the door together?"

He didn't move. "No, go ahead. She's not expecting me."

O-kay. She gave another nod his way and continued up the driveway. To her annoyance, she was too conscious of his gaze to assess the house or yard as she walked, or to organize her thoughts.

She rang the bell, and the door opened so quickly, Suzanne had to have been hovering nervously in the entryway. She looked just like the photo in the file, pretty and petite with warm brown eyes and thick, glossy dark hair bundled on the crown of her head with a scrunchy.

Smiling, Suzanne said, "Hi, you're Ms. Wilson?"

"Rebecca, please." They shook hands. "What a nice neighborhood! And I see you have a bit of a view."

Suzanne laughed. "That's a generous way of describing the fact that if you stand at the very edge of the porch and crane your neck you can see a sliver of blue." Her gaze went past Rebecca. "I wonder who that is."

Rebecca looked over her shoulder. "The guy with the bike? He says…" Wow, she felt silly even saying this. "He says he's your brother."

She could never have expected the reaction she got. A tiny whimper escaped the woman who'd greeted her with such friendly poise and Suzanne gripped the door frame, face suddenly pale. "My…brother?" she whispered.

"Well, he said you're his sister, but he

doesn't know what you look like. I didn't take him seriously...."

As if she didn't hear her, Suzanne brushed past Rebecca and hurried down the steps and then the driveway.

The man, who'd been half sitting on his bike, legs casually crossed, rose to his feet.

"Lucien?" Rebecca heard Suzanne say, voice high-pitched, shocked.

"So I'm told. Gary now."

Rebecca watched, openmouthed, as Suzanne Chauvin threw her arms around the dark stranger. Even from this distance, she could see that he was startled and didn't know what to do. After a moment, he awkwardly lifted his arms from his sides and patted her back as she apparently sobbed on his chest.

The scene was so bizarre, Rebecca didn't quite know what to do. Leave and politely deny the application? Wait to hear an explanation? She was fairly new at this, but she'd never had an applicant so completely lose interest in her arrival for a home study. Anyone who wanted to adopt knew that this visit was make-or-break.

Finally, sniffling, Suzanne stepped back. She and the man spoke for a moment, the words indistinguishable to Rebecca. Then she gasped and turned toward Rebecca. She said something else to him, and finally they both came up the driveway to where Rebecca waited on the porch.

Tendrils of dark hair had pulled from the knot on Suzanne's head, and her face was blotchy and wet. "I'm so sorry!" she exclaimed. "You must think I'm crazy!"

The thought had crossed Rebecca's mind, but she murmured, "No, no."

"I said in my application that my parents died when I was young and my siblings and I got split up. Lucien…" She glanced quickly at the man next to her. "Gary was adopted out. I haven't seen him since he was three years old."

"No wonder you didn't recognize each other! How on earth did you find her?" Rebecca asked him.

His mouth tilted in what might have been a smile. "She found me."

"Months ago," his sister filled in. "But he said he wasn't interested in a reunion, so I tried to resign myself to never seeing him again. And then…and then…"

"He showed up out of the blue." Rebecca's eyes met his, completely unrevealing. Why had he changed his mind? Why decide to just drop out of the sky like this?

"Yes." Suzanne dashed at her tears. "Oh, gracious! I so wanted to impress you, and then I fall apart like this!"

"Getting a little emotional is certainly understandable, under the circumstances." So why wasn't *he* getting emotional? she wondered. "Suzanne, meeting your brother for the first time in…"

"Twenty-six years." New tears filled her eyes.

"…twenty-six years should take precedence," Rebecca said. "Why don't you and I reschedule?"

"Oh, I can't inconvenience you like that!" Suzanne Chauvin was trying to hide her alarm, but failing.

Rebecca understood that convenience wasn't what they were talking about. Suzanne feared she'd just blown her big opportunity.

Rebecca smiled. "No, I really mean it. You'll be torn two ways if you and I try to sit down to talk. I can easily come back next week. Maybe even later this week. Let me check my schedule. We can talk tomorrow. Okay?"

Suzanne smiled shakily and then gave her what appeared to be an impulsive hug. "Bless you. This is…" her gaze strayed to the impassive man standing beside her, "so amazing."

"Well." Rebecca smiled at him, too. What the heck. "Nice to meet you, Mr.…?"

"Lindstrom." He held out a large hand. "Ms.…?"

"Wilson," she replied, as she clasped his hand.

They shook. "Pleasure," he murmured.

"I'll call," Rebecca promised, and left without ever going in the house.

As she drove away, she reflected on what the odds were that her appointment would coincide with the arrival of a long-lost brother.

She briefly wondered if the scene could have been staged, but remembered the shock and blaze of joy on Suzanne Chauvin's face and dismissed the possibility. Besides, what would have been the point?

No, it was just one of those things.

A minor irritant, like the red light flashing at a railroad crossing when she was in a hurry.

Rebecca smiled. Hey, an optimist would say it was serendipity!

THE REDHEAD REMINDED Gary unpleasantly of his ex-wife. She was prettier than Holly Lynn, and also—judging from her freckles— a genuine redhead, which Holly Lynn wasn't, as he'd discovered the first time he undressed her. No, it wasn't the hair that brought back thoughts of his little-lamented ex, but rather the judgmental, holier-than-thou air both wore as if it were Chanel No. 5.

He wondered why she was interviewing Suzanne. Was she a pollster? Loan officer? Journalist? He leaned toward the loan officer explanation, because Suzanne had seemed damned anxious not to offend her.

Ah, well. What difference did it make what the redhead did for a living? Although… He turned and watched her circle her car. She did have spectacular legs, he decided with appreciation.

The woman beside him—his sister—said, "Come in, Lucien. Gary. Oh, I can't believe you're here!"

She'd taken him aback with that sobbing embrace. He didn't think any woman had ever cried on his shoulder before. Certainly not Holly Lynn, who'd departed hissing and spitting but dry-eyed.

He nodded and stepped into the small living room ahead of her. "I hope this wasn't a bad time."

"Not if she meant it about rescheduling. And I think she did. Don't you?"

What the hell did he know about it?

"Sure," he said with a shrug.

She shut the door and they stood there for a minute, appraising each other.

He saw a dark-haired, dark-eyed, attractive woman whose face gave him a weird, uncomfortable sense of familiarity. It wasn't that he was seeing his own face. No, while they did bear a superficial resemblance, their coloring similar, he didn't think it was that.

That wisp of memory, the dark-haired, laughing woman, slipped in and out of his consciousness and he felt a jolt. There it was. She *was* that woman. Except of course she couldn't be.

"Do you look like our mother?" he asked abruptly.

Tears brimmed in her eyes again and she nodded. "And you could be Daddy. It's…extraordinary. Seeing you like this. You have his nose, the shape of his face, his eyes…."

The observation felt like a rough-hewed shim wedged in somewhere, the potential for slivers both making him wary and irritating him. Last he knew, his nose and eyes were his, not someone else's.

But he knew his discomfort was irrational. Why was he here if not to figure out where he came from and whether he wanted to have any ties at all to these two women who were close blood relatives? So, okay, now he knew he looked like his father.

Check.

"I'm being a terrible hostess," she exclaimed. "Can I get you something to drink? Why don't you come back to the kitchen? We can talk there."

What he'd have preferred was a beer, but he accepted a glass of lemonade and followed her to the kitchen table, sitting and looking at her some more.

"Your sister...*our* sister," he corrected himself. "Does she look like you?"

"Yes, amazingly so. Except Carrie is obviously younger. She was the baby, you know."

He shook his head. "Actually, I don't remember much. There was a woman. Uh, and a skinny dark-haired girl."

"Me."

Wow. Yeah, he guessed it had been her.

"And the baby."

"Carrie."

"She and I went to a foster home together. Right?"

"Right. It was awful." Remembered grief filled her eyes. "You were sobbing, your face pressed to the car window...."

God. No wonder he'd never been all that eager to recall his oldest memories. That one…well, a twisting in his gut told him it was filed somewhere in his head. Just like her face, he recognized her description of that scene.

"So, you were the lucky one, huh?" he said with what he knew to be insolence.

Her expression shadowed again, but he wasn't so sure it was his tone that caused it. "I suppose so. Uncle Miles and Aunt Marie… Mom's sister and her husband," she explained. "They already had two kids, and didn't see how they could take in three more. Since I was six and had the best sense of what was happening, they felt…obligated."

The tiny pause was telling, and Gary had his first hint that maybe she hadn't been so lucky after all. Or maybe she just had a sob story prepared so he couldn't cry her a river.

"I think they truly believed you would both be adopted quickly," she continued. "You were so young. I hoped all those years that you'd been able to stay together. I was upset when I found out you were adopted separately. And that you didn't get a home for over a year after our parents died."

"So that part was true?" His voice came out

rough, as if it needed oiling. He didn't like thinking about any of this.

"Your adoptive parents told you that much?"

He nodded. "They said my mom and dad were killed in a car accident."

"It was so sudden. They'd gone to a play, and we were home with a babysitter. I remember a police officer coming to the door." She seemed to look right through him. "The doorbell woke me and I thought, Why would Mommy and Daddy ring instead of coming in? So I got out of bed and went to the window. I can still see the police car in the driveway, lights flashing. Red and blue and white, hurting my eyes. I think maybe I knew." She fell silent.

Questions crowded his tongue, but he found he was hesitant to ask any of them. He didn't like being the supplicant, and that was a little what he felt like right now. *Please, please, please, tell me about my mommy and daddy.* The questions tangled together, too, until he didn't know how to lay them out singly. How did you ask what kind of people those parents were? Whether they loved their children? Whether he'd be a different man if they'd lived?

"I have pictures," Suzanne said, as if reading his thoughts. "But first… What changed your mind? Why now? Why *not* then?"

"I never wondered much about my real parents." Not true—once he hit ten or twelve, he quit wondering. Gary shrugged. "If I didn't remember them or you, what would meeting you mean?" Seeing her expression, he elaborated, "I grew up the way I grew up. Nothing will change that."

He could tell from her face that he hadn't improved on his first bald statement.

"We're family," she said, as if the fact was so obvious he was a simpleton for not having seen it from the first. "We share blood. Genes. Not to mention early experiences and memories."

"You have more of both of those than I do."

"I know," she agreed. "And I hope you'll let me share what I do remember with you."

Fair enough. That's why he'd come, wasn't it? It was like, say, getting the provenance on something you were buying. Nice to know where it had been and how it had been treated.

"Where are you staying?" she asked.

"Came straight here." He shrugged. "There must be a hotel here in town."

"Would you like to stay with me?" She bit her lip. "You don't have to. I don't want to put pressure on you if you'd like some space, but... I'd love to have you."

Yeah, he wanted space, but he found

himself strangely reluctant to hurt her by refusing. What the hell? he told himself. A few days, a week. Why not?

"You sure it wouldn't put you out?" Gary asked.

Pleasure brightened her face. "I have a guest room. Oh, this is wonderful! I can hardly wait to call Carrie! Shall I?" She half rose. "Or would you rather I wait?"

"Can we take this a little slow?" he asked.

"Oh." She sank back to her chair. "Of course."

She sounded so damned disappointed, he felt like a crud.

Even so… Two of them, both weeping and wanting to clutch at him. Both gazing at him with a look so needy, he shifted in his chair at the very idea.

"So why did you change your mind?" this sister asked suddenly. "You never said."

"You know your…uh, Carrie called me."

She nodded.

"I kept thinking about her voice…." Her scorn. "Her talking about how much it would mean to you to meet me."

Her face softened. "She said that?"

"She said it would be a kindness if I were to call."

Once again, he'd apparently stumbled, because her expression became warier. "So that's what you're doing? A kindness?"

He was almost embarrassed to realize he rarely cared enough about what other people thought or felt to do a kindness.

"No," he admitted. "I suppose…I was curious."

"Oh." She relaxed.

"Also, I had an accident." While she exclaimed in horror, he told her the facts without mentioning the pull the abyss had exerted on him. "Just got the cast off my leg two weeks ago."

She was shocked that he'd been able to ride crosscountry so soon and fluttered some more. Once again, Gary was mildly surprised at his tolerance. He didn't go out of his way to hurt people's feelings, but he didn't usually put himself out a great deal to prevent doing so. Maybe there was something to this blood and genes thing.

Or maybe a near-death experience softened a man up.

"Are you married?" she asked finally. "Do you have kids?"

"Divorced. No kids."

"A girlfriend?"

"Not lately."

"What do you do? I mean, for a living."

He hesitated. Would it affect in some way how she felt about him? How worthy she found him?

"I've been working in coffee."

Instead of reacting to the modesty of his job description, she laughed. "You mean, our Northwest mania for fancy coffee has spread to the Southwest?"

"Big time." Coffee was damn profitable in New Mexico these days. Hot or iced, flavored or dark and bitter.

Her smile became kind. "Well, I'm sure if you'd like to get a job locally, you won't have any trouble."

"I won't be staying that long."

"Oh." She looked disappointed. "I'm sorry. I hoped…"

"I own the coffee shop," he explained. "And the roasters."

"I don't know what made me think you'd come to stay anyway. Of course you have a life! I'm just so glad you're visiting. New Mexico isn't that far away."

Not that far away? he thought in mild alarm. Was she imagining holidays with the whole family gathered around the table, holding hands and saying grace? The image made him queasy.

"What about you?" he asked. "Are you married?"

Echoing him, she said succinctly, "Divorced. No kids."

"Job?"

Pride filled her voice. "I just opened my own business, too. We must be an entrepreneurial family. I opened a yarn shop three months ago, right here in town. Knit One, Drop In."

"Yarn shop?"

"Knitting. I sell supplies, give classes. Business is taking off really well."

Knitting. He hadn't known that anyone younger than eighty did it.

"I sell my own work, too," she continued. "And I've had a bunch of patterns published. I'm hoping for a book of patterns one of these days."

"Do they sell well?"

"Hugely," she assured him. "The thing is, they don't go out of print the way the average novel does. They sell and sell and sell. For years. I've made thousands just on a single pattern."

Who'd have thought?

"You have employees?" he asked.

She wrinkled her nose. "Not really. I'm working long hours. I open, eat lunch and run to the bathroom during lulls, close, then do the books."

He remembered those days. You didn't make it with a small business if you weren't prepared to put in twelve-hour-plus days and maybe go months on end without taking a day off.

"A couple of my customers are experienced knitters who live locally and enjoy working a few hours here and there, so I have women to call if I'm sick or need time to get to the bank. Today, one of them is filling in because of my appointment."

"With Ms. Wilson?" He put the faintest of emphasis on Ms.

"Yes. I'm trying to adopt a child. Today was my home visit."

He'd been rocking back in the chair. Now all four feet clunked down. "She's a social worker?" Lawyers and politicians were commonly despised. He saved his loathing for the group of managing, high-minded people who were determined to tell everyone how to live. "Home visit?" His mouth curled. "You mean, she was here to decide whether you were good enough to be a parent?"

"Don't you think an agency *should* be sure

they're placing children in homes where they'll be loved and well taken care of?"

His laugh wasn't pleasant even to his ears. "And you think they can tell from one visit? Lie halfway decently, you can fool 'em. Haven't you read about all the kids raped by their adoptive daddies or hurt by the woman who was so sweet when the social worker interviewed her?"

Suzanne's eyes had gone wide. "You weren't…" she whispered.

"Raped?" He made himself lean back and ostensibly relax. "No."

"Or…or…?"

"Hurt?" He shrugged. "Harold used his belt or his fists sometimes, sure. He didn't put my hand on a hot stove, if that's what you mean."

Damned if her eyes didn't start brimming with tears again. "Oh, Lucien! I would have done anything… Anything…"

Abruptly, his throat closed and he couldn't breathe. He lunged to his feet.

"Listen, I've got some things to do. I'll, ah, be back later. If that's okay."

She rose, too, staring at him as if he'd gone loco. He didn't care. He had to get out of here, away from her affection, from her sympathy, from her tears. He was feeling smothered.

"Of course it is." She hurried around the counter into the kitchen and fumbled in a drawer, coming back with a key held in her outstretched hand. "Here. In case I'm not home. The first bedroom on the left is yours."

"I...thanks." He lurched toward the living room, his leg almost giving out on him. "I'll just be an hour or two." Or three or four.

With more dignity than he'd expected, she said to his back, "I told you if you needed space that was okay. While you're here, consider this your home. You don't need permission to come and go."

At the front door, his hand on the knob, he paused with his head bent and his back still to her. "I'm sorry."

Voice gentle, she said, "Don't be. You've given me a gift today. You never, ever, have anything to be sorry for."

After a moment, he nodded and blundered out, wishing that was true but knowing it wouldn't be. He hadn't yet had a relationship with another human being that hadn't meant being sorry most of the time.

He doubted shared genes were going to change that.

CHAPTER THREE

WHAT IN THE HELL had happened to him back there?

Gary rested his elbows on his knees and stared out at a body of water that smelled like ocean but seemed to lack waves. He'd hoped there was a beach and had ridden downhill until he found the ferry landing and—sure enough—a public beach, mostly empty if he ignored the dock fifty yards to his left and the idling cars and people leaning on the railing.

If he looked straight out, he could almost imagine he was all alone. The hoarse cries of seagulls suited his mood, and he liked the smell of salt and drying seaweed and rotting fish carried by the cool, strong breeze. Once he thought he saw a dark head crown the choppy water. A seal or sea lion. He didn't know one from the other.

Feet crunched on gravel but passed behind

him without the owner feeling compelled to initiate cheery greetings, for which he was grateful. Not much given to self-examination, Gary knew he needed to make an exception.

He valued his ability to stay in control of himself, his emotions, his destiny, above all else. Holly Lynn had accused him of being a cold son of a bitch, which had irritated him no end. Why did she marry him if she wanted all that crap? He hadn't changed because he put a ring on her finger. He felt; he just didn't like to lay himself open.

Gary envisioned emotions as oil spewing from a well, thick and black. It would shoot skyward and splatter the landscape with gummy blobs if you didn't cap it. If he'd learned one lesson growing up in the Lindstrom house, it was to cap every sickening gush of rage and fear.

But today… Damn it, he'd panicked! A man who was better at being reckless than cautious, he'd run like a scared bunny rabbit.

And he didn't even know why.

He'd been doing okay, talking about the parents who'd died without making adequate arrangements for their children, getting a sense of a sister who was unlike any other woman he'd ever known, telling her a little about himself. After the way he'd acted, what was she thinking to give him a key to her house?

It wasn't even the subject of social workers, although he did detest them, or Harold's belt, that had gotten to him. Brooding, Gary realized it was her reaction. She'd wanted to go back in time and leap between him and his adoptive father. Her instinct had been to defend *him*.

Why? He was genuinely baffled.

He was also freaked. This woman he didn't know felt something for him he didn't understand. Something no one else had ever felt. Not even his adoptive mother, who had at least pretended to love him but deferred to her husband's harsh brand of discipline.

So, okay. The way things happened, he could see some emotions getting frozen in time. The last time she'd seen him, he'd been a little kid, and she was the big sister. Maybe she still thought she needed to protect him.

What he didn't get was why her trying had sucked all the air out of the room and made him feel… He drew a blank. He didn't even know what he'd felt. Thinking about feelings wasn't something he did much. Capping them, sure. Conducting analysis on them…not so much.

All he knew was, she'd scared the crap out of him.

He wanted to head back to Santa Fe. Leave her a phone message saying, *You're a nice woman, but I'm not the little boy you remember. Nothing to do with you, but I just don't see this reunion going anywhere.*

Two reasons he knew he wouldn't. Couldn't. One was the curiosity she'd aroused, and the other was his memory of that pang of regret because he hadn't died.

A week, he reminded himself. Maybe two weeks. Look at the pictures, get to know the sisters, then promise to exchange Christmas cards. Everybody would be satisfied, including him.

Inhaling a deep breath of sea air, he nodded. Yeah, a week. He could do that.

That moment of…whatever it had been— it was natural. Normal. His version of his sister's tears.

Giving a grunt of amusement, he thought, *What d'you know, Holly Lynn. I do get emotional.*

NO ENORMOUS BLACK-AND-CHROME motorcycle sat in front of her house or in her driveway.

Suzanne got out of her car and looked at the blank windows of the house. Had she imagined that her brother had been here at all?

"Hey," her neighbor said behind her. "How'd it go?"

She hadn't heard his truck or a door, but there he stood, just on his side of the property line. Today he wore a gray suit, white shirt and dark tie. Lowering her gaze, she saw that his black shoes gleamed. Of course.

"It?"

His brows rose. "Wasn't that woman from the adoption agency coming today?"

Of course that's what he was talking about! He didn't know about her brother.

"We…had to reschedule," she said. "I had an unexpected visitor. You may, um, see him around. He'll be staying here for a couple of weeks."

She hoped.

Her neighbor's eyes narrowed slightly. "Your ex-husband?" he asked, with noticeable reserve.

Her cheeks heated at the very introduction of a topic they had never discussed, and never would if she had anything to do with it.

"My brother."

The brows went higher. "I didn't know you had a brother."

"I haven't seen him in a long time. Years."

"Ah." He nodded. "I'm glad that you mentioned he's here. In case I see a stranger going in and out."

"Thank you again for mowing the lawn," she said to his back as he started toward his house.

"Any time."

He'd gone in his front door before Suzanne shook herself and went up the walk to her own door. When she let herself in, the house felt like always: empty.

Gary hadn't returned.

She peeked in the guest room to see if he'd come and gone, perhaps leaving a bag here. But it looked just as she'd left it.

What if he *didn't* return? Had she somehow scared him away? She didn't know how, except maybe for the tears she'd shed on his chest. His stiffness had told her he wasn't used to comforting women in the midst of emotional storms.

But he hadn't left then. So why the panic later?

She wandered restlessly, unable to settle down to knitting or even television. She'd been so eager to see Gary again, she hadn't even taken the day's receipts by the bank— she'd just thrown the money in a bag and brought it home.

It was getting easier to think of him as

Gary instead of Lucien. Lucien still was and probably always would be the little boy of her memory, skinny, quick, full of energy and intense highs and lows.

Her mother would try to put him down for a nap and, by the time he was a year old, invariably fail. "Just a short nap," she'd beg, and he'd giggle or scream, depending on his mood. Suzanne had thought it was funny, only now as an adult understanding her mother's exhaustion and frustration. How brave she'd been to have another baby so soon! Or perhaps she just hadn't used birth control because of her faith. Suzanne didn't think of her parents as devout, but they had considered themselves Catholic and gone to church now and again.

If they'd lived, would they have kept having babies? Maybe she'd have been the oldest of eight, or ten. If so, she would have spent her youth diapering and babysitting instead of mourning and rebelling.

She would have to ask Aunt Marie sometime. She might know if her sister took birth control pills or considered them a sin. If nothing else, she'd undoubtedly cleaned out the medicine cabinet along with the rest of the house when it was to be sold.

Suzanne checked her voice mail, but there was no message.

The phone in her hand, she hesitated. Gary hadn't wanted her to call Carrie right then, but there was no reason not to now, was there?

Her mind made up, she dialed.

A boy answered. "Hello, Kincaid residence," he said by rote.

"Hey, Michael. It's Aunt Suzanne." As always, she marveled at being an aunt. Okay, not by blood, but what difference did that make? Michael was one of the world's great kids. She asked about his day and they talked for a minute before she asked, "Is your mom home?"

"Yeah! Mommy!" he yelled.

Suzanne winced.

A moment later, her sister came on. "Hello?"

"Hey," Suzanne said.

"How did it go?" Carrie asked eagerly.

There was that "it" again. No surprise that Carrie thought she was going to get a report on the dreaded, but eagerly awaited, home visit. "It was postponed," Suzanne said.

"Oh, no! What an awful thing to do to you! Now you'll have to keep worrying, and clean again, and—"

"It wasn't them, Carrie," Suzanne interrupted. "She came."

"Then…then what happened?" her sister asked in puzzlement.

"When I answered the door, I noticed this guy sitting on his motorcycle out front. I commented, and Rebecca—the adoption counselor—said, 'That guy says he's your brother.'"

A quick rush of breath told her Carrie guessed.

"Lucien?" she whispered.

"It was him." Her voice caught. "I started to cry and flung myself into his arms. Rebecca said she'd call me to reschedule."

"He really came? Just like that? No warning? No…" Amazement was morphing into indignation.

"Who needs warning? He came, Carrie." Wonder spread in Suzanne's chest, a warm glow. "I hugged him. We talked."

On a note of alarm, Carrie asked, "Why are you saying that in the past tense? He's still there, isn't he?"

"He said he was going to stay for a few days. I gave him a key to the house. But I had to go back to work, of course, and he isn't here. I hope…" She swallowed. "I think I overwhelmed him."

"What's he like? Is he nicer than he sounded on the phone that time I called him?"

"I don't know yet. He's cautious. He rides a big, black motorcycle, and he told me he had a bad accident a few months back when he lost control on a mountain curve. He just got out of a cast last week. His hair is longish, and he's sinfully handsome even if he is our brother…"

"You mean, *since* he's our brother."

Suzanne laughed. "Right. He has to be, doesn't he?"

In her mercurial way, Carrie shifted gears. "Why didn't you call me then?"

"I assumed you'd be in class. Also…he wanted to take it slow. I think the idea of two of us scared him."

"I can see that. Wow. He sounded so…indifferent. To the point of cruelty. I thought if he ever made contact it would be years from now."

"I know!" Suzanne heard an engine and hurried to the front of the house, only to be disappointed by a glimpse of the back of a souped-up pickup she recognized as belonging to a teenager in the next block. "He seems genuinely curious, Carrie. But also… I don't know. I got the feeling he wishes he wasn't."

Her sister was silent for a moment. "Boy, do I understand that."

They'd become so close, Suzanne some-times almost forgot that Carrie had been less than thrilled to find out she was adopted, and had taken weeks before she was willing to talk to Suzanne. So it made sense that she, more than Suzanne, truly understood that their brother, too, felt con-flicted.

"Why hasn't he come back?" her sister asked in frustration. Carrie was more impul-sive, less patient than Suzanne.

"I don't know. I told him if he needed space not to worry, so I can't exactly call the cops and ask them to put out an APB."

"Suzanne…you're sure this guy *is* Lucien?"

"You mean, versus some con man trying to take me for everything I'm worth?" It felt good to laugh. "I'm sure. He looks so much like Daddy, it…shook me."

"Do you want Mark and me to come up this evening?"

Suzanne hesitated. "You, maybe," she finally said, slowly. "Can you come?"

"The minute Mark gets home to be with Michael. He's due any minute. Do you want me to call when I'm going out the door?"

"No, I'll just expect you when I see you." She paused. "Thank you, Carrie."

"Are you kidding? I can hardly wait to meet him!"

After they'd said goodbye, Suzanne took the phone back to the kitchen, then peeked out the front window again before deciding she didn't want Gary to catch her waiting there like some parent annoyed because he'd violated curfew. She would just…get on with her evening, she resolved. Pretend her long-lost brother hadn't popped into her life before fleeing out of it again. Pretend she wasn't waiting for the sound of a key in the lock with as much anxiety as that terrified parent.

Or the big sister she'd always been.

GARY EASED HIS BIKE down the street and to the curb in front of Suzanne Chauvin's house. Dusk had come and gone, and now he was a little embarrassed that he hadn't come back sooner. He hadn't wanted to assume she'd feed him, so he'd grabbed a bite out, but he found himself worrying that Suzanne had plunged into an orgy of cooking, like women did, and was in there gazing sadly at too much food gone cold.

A strange car was in the driveway, a bright blue Miata, which meant his sister had company. Gary was pretty sure he knew who it was.

His anxiety had heightened the closer he got to Suzanne's house, but he'd made up his mind to see this thing through, so he grabbed his bag and walked up to the door. There he hesitated, then rang the bell.

Suzanne came to let him in and exclaimed, "You don't need to ring! Pretend you live here."

"Thanks." He stepped in with a wary glance. "You have company?"

"Carrie's in the kitchen." She gave him an apprehensive look. "I hope you don't mind that I called her."

What could he say? "No, that's fine."

"Why don't you go put your bag in your room, and then come meet her. Have you eaten?"

"Yeah. I hope you hadn't planned dinner," he said awkwardly.

She flapped a hand. "Don't worry. I know all of this feels strange."

Strange? That was one way of putting it, he decided, depositing his bag on the bed in the guest room, then starting back to the kitchen.

At first glance, the two women sitting at the table looked so much alike he couldn't have guessed which was Suzanne if he hadn't just seen her and known what she was wearing. Two dark heads were bent toward each other, two fine-boned hands fingered wineglasses. Dinner plates were pushed to one side. From the smell, he guessed they'd had spaghetti.

He must have made a sound, because both heads lifted in unison and he found himself being inspected critically by his little sister Carrie.

Yeah, he could tell them apart after all. Her hair was curly, he saw, but more important was the challenge in her brown eyes, the tilt to her chin. Little Carrie was feistier than her sister, less inclined to trust. And to weep, thank God.

"Carrie," he said, trying out the sound of her name.

She stood. "That's me."

Her gaze seemed to take in the scuffs on his boots, the deliberately relaxed way he held his hands at his sides to hide his tension, the set of his shoulders, the length of his hair. He doubted she missed a thing.

"So, you decided it wasn't too late, after all."

He recognized her reference to the phone call she'd made to try to persuade him to make contact with Suzanne. Far as he'd been concerned, the overture had come too late to mean jack.

But it would seem he'd been wrong.

"Getting chewed out makes a man think."

If he'd expected her to blush, he'd miscalculated.

"Good," she said with satisfaction.

"So you're the baby."

She planted one fist on her hip. "If by that you mean your baby sister, yes, I am."

"Linette." He sampled the taste of that name, too.

"Lucien," she fired back.

"Let's go with Gary."

His leg ached today, but he tried to disguise his limp as he crossed the kitchen.

"Wine?" Suzanne asked, lifting the bottle. An empty wineglass sat at the third place set at the table.

He nodded. "Thanks."

All seated, the three looked at each other. Damn, he thought, with a feeling of unreality.

As if she'd read his mind, Suzanne said, "We haven't been together like this in twenty-six years. And then, you were in a booster seat and Carrie in a high chair."

"Probably rubbing peas in my hair," his little sister agreed, unruffled.

He had absolutely no idea what he would have been doing. Flicking whole peas at his bossy big sister? Hanging on her every word? Kicking his heels in boredom? Funny thing, not to know what you were like as a small child. Seemed like a natural memory to retain, a part of your sense of self.

"You'd have been squirming," Suzanne told him, her gaze perceptive. "Nowadays, a doctor would probably have labeled you as hyperactive. You couldn't sit still to save your life."

"I'm still not much good at sitting," he admitted.

"You're doing just fine right now," Carrie said.

"You haven't bored me yet."

"Well, don't I feel special to hear that."

A laugh in her voice, Suzanne said, "Listen to you two, squabbling as if you'd been doing it all your life."

With shock, Gary realized she was right. And it wasn't as if he'd ever had any practice. She'd just been a baby the last time he saw her. She wouldn't have even said her first word yet. And he hadn't had an adopted brother or sister.

"I'm just testing you." His little sister grinned, then held out a hand. "Truce?"

"Truce." He shook.

Sipping wine, they asked questions about

his life, which he gave sketchy answers to. They seemed to notice how much he wasn't saying, but didn't comment, which he appreciated. He told them briefly about Holly Lynn, a city health department official of all damn things.

"I guess I'm not made for marriage."

"Carrie seems to be the only one of us who is," Suzanne commented.

His little sister's face softened. "I wasn't so sure I was, either, until I met Mark. You've talked to him," she said to Gary. "The P.I.? Did Suzanne tell you I married him? He's a good guy."

"He seemed decent when he called."

If she was underwhelmed by this accolade, she ignored that, too. "Mark has a son, Michael. He's six, in first grade this year. He's accepted me wholeheartedly, for which I feel blessed."

"His mother?"

"Died when he was two. He barely remembers her." She paused a beat. "Mark and his wife adopted him."

A lot of that going around.

"Tell us about your adoptive parents," Suzanne suggested. "Mark said you grew up in the central valley in California?"

"Outside Bakersfield. Harold is a farmer. I was driving a tractor by the time I was ten."

"Really?" She looked appalled.

He shrugged. "Farming families need their kids. He and…" Mom. He'd almost said Mom. "…Judith couldn't have their own little worker, so they went out to find one."

Both sisters stared at him. "You think they adopted you just to provide labor for the farm?"

Voice devoid of emotion, Gary said, "Harold told me he wanted to get an older boy. He was indulging his wife to bring home one as young as I was."

"That's awful!" Carrie breathed.

He shrugged again. "Some people take home a kitten so they can cuddle it and have something to coo at. Some just want a mouser."

"And you were the mouser. Oh, God." Suzanne pressed a hand to her breast, her eyes huge.

He hoped like hell she didn't start to cry again.

"My adoptive mother was nice enough, until she got fed up with Harold and just upped and left one day. It wasn't so bad." *Until then.* A part of him had died that day.

"I thought adoption agencies were supposed

to be picky! How could they have let those people take you?" Carrie demanded.

"Maybe Suzanne should ask Ms. Wilson," he suggested. "My guess is, she'd use a bunch of statistics to claim that most adoptive homes are happy."

"I would give anything…" Suzanne began.

He shifted in alarm. There she went again, ready to fling her body onto the tracks to stop the train.

Too bad the train had derailed twenty-six years ago.

"It's over and done," he said flatly. "That's what I tried to tell you when your P.I. contacted me."

"We can't change the past," Suzanne argued, "but we can make the future better. We can be a family again."

Since he had only a distant acquaintance with the whole concept, he wasn't all that sure what she had in mind, except he guessed holiday get-togethers figured in it somewhere. He'd probably better find out just what she *did* envision, before he found himself sucked in.

When he didn't comment, she said, "Do you want to see pictures now?"

He gave a clipped nod, less than sure he really did.

She fetched a big photo album bound in green leather and wordlessly set it in front of him at the table. Then she sat again and both sisters gazed expectantly at him.

Throat constricted, he opened it.

On the first page was a wedding photo. God almighty, Gary thought in shock. He could have been the groom. Dark, lean, a dent in the cheek because the man was smiling at his bride. *She* looked like Suzanne and Carrie, startlingly so. Pretty, brunette, delicate to the point of being ethereal.

His mother. His father.

People who might have loved him.

Very softly, his big sister said, "Do you see why I burst into tears at the sight of you?"

He lifted his gaze but didn't really see her. "Yeah," he said, voice hoarse.

More wedding photos followed, some including another young woman who resembled the bride as well as an older woman who must be…his grandmother?

Silent, staring with a hungriness he didn't want either of his sisters to see, Gary kept turning pages. He saw the young couple with a Volkswagen Beetle, then a tiny house, run-down in the first photo but painted and edged with a white picket fence in later ones. The woman acquired a radiance along with an enlarging belly, and then suddenly a shrivelled, frowning infant appeared. He had to look up after seeing that picture, as if to measure it against the beautiful woman who sat at the table, the one who'd been that infant.

He could see it better as she became a laughing toddler and a stick-thin girl with pigtails tied with red bows. Gary tensed when he saw that the woman was pregnant again, but still felt unprepared when he turned a page to reveal a photo of another newborn baby, this one wrapped in a pastel blue blanket.

That was him. He stared for the longest time, then shifted his gaze to the cluster of photos on the next page, all showing the baby at the center of attention. The woman held him against her shoulder and had her head turned. She looked at him with so much love, it tingled in the air. The pigtailed girl making a horrible face at him in one photo, cradling him in another for a staged picture. The man—his father, giving him a bottle, smiling down at him.

In a daze, he turned the page again and saw himself sitting up, eating in a high chair, crawling, in virtually every picture guarded by his big sister. He was walking when they apparently moved into another run-down place, but a bigger one. It was decorated in colors that reminded him of the famous Painted Ladies in San Francisco, Victorian houses that flaunted their lacy trim and gaudy hues. A garden bloomed in a yard that had been bare in the first picture. He was running around, soaring on a swing set, crouching in a sandbox frowning with intense concentration at something out of sight.

The mother was pregnant again, and he tensed at how close the story was to over.

This newborn looked like the others, red-faced and raisinlike, but he and Suzanne seemed to find her fascinating nonetheless. A studio portrait appeared in there, the three kids dressed up like dolls and posed, with him sitting next to his baby sister and Suzanne hovering protectively over both.

His third birthday choked him up. His face held such wonder as he stared at a birthday cake with three lit candles.

On the next to last page, Gary—Lucien— rode a fire-engine-red tricycle down the sidewalk toward his father, who seemed to be saying something to him.

Hand not quite steady, Gary turned the final, stiff page to see mother and kids around a dining room table that looked a hell of a lot like the one he sat at now. The father must have been taking the picture. Baby Linette appeared to be banging a spoon on the tray of her high chair, Suzanne to be talking, him to be stuffing a cookie in his mouth, their mother smiling lovingly at them.

The End, he realized. As if he were unmoved, he closed the cover, but kept his hand splayed over it. It seemed as if through his fingertips he felt the life within, so much he didn't remember but had ached for since he was little.

"It's yours," Suzanne said. "I made one for Carrie, one for you. There are other pictures we can look at some day, but I made copies of the best ones."

He swore and scrubbed a hand over his face. "Thank you."

Carrie's smile was painfully like their mother's in some of the photos, gentle and caring. "Feel wrung out?"

Startled, he said, "How…?" then knew. She'd looked at an album just like this—her album—not that long ago. He met her eyes and saw in them a complete understanding of everything he felt. Nobody had ever, in all his life, seen inside him the way she did at that moment. It was the weirdest damn feeling.

"We looked…close," he said, glancing down again at the closed book.

"We were," Suzanne said. "Mom and Dad would have hated more than anything in the world to think of us all split up, not even knowing each other anymore. I hope they can see us now, together again."

"I hope so, too," Carrie murmured.

Gary wasn't so sure he liked the idea of these parents he didn't remember gazing down on them with saintly smiles. If they could see them now, what about the rest of the time? Had they seen him, locked by his adoptive father in the old outhouse for punishment, spending the night bloodying his fists trying to beat his way out? Had they seen him screwing women and leaving before first light? The idea both angered him and encroached on a sense of privacy that was important to him.

"When you're ready, I'll show you a packet of love letters that Dad wrote Mom," Suzanne told him. "And Mom kept baby books for each of us with the dates of milestones. You know. First smile. Rolled over. Crawled. For you and me, first word. They even have locks of our hair from our first haircuts."

The panic that felt like claustrophobia had been nudging at him, but now it swelled to fill his chest again. He took a hasty swallow of wine. Shouldn't he be *happy* to know that he'd been loved as a little boy? Why did the knowledge fill him with resentment and something too much like the fear he'd felt when he lost it on that curve?

"If you want to go settle in…" Suzanne suggested.

He shot to his feet. "Yeah. Yeah, I think I'll do that." He meant to leave the album on the table for now, to show himself if not them that it didn't mean that much to him, but he couldn't do it. "Thanks for, uh, doing this." He gripped it, white-knuckle tight.

Carrie rose, too. "I'd better get going. But I'm sure I'll be seeing you in a day or two." She held out her hand.

He shifted the album to his other hand so he could shake.

"Big brother," she said, with a saucy grin, then kissed Suzanne on the cheek. "Wow. This is amazing."

"Amazing," Suzanne echoed.

Okay. Yeah. He guessed it was. Suzanne

hadn't been that old in the last photo, and yet she'd held tight to a memory of them all together.

He envied her that memory, but was glad he hadn't kept it to taunt him all those years.

He escaped to the bedroom while the sisters said goodbye and made plans for what to do with him while they had him. In the quiet after he shut the door, he set the album atop the dresser, lay on the bed and stared at the ceiling, his gut churning.

Give him a choice between another day like this and a dive from his Harley at seventy miles an hour, he'd take the dive. Without a second thought.

CHAPTER FOUR

REBECCA WAS SAILING down I-5 when her car died. Just like that, with the car still going sixty miles an hour, the power steering and brakes were gone.

Swearing, she wrestled with the wheel to steer onto the shoulder while she stamped on the brake pedal. She hated to think what a dead car in one lane would do to traffic. The wheel moved as if the column had rusted fifty years ago, but it did turn. The car slowed and finally came to a stop on the shoulder.

Whispering her thanks for small mercies, she sat shaking, adrenaline coursing through her body. It was several minutes before she felt steady enough to turn the key and try to start the engine again.

Absolutely nothing happened. It didn't even make an effort. Did that mean her starter was out? But then why would the engine have died? Something electrical, she supposed. All she knew about cars was how to drive one and how to fill it with gas.

Great. Wonderful. She was stuck on the shoulder of the freeway halfway between Lynnwood and Edmonds, traffic whizzing by. Thank God for cell phones. Hers had sunk to the bottom of her purse, but she found it and called information, asking for a nearby towing company.

"Fifteen, twenty minutes," the dispatcher promised.

Now she'd have to cancel the home visit at the Coopers. Rebecca opened her briefcase and pulled out their file. The phone number was in here.... She found it and pushed the keys. Before she completed the number, the roar of a motorcycle brought her head up.

A huge Harley-type bike was easing to a stop behind her car. Her adrenaline surged again. As she hit the lock button on her door, images of rape and murder flashed through her mind. Forget the fact that it was broad daylight and they were in plain sight of busy freeway traffic. She wouldn't even crack the window, she'd just give her head an emphatic shake *no*.

The driver, in jeans, boots and a black leather jacket, set the stand and took off his helmet, revealing long dark hair and a face she recognized. She'd met him, she knew she had.

Her mind raced as she peered in the rearview mirror. Where did she know him from?

Suzanne Chauvin's. That was it. He was the long-lost brother. The one whose mouth had curled ever so slightly when he said, "*Ms.* Wilson."

Why had he stopped? Did Good Samaritans come in the form of bikers in black leather?

He swung his leg over the seat, hung the helmet on the handlebar and strolled toward her passenger door. A semi thundered by in the outside lane, whipping his hair, but he didn't even glance sideways.

When he reached the car, she hesitated, then unlocked it. He opened the door and bent to look in. "Ms. Wilson."

Damn, he was handsome. Chocolate-brown eyes and a narrow face with spectacular cheekbones might have made him movie-star sexy, but a mouth that didn't seem to be made for smiling erased any hope of charm.

"Mr. Lindstrom." Now, why had his name popped into her head so easily? she wondered with surprise. Usually, she had an awful time remembering names.

"Flat tire?"

She shook her head.

"I was driving and my car just...died."

His heavy brows rose. "Power steering?"

She nodded and realized she still felt shaky.

"Have you tried to start it again?"

"Yes, but it won't even turn over."

"Then it's not likely to be anything I can take care of here."

"I've called for a tow truck. I'm just waiting for it."

His gaze flicked to her plum-colored blazer and skirt. "Working?"

"Yes, I had a home visit scheduled." She lifted her cell phone. "I was about to call and cancel."

"Where do they live?"

"Mountlake Terrace." She could see the exit up ahead. So close.

"I could give you a lift," Gary Lindstrom suggested.

She was embarrassed by the knowledge that her eyes had widened. "On your motorcycle?"

The very corner of his mouth lifted in the sketchiest smile she'd ever seen. "You can wear the helmet."

"The tow truck..."

"Call them back. Tell them you're leaving your key."

She did hate to cancel. She knew how eager couples were at this stage, how long they'd yearned for a child, how much time they probably spent getting their house to a point of perfection whether they'd deny it or not. Still, to arrive, windblown, on the back of a Harley-Davidson, her arms wrapped around the waist of a perfect stranger who happened to be dark, sexy and a little scary...

Oh, heck. It was a fantasy come true.

"If you mean it," she capitulated. "I can call a taxi to take me home..."

"I mean it."

While he waited, she phoned and arranged to leave her key under the driver's side floor mat. There wasn't anything in the car to steal, and unless they could throw it over one shoulder and carry it, no one would be taking her Tercel today.

A moment later, carrying her purse and briefcase, she followed him to his motorcycle.

"You don't have to give me the helmet."

Even though his mouth had only that faint crook, his eyes narrowed in amusement. "You're prepared to risk life and limb?"

"It's not very far to Mountlake Terrace."

"Wear the helmet anyway. You'll feel safer." He unhooked it from the handlebar, brushed

her hair back from her face and settled the
helmet on her head. She clutched her briefcase
to her bosom and stood like a child being
dressed as he matter-of-factly fastened the
chin strap and then stepped back. "You may
have to hike your skirt a little to get on."

A dignified, professional woman wouldn't
be nodding obediently and letting him stow
her briefcase in a leather bag that was
strapped to the motorcycle carriage. He
climbed on and watched as she lifted her
snug skirt, first a little, then more. Cheeks
hot, she finally freed her leg enough to get on
with all the grace of a newborn colt trying to
stand for the first time.

"Hold on," he said, and started the engine
with a roar that made her jump.

Her first grip at his waist was tentative, but
as the motorcycle started to move, she
grabbed hold tight while still trying to keep
some distance between them. By the time he
reached freeway speed, she was plastered to
his back, her cheek pressed to him and her
arms locked around him.

She'd no sooner dared open her eyes than the
bike headed onto the exit and began to slow.

At a red light, she loosened her grip and
pulled back.

"Doing okay?" he asked over his shoulder.

"Fine," Rebecca said, as if she rode one of these every day instead of never. Her mother would have a heart attack if she could see her.

"Good. Hold on," he warned, as the light changed.

She grabbed tight again as he accelerated. For a moment they proceeded sedately, but then he swerved and shot through a gap that seemed frighteningly small to her to pass the car in front of them.

"Where are we going?" he shouted.

She yelled directions at the back of his head, and he nodded. Half a dozen turns, and he drove slowly down a winding street lined with modest but well-cared-for houses. Lawns were neat, and jack-o'-lanterns, scarecrows and dried cornstalks decorated doorsteps. The Coopers didn't make a great deal of money, she knew; the husband drove a bus for Snohomish County Transit and the wife was a hairdresser. Neither was especially articulate, but she'd liked their answers on the questionnaire in the file. They sounded like good people.

Fortunately, she'd memorized the street address, and he pulled to a stop on the gravel strip in front of a white-painted rail fence. He turned the engine off.

"Safe and sound."

She felt the rumble of his words in her hands, locked around him. She let go and straightened. "Thank you. This was really nice of you…."

He turned, eyes narrowed and the skin crinkled at the corners in what she thought was a smile of sorts. "Want me to give you a lift back to the office or home, too?"

In the act of lifting the helmet off, she stared at him. "You'd wait for me?"

"Come back," he corrected. "I have a cell phone. You can call."

"I can get a taxi."

His voice was sexy, too, husky and tempting. "But they're not nearly as much fun."

No. They weren't.

"You're serious?"

"I don't have anything better to do," he pointed out. "I can't do much for Suzanne at her knitting shop."

A tiny giggle rose in her throat at the image of him sitting with a circle of ladies, demonstrating the purl stitch. "No, I guess you can't."

"So, what do you say?" One brow rose. Of course he was the kind of man who actually *could* lift one eyebrow.

"If you mean it," she said weakly.

He took the helmet from her. "Got something to write with? I'll give you my number."

"Oh. Okay." Horribly conscious of him watching, she scrambled off the bike and then tugged down the hem of her skirt before she pulled her briefcase and purse from the leather bag. When she found a pad of paper, he scribbled the number in dark, slashing lines. "I usually spend at least a couple of hours," she warned.

"No problem." His mouth crooked. "You might want to brush your hair."

Her hand went to her head in instant reaction, and he grinned, then put the helmet on his own head and started the motorcycle, raised a hand as if to say, *See ya,* and took off with a small spurt of gravel.

She was left gaping after him, stunned by that smile. She'd been wrong. Oh, so wrong. His smile was devastating. Cocky and yet also somehow *sweet.*

Which was a very strange word to use about a man who looked as tough and self-sufficient as he did.

Shaking her head, Rebecca walked to the front door and rang.

The Coopers were as nice as she'd anticipated, accepting with apparent equanimity her explanation of a car breakdown and a chance ride to explain windblown hair. Beth Cooper showed Rebecca to the bathroom where she discovered her skirt had swiveled so that the zipper was to one side instead of in back where it belonged. She turned it, smoothed wrinkles without much success and brushed her hair, then returned to the living room.

Beth smiled. "Can I get you a cup of coffee?"

"I would love coffee," she agreed, with more fervency than was probably appropriate.

Her hostess laughed and went to get it, leaving Rebecca to chat with Ronald Cooper.

In the next couple of hours, she coaxed them to talk about their own childhoods, their parents and the family gatherings that Beth admitted had begun to depress her these last five years as they struggled to get pregnant and her two sisters had three kids each.

"Mary Ellen once said just *thinking* about getting pregnant is dangerous for her."

Her husband rumbled.

"She didn't mean to be tactless," Beth said hastily. "But it stung. Because *I'm* the one with the problem."

Ronald laid his hand over hers.

Rebecca knew from their file that Beth

couldn't carry a baby to term, so in vitro fertilization wasn't an answer for them. "Did you consider finding a surrogate mother?" she asked. "Perhaps one of your sisters?"

"They haven't offered," Beth said.

Her husband said firmly, "I don't care that much about having a son who is mine. You know? We just want a child."

"Do you have a preference as to gender?" When they didn't answer immediately, she amended, "A girl or a boy?"

Their heads shook in unison. Neither cared. Yes, they'd consider a child of mixed race, although they guessed their druthers were for a Caucasian baby just so he or she didn't stand out at those family gatherings and so people weren't always thinking, *Oh, she must be adopted,* when they saw the Coopers together.

The agency's policy was to, whenever possible, place babies with parents of their dominant race. It took unusually committed parents to provide a child of another race some sense of identity with his biological roots. In the 1970s, many black children had been placed with white parents, but in the decades since, there had been a shift in attitude. In any case, too few babies of any race were available for adoption to satisfy the hunger of childless couples. Many, frustrated, chose to go overseas.

Beth's parents had been sterner than Ronald's, but the couple agreed on how they wanted to raise their children.

"We've spent years shaking our heads and saying we wouldn't say that or do that, so confident we'd be having kids when we were ready," Beth confessed. "There's never been any doubt that someday we'd have a family. We've saved so I can stay home for a few years, until they're school age, for example. We talked about using that money for a foreign adoption, but then I'd have to go back to work and put the baby in day care, and we just never wanted that. Not if we could help it."

They showed her around their small trilevel, including the bedroom upstairs right across the hall from theirs that would be the nursery. It was a big, sunny room, the walls painted yellow, a twin bed, child's table and chairs and toy chest the only furnishings.

"Our nieces and nephews spend the night sometimes," Beth said. "We enjoy having them."

Rebecca guessed the pleasure was bittersweet, a chance to sample what was denied to them, but she smiled in agreement.

"We haven't really decorated," Beth continued. "In case we never—" She stopped, pressed her lips together. "This could be a sewing room."

Rebecca talked to them about the birth mother's role in choosing the placement for her child, and the profile birth parents would be shown of the couples like the Coopers who were waiting. She warned them of how long the wait might be before they were likely to be offered a baby. Faces shining, they assured her they'd wait ten years if they had to.

"Does this mean you're approving us?" Ronald asked, voice gruff.

She smiled at them both. "I think you'll make wonderful parents. I have no hesitation in recommending that you go on our list."

She was moved to see that Ronald's eyes got as damp as his wife's before he harrumphed and wiped at them. It made her wish she could call them tomorrow and announce that a newborn was ready to go home to them. Unlike some older couples, though, they had time; they'd started trying to get pregnant when Beth was twenty-four or -five, so now she was thirty-three and her husband only two years older.

Rebecca used her cell phone to dial the number Gary had given her. He answered with an abrupt, "Lindstrom."

"Hi, this is Rebecca Wilson. Um, if you're still willing—"

"Five minutes."

Dead air told her he was gone. Well! So much for her prepared speech about how it was fine if he'd gotten busy doing something else, getting a taxi was no problem, etc., etc.

Next she called the auto repair shop where she had asked that her car be towed.

"Can't get to it until tomorrow," she was told. "Check with us, say, eleven o'clock?"

Yes, fine, she could do that.

Obviously, she needed to rent a car. She had an appointment in Seattle tomorrow morning and had promised to go to dinner at her mother's house in Woodinville that evening. Instead of having Gary take her back to the agency, maybe she'd have him deliver her to a car rental office.

She borrowed the Coopers' phone book to look for the handiest location, finding one not a mile from her agency. By that time, the distinctive throaty roar of a motorcycle outside gave notice that her ride had arrived.

The Coopers thanked her profusely and waved goodbye from the doorstep as she left.

When she reached the street, her cynical Good Samaritan nodded toward them. "Are they still trying to convince you that they're great people? Or did you make them happy today?"

"They can't just be friendly?" She took the helmet from him, both relieved and a little disappointed that he wasn't going to put it on again for her.

"It would be normal to go back in the house now. Don't you think?"

She turned and gave a reassuring wave at the couple, who waved back. Yeah, okay, it *would* be normal for them to go back in the house. Instead, they stood side by side, holding hands, smiling at her.

"I gave them hope." She settled the helmet on her head and fumbled with the strap.

He lifted a tanned, calloused hand and fastened it for her. "They're going to get a kid?"

"They may have to wait for a couple of years, but probably."

He nodded. "So you made 'em happy. Is that why you do this?"

"Partly."

He waited until she settled herself behind him before asking, "So, ma'am, where will I be taking you?"

"Maybe I should get you a uniform."

"I was picturing a peaked cap."

"Sorry, you don't look the part," she told him.

"What, you won't give me hope?"

Although his tone was light, she heard a peculiar note that made her wonder.

"You think I can pass it out like…Easter eggs?" she asked.

In profile, she caught another glimpse of that deftly raised brow. "Don't you?"

She thought of the children she'd tried to protect in her last job, the mothers who were too desperate for the next drink or fix to notice that their kids had gone unfed for days, that the baby's bottom was raw from a diaper soaked with twenty-four hours' worth of urine and feces. She saw again the mothers' terror and grief when she took their children and they realized what they'd lost.

"No. If only."

Gary Lindstrom gave her an unreadable glance. "So, where do you need to go next?"

"Hm? Oh. I'm going to rent a car."

"Have time for lunch first?"

To hide her startled jolt of pleasure, Rebecca teased, "You *are* bored."

"Yep, just about any company is better than none right now."

Rebecca punched his back and enjoyed the sound of his laugh. "And, yes, since you ask, I was considering picking up a sandwich somewhere after I rent the car."

"Good. Edmonds okay?"

A little out of the way, but why not? She didn't have a commitment until three. She could work at home tonight to catch up on paperwork.

"Sure."

This time, she grabbed a more secure hold when he started the motorcycle. At freeway speeds, she had to close her eyes in sheer terror when he wove through traffic, but at the slower speeds she began to find the ride exhilarating. She wondered what people thought of the sight of a biker in black leather on his Harley with a woman in a business suit and heels behind him. Imagining heads turning, she smiled. Sometimes it was nice to do something unexpected.

He took her to a place called Olive's Cafe & Wine Bar in downtown Edmonds. The walls inside were painted a warm terra-cotta color and hung with art. Gourmet sandwiches and salads seemed to be the lunchtime specialties. After they were seated at a small table, Rebecca ordered a Mediterranean salad, and was intrigued when Gary chose a grilled panini with mozzarella, tomato, fresh basil and balsamic vinegar.

"Are you vegetarian?" she asked.

"No, but I'm not a big meat eater. Taste more than conviction."

She smiled absently at the waitress who brought them their drinks, then when they were alone again tilted her head. "Okay, I'm curious. Do you always stop to help travelers in distress? Or did you somehow recognize my car?"

"Recognized your car. It was the Pessimism Will Never Work bumper sticker that did it."

She'd almost forgotten she had it. She'd been driving this car since she was a graduate student at the University of Washington.

"Your sister and I rescheduled for Tuesday."

"I heard."

She wished she could read him better. A suspicion had been niggling ever since he'd invited her to lunch. Set it right there on the table between them, she decided. "Is the meal meant to butter me up on her behalf?"

A flare of anger wouldn't be unexpected.

Weirdly, his blank look of surprise coupled with something she could only call indifference did startle her.

"Why would I do that?"

"She's your sister?" Rebecca suggested.

He shrugged. "I met her a few days ago for the first time. I imagine she'll make a good mother. She seems the type. Why she wants to adopt instead of having a kid herself must have something to do with what happened to us, but I'm not sure I get it."

His tone implied he didn't much care, either, which amazed Rebecca. Her curiosity about why other people did what they did was bottomless. She felt concern when a stranger at a bus stop muttered, "This day sucks." She could spend the next half hour speculating on why the day sucked and whether she ought to move to that empty seat next to him and express sympathy.

"Have you asked?"

He shrugged. "Not my business."

Rebecca sipped iced chai tea. "Why did it take so long for you all to find each other? Were you too young when you were separated to remember that you had sisters?"

"I was three. I guess I vaguely knew." Knew but hadn't cared, another shrug suggested.

"Were you excited when she found you?"

He gave a soft laugh. "Nope. More irritated. Who was this woman, and what did she want with me?"

Rebecca stared at him. "You're kidding."

"No. I told the P.I. I wasn't interested. Then Carrie, my younger sister, phoned too and basically told me I was being a selfish bastard and it wouldn't kill me to call Suzanne because it would mean something to her."

"So that's why you're here," she concluded.

"Nope," he said again, the corners of his eyes crinkling in amusement. "That was almost six months ago. I intended to put them out of my mind."

"But you couldn't."

"Seems not."

The waitress brought their lunches. After she left, Rebecca picked up her fork. "So? Go on. What happened?"

"Happened?"

"Yeah. Why didn't you call? Why did you just show up?"

Picking up his sandwich, Gary said, "Don't you find phone conversations unsatisfying? I decided I was curious. I wanted to see her. So I came."

Rebecca shook her head in amazement.

O-kay. Still, maybe he was just being a guy, not overintellectualizing everything. You decide to do something, you do it. Much easier than worrying it until your original intentions are tattered.

"Tell me about you," he suggested. "It's got to be more interesting."

"Oh, I seriously doubt that." She watched as he ate with apparent hungry pleasure. "Anyway, I still don't know anything about you. Where you're from. What you do." *Whether you're married or have a girlfriend, children.*

"Nope. Your turn," he said between bites.

Giving up, she talked at random about herself while she ate. Degree in psychology from Reed College in Portland, her year of working in personnel at a major software company—horrible—and her decision to go back to school for a master's degree in social work.

"All so you could find the perfect homes for poor, abandoned children?" he asked, tone ironic.

"No, I had higher ideals than that. I thought I could make this huge difference in the lives of impoverished families. I'd connect them with resources, make it possible for them to stay together. Other caseworkers just hadn't cared enough, or they'd quit caring, I convinced myself." How naive she'd been! "I graduated and went to work for the state department of social and health services monitoring kids who'd become wards of the court for some reason."

"And found out it wasn't quite so easy?"

"Oh, yeah." Rebecca sighed. "I ended up at Child Protective Services for a year, where I actually had to decide whether to take a child out of a home. You know, if you make the wrong decision, you'll spend the rest of your life second-guessing yourself. But thinking like that can be paralyzing. You do the best you can. I hated it."

His eyes were astonishingly perceptive. "So you decided to dispense hope instead."

"Something like that," she admitted, making a face.

"You know, you look like a do-gooder."

She blinked. "How so?"

"That air of determination, the faith that you can overcome all obstacles shining in your eyes."

Beginning to be offended, she set down her fork. "I just told you that I'd realized I *couldn't* overcome all obstacles."

"But do you really believe that?" he asked

softly. "Or are you just suffering from temporary discouragement?"

Rebecca was momentarily silenced, stunned to discover that he was right, of course; her discouragement *was* temporary. She'd acknowledged it to be temporary with her belief that one of these days she'd be ready to go back to the trenches.

"You make me sound foolish."

"No. I don't mean to. Most people would admire your ability to sustain that kind of faith."

"But not you?" she asked.

His voice became silky, even dangerous. "Ah, but you see, I hold grudges."

Understanding dawned. "You weren't happy. I mean, in your adoptive home."

"No. I wasn't happy."

She opened her mouth to ask about his home, but didn't get the chance to say a word.

"Can we talk about something else?" he asked abruptly.

Embarrassed, Rebecca picked up her fork again. "Sure. I'm sorry. I'm nosy, and I don't always think."

After a discernible pause, he said, "If you really want to know, I'll tell you another time."

She wasn't altogether sure he meant it, but appreciated the fact that he was trying to let her off the hook. Anyway, it wasn't likely there'd *be* another time.

"This salad is wonderful." Which it was, even if she'd been more conscious of the man across the table from her than she was of the food. "So tell me, Gary. Do you ever drive a car? Or is it always a motorcycle?"

He admitted to having a pickup back home in Santa Fe, and told her about his hobby, which she gathered was sometimes profitable, of restoring vintage motorcycles, mostly Harleys.

"Finished one just a couple of months ago." He shook his head. "Then I totalled it in a crash. Too damn bad. The engine was running so sweet." He sounded like he was talking about a woman. "Just purred." Another regretful shake of the head.

"You totalled it? What about you?" Rebecca asked, appalled.

"Broken leg, cracked ribs, concussion. I survived. It didn't."

"How terrifying!" Her enthusiasm for climbing back on behind him dimmed. "Did somebody hit you?"

"No, just riding a winding road for fun and didn't judge a bend right."

"Fun."

He flashed a breathtakingly wicked smile. "I'll convert you someday."

"Uh-huh."

"Say, tomorrow night. We could go for a ride, stop and get a bite somewhere."

She shouldn't date Suzanne Chauvin's brother. Although he wasn't making any attempt to influence her. To the contrary. Still...

"Will you misjudge a bend in the road?"

"I'll drive like a little old lady. Cross my heart." He sketched the motion.

"I don't like the 'hope to die' part."

Another laugh. He lifted a finger to signal the waitress, who jumped as if Bill Gates himself had summoned her.

It struck Rebecca then how comfortable, even assured, Gary Lindstrom seemed to be in this chic little café, despite his heavy boots, leather jacket and too-long hair.

Life lesson: don't assume everyone who wears black leather and rides a Harley-Davidson is also missing front teeth, has tattoos from wrists to neck, and spits tobacco.

Rebecca held out her hand. "Let me take care of that. In recompense for the rescue."

Gary frowned at her. "I invited you to lunch."

She waggled her fingers.

After a moment, he handed it over. "I'm

conceding only because I don't want you to think you owe me."

She dug in her purse for a credit card and handed it to the waitress. "Okay, we're even."

"Tomorrow night?"

"If you won't be in town long, shouldn't you be spending your time getting to know your sisters?"

A shadow crossed his lean face, and she suspected she'd hit a nerve. After a moment, he said, "I'm not used to having family. It can be a little overwhelming."

So she was to be his escape. After a moment's reflection, she decided that was okay with her. A slightly daring evening on the back of a Harley; wasn't that an escape, a modest adventure, for her? The man lived in New Mexico, for Pete's sake! This relationship, if you could call it that, had nowhere to go.

She signed the bill and tucked her credit card back into her purse. "Why not?" she said, recklessly.

CHAPTER FIVE

GARY HADN'T SPENT as much time with another person since Holly Lynn told him he wouldn't notice when she was gone anyway and walked out for the last time. He wondered if Suzanne had any idea how stifled he felt during their cozy evening chats.

Tonight she sat at one end of the couch with her legs crossed yoga-style. The minute she sat down, she reached for the basket that held her knitting and took it out. It seemed to him to be unconscious; her butt went down, her hands *had* to have those needles in them. He'd mostly gotten used to the incessant click, click, click, but sometimes it still irritated him.

She'd been working on an afghan, but tonight she took out some tiny, tubular thing on a circular single needle with points on each end. The yarn was lime-green, although as he watched she picked up a buttercup-yellow strand and added it in.

What in hell was she making? A sweater for a goddamn boa constrictor?

No, too big, he decided. A sweater for… oh, crap. A kid. She was knitting for a baby or maybe a toddler.

And Rebecca Wilson hadn't yet dispensed her brand of hope to Suzanne. What if Rebecca said, gosh, sorry?

"What are you knitting?" Gary asked, hoping he was wrong.

"Hm?" She glanced up. "Oh. A sweater. See?" She turned it, which told him precisely nothing except that the lime-green tube was gaining a half oval of yellow. "It's going to have a daisy on the front."

"A baby present?" People gave those, he knew, although he'd never been called upon to do so.

"No, I'm working out a pattern." She started talking about stitches, but he tuned out that part. It was something new for the pattern book she was planning, apparently.

"This isn't for, uh, the kid you're hoping to adopt, then?"

"Heavens, no!" She laughed. "No, I couldn't handle a baby right now if the stork brought one, not with working eighty hours a week. Lord, no!"

Deciding he believed her, Gary nodded. He'd debated after leaving Rebecca in front of the Enterprise Rent-A-Car place whether to tell Suzanne he'd seen her, but finally decided he had to. Rebecca was bound to mention him when she came on Tuesday for the home visit.

"Saw that social worker today," he said. "The one from the adoption agency."

Her hands stilled and her head came up. "Really? Where?"

"Her car had broken down on I-5. I stopped and gave her a ride to her next stop."

"How lucky for her that you saw her!" Then her eyes widened. "She got on your Harley?"

Suzanne had so far declined to be taken for a ride. Carrie, in contrast, had accepted his offer with delight and appeared to love riding behind him when he'd picked her up a couple of days ago in Seattle and dropped her at the UW for a class.

"It was my Harley, or miss a home visit." He took a sip of Suzanne's piss-poor coffee and avoided wincing. He'd called today and was having some of his own roast FedExed from Santa Fe. It was time she found out what coffee *should* taste like.

"Oh. Well, that was nice of you."

He sipped again, let a pause develop. "We had lunch, too."

"Really?" She sounded shocked. "You mean, as in…"

"We're having dinner tomorrow night. Is that a problem?"

Her mouth opened and closed a couple of times. "I suppose not," she finally said, hesitantly. "I mean, I hope not."

"I promised not to try to influence her about your application."

"It isn't that. I'd be a little worried if it blows up between you two she'd associate you with me."

Another oh crap. He hadn't thought of that. *Was* she the kind of woman to take anger at him out on Suzanne, if it came to that?

"She wouldn't do that," he decided. "She's too well-meaning. Too sincere about her job. If she thinks you'll be a good mother, she wouldn't be petty."

He could tell Suzanne wasn't entirely convinced, but after a moment she nodded. Nice woman that she was, she didn't say, *I hope you're right,* in that grudging tone that implied she already knew someday she'd be throwing at him an *I told you so.*

Holly Lynn never could resist saying *I told*

you so. It had gotten real old, especially since most of the time she *hadn't* told him. She just liked to be right, and in hindsight she always could be. If he contradicted her he was both wrong and a bastard.

Why couldn't he ever seem to remember the good things about Holly Lynn? The reason he'd married her?

To change the subject, Gary asked, "How was your day?"

She sighed. "Slow. Despite which, my till didn't add up and I couldn't figure out why."

"This your first business?"

"Yes, and for some reason when I dreamed about having it I pictured the yarn and the customers and the classes, but never gave a thought to the money part." She gave a rueful laugh. "Well, except for a few worries about not having enough of it."

He nodded. "I remember those days."

"Right. I keep forgetting you have a business, too. Is it a sit-down coffee shop, or one of those cute drive-by ones?"

Gary didn't know why he'd been evasive about his livelihood. He guessed being secretive had just become a habit. A way of fending people off. The more these unknown blood relatives knew about his life, the more entangled in it they'd be. But he was starting to like Suzanne, and there didn't seem to be any real reason *not* to be honest.

"Actually," he said, "I opened my first coffee shop when I was twenty-two. I have eleven of them now."

Her knitting fell to her lap and her mouth opened and closed like a fish's. "Eleven?" she finally bleated.

"I'm looking to expand into the Phoenix area."

"You own a *chain?*"

"Getting there," Gary admitted. "We also sell our special blend roasts to some gourmet grocery outlets. Whole Foods, for example. I see you have a couple in this area."

"But…that means you're a *mogul.*"

He shifted, uncomfortable. "I wouldn't say that. These are little places. It's not like a string of Kmart stores."

She gave her head a shake, as though dazed. "Still, that sounds pretty successful to me."

"I'm happy enough with the way it's going." He was, in part because the bigger the company got, the more it freed him from doing everything himself. Three years ago, he wouldn't have been able to take a few weeks to come out here. Hell, he couldn't take a *weekend* off those first few years.

He'd plowed most of his income back into the business and continued to do so. Honestly, he wasn't that interested in the trappings of wealth, anyway. He'd bought a house a couple of years back, but it was pretty bare inside. Occasionally, exasperated by the demands of his growing empire, he wondered why he did it. Although not usually given to self-analysis, Gary had finally concluded that his drive for success had something to do with a need to silence his adoptive father once and for all. Not literally, of course; Gary hadn't spoken to Harold since the moment he hitched out of town. But from the time his adoptive son was ten years old or so, Harold had decided he was worthless and would never amount to anything, and said so often. That voice had lingered in Gary's head, and it was damned hard to shut up.

Now, Suzanne shook her head again. "Wow! I'm speechless."

A little bit amused but also burned by her stupefaction, he said, "I take it you don't think I look the part."

"It isn't that!" Flustered, she blushed. "Well, maybe a little. I mean, businessmen are supposed to wear suits and ties! And shouldn't you drive a Lexus or a BMW or something instead of a motorcycle? But it's mostly that you never said anything!" She paused; her brow crinkled. "Why *didn't* you say anything?"

It was the kind of thing Holly Lynn had often asked with that same genuine puzzlement. Gary had come to suspect that he lacked some basic knowledge of social intercourse. Maybe, working on the farm, never being able to play sports or go to friends' houses after school, he'd missed some classes. How To Talk To Cool Kids 101 and How To Blend In: Be As Cool As You Can Be 301.

What was wrong with not running off at the mouth? Not sharing your business with anyone who'd listen? He hadn't lied; he'd said he was in coffee, owned a shop. Suzanne and probably Carrie had just interpreted that the way they wanted. Apparently, in a way that went with the length of his hair and the fact that he rode a Harley.

He shrugged. "It didn't seem important."

"But we asked what you did for a living."

"And I told you."

That stopped her; she thought back, eyes narrowed in suspicion. "Okay," she finally admitted. "Maybe you did. Just not very expansively."

"I guess I tend to be closemouthed."

"Not by nature," she told him. "Once you started talking, you never shut up! You loved people. Aunt Marie tells me I was the more suspicious one. It's sad that you—" She stopped, her gaze flashing to his.

His most distant memories were of being more volatile, of joy and fear and temper. He dimly realized that he'd been forced very early to learn to tamp down his enthusiasm and all other extremes, leaving him wary, with an inability to feel as much as other people seemed to.

"Personalities do change," he said.

"Outside forces change them."

He remembered dinners, mostly silent. If he chattered too much, Harold would slam his hand onto the table, making dishes jump, and roar, "Goddamn it, I can't hear myself think!" By the time Gary was twelve, he privately doubted that one heck of a lot went on in Harold's head that would require silence to come to fruition. About the only news he paid attention to was weather and anything that might impact his taxes. He read an occasional western,

usually Louis L'Amour, each book taking
him a couple of months of time spent on the
can. He was not just a son of a bitch, he was
a boring one.

"I wasn't encouraged to talk."

He regretted saying that much the minute
he saw his sister's expression. "Oh, Gary!"

If there was one thing he hated, it was anyone
feeling sorry for him. He'd have said something, except he sensed how complex Suzanne's
pity was, comprised of guilt and unnamed what-
ifs. Understanding that much kept his mouth
shut. She couldn't fix the past, and he didn't
have to make that fact worse for her.

He shrugged, and she struggled with her
sorrow for a minute, finally determinedly
picking up her knitting again.

"So, what's your company called?"

"Chimayo Coffee Company."

Her mouth dropped open again and the
needles quit clicking. "I've seen that!"

"At Whole Foods," he said patiently.

"Maybe. No. Trader Joe's, I think. *You* make
that?"

"Haven't roasted it myself in a couple of
years, but…yeah. It's the best coffee you can
buy." Fact, in his opinion, not bragging.

"Wow," she said again.

He grinned at her. "It's always good to shake someone up."

"You've done that. Big-time. I'm stunned. I've been feeling awful because I know you ended up running away from home at sixteen, and I figured you'd never had the chance to go to college, so I just thought... well..."

"That I'd never amount to much," he said flatly.

Her brow furrowed again. "No. That you haven't yet had the chance to find a real career. I don't equate 'amounting to much' with the job you hold."

He felt his face relax. "You wouldn't, would you?"

His sister bristled. "What's that supposed to mean?"

"Don't get your back up. I meant that you'd put things like family and friends ahead of financial success."

Funny, he thought; he didn't value financial success all that much himself beyond the personal satisfaction of knowing he was doing something well, but he wasn't so good at the family and friends thing, either.

Gee, could it be that's why he got to the point he didn't care whether he lived or died? No big revelation there.

After a moment, he asked, "How did you know I ran away from home at sixteen? I don't remember telling you that."

"Mark called your adoptive father. He said you had and that he hadn't heard from you or seen you since."

Gary nodded. He hadn't thought through how the P.I. had found him. It was logical that he'd started with Harold.

Suzanne's knitting dropped to her lap again. "How did you survive on your own that young?"

Short answer: "Hitchhiked until I got to New Mexico, then got a job in a mechanic's shop."

Longer answer: Went hungry one hell of a lot of the time, escaped an insane knife-wielding trucker intent on rape, and slept under bushes in public parks. He'd begged and shoplifted, both of which went against his nature. He hadn't gotten lucky for almost a year, when he'd seen that Help Wanted sign and gone in. One thing he had learned on the farm was to work on machinery. He'd admitted most of his expertise wasn't on cars, but when McGinnis heard Gary could keep a harvester running, he figured he could learn most any engine.

"That's where I first worked on Harleys,"

Gary continued. "My boss owned two businesses, one for car repair, the other for motorcycles."

"And the coffee?"

"A friend wanted to try roasting. I offered to help build the roaster. He was the coffee guy, I was the one who knew how to build. We started as partners, but he lost interest and joined the marines. Died in Iraq."

That had hit him hard, hearing Billy had been killed by a suicide bomber at a checkpoint. If he'd just stuck to coffee... But he hadn't. He'd wanted adventure. So he'd died the same day Gary mailed him a package of his latest blend, and two weeks before Gary opened the sixth shop.

"That's sad," Suzanne said, her voice soft as if she meant it. Gary figured she did; if he'd learned anything about her, it was that she had a big heart. He didn't let himself dwell on it, but he was starting to wish real bad that he'd had the chance to grow up with her as his big sister.

As if sensing he'd had enough of emotionally sensitive topics, she asked then if he knew Quicken accounting software, and when he said he did she had a bunch of questions. She'd taken some kind of online course that had left holes in her knowledge, and she was now learning as she went but getting frustrated. He offered to help, and they spent the rest of the evening side by side in front of her computer. Afterwards, he went out like he'd taken to doing every night, sometimes for a ride, sometimes—like tonight—just to walk and be alone.

The next morning, Suzanne had left to open shop before Gary woke up. He ate a bowl of cereal at the table in the kitchen, thinking about his plans for that evening and wondering if it was a mistake.

He did have a way of being attracted to women who also made him edgy. Women in positions of authority. Women who could both giveth and taketh away, and not just their bodies. That was funny, because swimming in his fragmented memories of his youngest childhood were several women who he later understood were social workers. It was these women who'd controlled his fate, who'd driven him away from his home, who'd moved him from foster home to foster home, who'd decided that the Lindstroms should raise him.

He hated only two things in life: Harold, and those women. The *idea* of those women.

And now he was taking a woman who represented that idea out to dinner because she had fantastic legs, fiery red hair, freckles and eyes the color of moss. And maybe because he'd heard her laugh with pure delight when she was astride the Harley behind him. That laugh had been the sexiest damn thing he'd ever heard.

Clearly, this was a case of thinking below the waist. He sure as hell had been surprised when the invitation had burst out of him. And maybe more surprised when she said yes.

Freud would have told Gary he wanted to screw not his mother but instead the women who'd wielded such devastating power over his life. To master them. To end up being the one on top.

He frowned, not liking to think that his subconscious was cracking the whip. How could he be sure whether he just wanted to screw her, the woman with those long, long legs and that joyous laugh, or whether he really had some mysterious, subterranean motive?

Did it matter? Gary asked himself with sudden impatience. He wasn't going to be sticking around. At most another couple of weeks; he'd been thinking he could extend his stay a little longer than he'd intended, since he was already here. And he had a suspicion that Rebecca Wilson was the kind who didn't sleep with men she wasn't in love with.

So to hell with his subconscious, and Freud. She was just his escape valve; a little fun, maybe a few kisses if he was lucky. It was chance that the most attractive woman he'd seen in years happened to be a social worker who handled adoptions.

Standing to rinse his dishes, he gave a bark of laughter. Yep. And if he believed it was pure chance that he was attracted to a woman who was not only a social worker but actually handled adoptions, maybe he could sell himself a nice little lot in the middle of the Mojave Desert.

"HEY," Rebecca said, opening the door. "You're early."

"Sorry." He didn't sound repentant. "I thought I might have trouble finding your place. Since I don't know the area."

She stood back. "Come in. I was going to do something with my hair so it doesn't fly all over the place."

He reached up and gently fingered a strand that dipped over her shoulder. "I like your hair when it's flying."

Feeling breathless, she backed away. "You're not the one who has to get a brush through the briars later. It'll take me just a minute."

She heard a soft chuckle as she fled to her bedroom, leaving him standing in the middle of her living room, reminding her of that photo she'd seen the other day of a moose wandering down a city street in Anchorage.

Her taste ran to pretty but modern, Scandinavian lines but bright colors. Pillows made from vintage silk scarves, cranberry and aqua-colored art glass vases filled with bouquets she could never resist when she passed the Vietnamese woman who set up on a nearby street corner, paintings with hues and shapes that pleased her eye. Rebecca admired simplicity, but knew her decor was still very feminine.

She'd never dated a man before who looked quite so out of place. Which ought to tell her something, she reflected, as she brushed her hair and began to plait it into a fat braid.

She just didn't know what that was. Especially since none of the men who *did* look as if they could belong ever made it as far as her bedroom.

Don't think like that! Rebecca ordered

herself, jabbing a pin into her hair hard enough to stab her skull. Gary Lindstrom was a novelty. A chance for her to play out teenage fantasies. But she was a grown woman now, and just because a guy would have stirred her hormones at sixteen didn't mean he was going to make it into her bedroom now, either.

Her hand went still and she stared at herself in the mirror. Sad to say, *no one* ever made it into her bedroom. Or hadn't in a very long time.

What was sad about wanting sex to mean something? she demanded of herself. Nothing! She wanted what her mother had never had: a man who stuck around, mowed the lawn, helped pay the bills, who assumed he too would get up in the middle of the night with the baby. Fly-by-night wasn't and never would be her style. She just hadn't found that guy.

She inspected her hair in the mirror, tilting her head this way and that, finally giving a nod. "I'm ready," she announced, returning to the living room.

Gary had been inspecting the DVDs on the shelf below the player. "*X-Men*? And *X-Men 2*?"

"I like Wolverine," she retorted, then felt a cramp of dismay. Damn. Long hair, leather, the occasional wildness of a feral animal in his eyes… Now, who did that remind her of? Double damn, she thought. Maybe Gary Lindstrom wasn't just a teenage fantasy; maybe he was her fantasy, plain and simple.

His eyes were knowing. "I like Wolverine, too."

"You would," she said.

He just grinned, a flash of white teeth. "I was thinking we head out toward Darrington. It looks like a good road on the map."

Rebecca nodded. "I haven't been up there in ages, but it's a pretty drive." She glanced pointedly at the window. "In daylight."

"It's going to be a clear night. Maybe a full moon. Empty, winding road." He spoke as if the bends in the road were more enticement than the full moon.

They might be, if she could forget the one he hadn't made.

Don't be a coward, she told herself.

"Are you planning to feed me, too?" she asked.

"There must be a café in Darrington."

She locked her door, tucked her keys in the pocket of her jacket, let him settle the helmet on her head and climbed onto the Harley behind him. Amazing how much easier it was this time to wrap her arms around his waist. Maybe she felt a little less prim and proper, now that she was in jeans instead of a linen suit and heels.

She liked the sensation of riding at night, she discovered; the swoops were less stomach-clench inducing and more exhilarating when near objects and the ground weren't so clear-cut. She had to trust him, and since she'd gotten herself into this, she had no choice, did she?

Once they left I-5 and took a jog through Arlington, the road to Darrington was a two-lane highway with a stripe down the middle and farms to each side. The bends in it were long and easy as it climbed into the Cascade Mountains. Traffic was sparse, the moon full or only a day or two shy of it, the air sharp with oncoming winter. Rebecca found herself sitting back and holding on to Gary more lightly, relaxing enough to enjoy the moonlit glimpses of mountains, the open river valley, the forested stretches, and the delicious sense of speed and power.

There were indeed cafés; a couple, along with some taverns. The Harley would have looked more natural sitting outside one of those, but Gary parked it sedately in the lot beside one of the cafés and they strolled in.

Given that it was a weekday night, the place wasn't real busy. They took a booth and ordered burgers, fries and milkshakes.

"Fancy first date," Rebecca commented, after the waitress brought the milkshakes and she'd taken a slurp.

"Second," Gary said, with only a narrowing of eyes to indicate he was amused.

"*I* paid for lunch," she argued.

"Doesn't make it any less a date."

She pursed her lips and thought about it. Okay, maybe not. Business lunches, friends having lunch, you each took care of your own bill. Nobody paid for anybody.

"Come on," he coaxed, "isn't this more fun than getting all dressed up and going out to someplace where you have to murmur and the waiters intimidate you?"

Yes, to her surprise it was.

"Do you ever go to that kind of place?" she asked.

"As a matter of fact, I do. I'm a businessman, you know."

"Actually, I don't know. You never said what you do for a living. I guess I assumed you have a motorcycle shop."

"That's my hobby. Coffee is my business."

She lifted her brows. "As in, shops? Roasting? Trading in beans?"

"Shops and roasting. I have a string of eleven coffee shops, and we sell our roast, too."

She wasn't as surprised as maybe she should have been. Perhaps it was his assurance at Olive's that had made her realize she could easily imagine him in a suit closing deals.

"Do you sell it out here?"

"Whole Foods. And my sister tells me it's in Trader Joe's as well. Maybe through an intermediary."

She was always experimenting, buying different coffees. "What's it called?" He told her and she nodded. "I just bought some. It's amazing coffee."

"Thank you."

"You roast it?"

"Well, not personally, although I used to."

She smiled. "How can you stand the coffee at the average restaurant?"

"Don't drink it most of the time."

Rebecca laughed. "Dare you."

He grimaced, then shrugged. "Hell, at least it's strong at a place like this. Bugs me more at some of those chains where image counts more than great coffee."

"Be careful," she warned. "Everybody would still be drinking the sludge that sits on the burner all day if it weren't for Seattle. Thank us for the coffee renaissance."

"You personally?"

"At least I'm a native."

"Appears," he said, "that I am, too."

"I guess you are. Wow. Maybe that's why you ended up roasting coffee."

His laugh was rich and strong, like the best brews. "It's in my blood? I'd agree with you, except Suzanne buys the most godawful coffee. Whatever's cheapest at Safeway, far as I can tell."

"Have you introduced her to yours yet?"

He grinned. "Last night. She asked me cautiously how much it costs. I told her it was all in the family, I'd keep her supplied."

"That was nice," Rebecca said.

His smile had died. "You know, it's funny. That's the first time I've ever said that."

She blinked. "Said what?"

"All in the family. About myself."

If that wasn't one of the saddest things she'd ever heard. "Your sisters. Do they *feel* like family to you?"

He nodded his thanks to the waitress who brought their food and he ate a fry.

Rebecca repeated her question and watched his eyebrows draw together.

After a moment he said, "Sometimes. It seems to come easier with Carrie—she's my younger sister. With Suzanne, it's a little harder. She remembers being my big sister, and sometimes she makes assumptions."

Between bites of a truly great hamburger, Rebecca said, "You feel like she's a stranger, but to her you're her little brother."

"Yeah, you got it." He ate in silence, a couple of lines staying between his brows.

"What did you expect?" she asked after a minute. "I mean, when you came out here."

"I guess I planned to look at pictures, learn a little about our parents, see what my sisters were like and then go home."

"Has that changed?" she asked quietly.

"No… Yeah." The furrows deepened to a scowl. "I don't know."

He felt a kinship and didn't know what to do with it, Rebecca diagnosed. "Do you have…well, family back in Santa Fe?" At his blank stare, she explained, "I mean, people you're close enough with that you have holidays with them, or assume you'd always be welcome to bed down at their place if you needed to. You know. *Made* family."

"I'm not big on holidays."

She waited while he dipped fries in ketchup and ate them.

Finally, sounding grudging, he said, "The first guy who hired me. McGinnis. I used to have Thanksgiving with him and his wife. They had a son, but he'd ended up in Maine and didn't come home much."

When he didn't continue, she prodded, "Used to?"

"McGinnis died a couple years after I left to open my first coffee shop. Lung cancer. Must've smoked three packs a day."

"Oh. How awful."

He shrugged as if the loss hadn't mattered, not to him, big tough guy that he was. "Wife moved a year ago to Maine to be near the son." He dipped another French fry and munched unconcernedly.

Rebecca studied him and wondered if he even knew how much it had hurt, losing a man who sounded as if he'd become a father figure. Or had he just buried the pain?

Kids who went through too many foster homes got really good at that. They didn't quit feeling; eventually, something would happen that stripped them bare. But they could fool the world and themselves for a long time.

"How about you?" he asked. "Any brothers or sisters?"

"Nope, just my mom and me. I don't even know my father."

His brows drew together again. "He ran out on you?"

"I'm not sure my mother even told him she was pregnant. I get the feeling maybe he was married. All she's ever said was that she made a huge mistake that didn't turn out to be a mistake at all, because she had me."

"You haven't minded, not knowing?"

Maybe it was strange, but she never had. Rebecca shrugged. "Mom and I were really close. *Are* really close. I didn't feel like I was missing anything."

"So you're predisposed to believe a single woman can do a good job raising kids."

"Uh-uh," she warned him. "That's forbidden territory."

"Yeah, that's right." He nodded at her plate. "Want dessert? The pies in the case looked good."

"I couldn't eat another bite. Well, I could steal maybe one or two if you have pie."

Or maybe three or four. They shared a

piece of Dutch apple pie warmed and à la mode. Watching him laugh at her as she stole yet another forkful, Rebecca marveled at her initial belief that this man didn't know how to smile. She was sticking by her original impression that he was closemouthed, but he did have a sense of humor and was fully capable of being charming.

So charming she was already wondering if he was going to kiss her good-night. Or maybe more accurately, what it would be like, having him kiss her. She had a feeling he'd had plenty of practice.

He paid the bill and they strolled out.

"I am so stuffed," she moaned.

"And here you look like the type who's always on a diet."

"I'm naturally skinny. I was a stick growing up. I do try to eat healthy foods."

"Not French fries, milkshakes and pie à la mode?"

Rebecca moaned again. "The cholesterol!"

"But it tasted damned good, didn't it?"

"You know it did. But let's not make a habit of this, okay?"

Gary straddled the Harley and waited for her to put on the helmet and get on behind. The streets were quieter than when they'd arrived, most of the parked cars clustered around the tavern down the way. In another mood, Rebecca might have suggested they go shoot some pool, but instead she gripped his waist and was glad when he accelerated out of town without slowing.

The moon was behind them now, but she caught glimpses off the river. The headlights of an occasional car hurt her eyes, but mostly she and Gary were alone with the dark and the moonlight.

Wind rushing against her face, she smiled. Blue jeans, a motorcycle ride, dinner at a greasy spoon café, and here she was thinking this was the most romantic date of her life.

CHAPTER SIX

AFTER PULLING INTO a visitor's spot in front of Rebecca's apartment building, Gary killed the engine of his Harley. He was sorry they were back. A man could get used to being cradled between Rebecca Wilson's thighs.

"Well," she said into the silence.

"I'll walk you to your door."

Without comment, she swung her leg over the back, then took off the helmet. He still regretted that she hadn't left her glorious red hair loose to spill out, but the fat braid had its charm. Unbraiding her hair, now that might be almost as good as undressing her. Working his fingers into the thick, glossy strands and freeing them, going higher and higher until he reached her scalp and could sink his hands into the silky mass. Yeah, that would be good, too.

He'd been pretty sure she wouldn't invite him in, and she didn't. Instead, she unlocked her door, then turned to face him.

She smiled. "I had a great time, Gary. Thanks for taking me."

"My pleasure," he murmured, savoring the sight of her cheeks, pink from the wind and, he suspected, self-consciousness. "Let's do it again."

"I'd like that."

He moved a step closer, crowding her, and the color in her cheeks deepened, but she didn't retreat. He liked that. She might feel shy, but she wasn't a coward.

He touched her jaw, smooth and beautifully sculpted, then let his fingers slip lower, to the pulse beating in her throat. When he wrapped his hand around the back of her neck, she tilted her chin up.

He'd been so aware of her all night, he was aroused just looking down into her face.

"You're beautiful," he said huskily.

"I have freckles," she argued, as if needing the last word.

"And they're cute." Sexy, too, especially when a man got to wondering where else she had freckles.

"Cute, okay. Beautiful, no."

"Let me be the judge," he suggested, just before his mouth closed over hers.

Her lips were soft, made for laughing—

and arguing. She should have tasted of hamburger and pie, but instead—oh, hell, tasted of *her*. Something a little tangy, a little exotic.

He'd meant to keep this kiss light. It was a strategy that had always worked for him.

Then she moaned. Just a breath of sound, and he quit thinking. He backed her against the door frame and plundered her mouth. His tongue sought hers, demanded a duel, got one. His hips crowded hers, and his free hand gripped one of her buttocks, squeezing and lifting her against him. It was damn near an assault, except she was kissing him back, her arms around his neck and her breasts flattened against his chest.

They both made small, desperate sounds now, dragged in frantic breaths, then went back to kissing. What glimpses he caught of her didn't help, with her color high, her lips swollen. If their clothes hadn't been in the way, he'd have lifted her, wrapped her legs around his hips and driven inside her. But shedding clothes took coordination and thought he couldn't manage. Not yet. One more kiss, one more taste…

The sound of the telephone ringing in her apartment behind her made both go still.

She wrenched back. "Oh, my God."

They stared at each other. If she'd looked, she couldn't have missed how hard he was. He saw panic on her face, and felt a fair share of it. What in hell had just happened here?

"I…I'd better go." She stepped back, stumbled over the doorjamb and flinched from him when out of instinct he reached for her.

He swore. "I'm sorry. Damn, Rebecca. I didn't mean…"

She closed her eyes momentarily, as though to regain composure. "No. It's okay. I just…didn't expect…"

She didn't finish the thought. Didn't have to.

He hadn't expected, either. Something, but not that.

"Yeah." He had to clear the rasp from his throat. "I really don't make a habit of…"

"No." She stopped him. "I don't either."

"I know you don't."

At his quiet words, she seemed to relax fractionally. As he'd suspected, she was a good girl who didn't indulge in wild, impulsive, short-term love affairs.

Just his luck.

He didn't suppose she'd be interested in moving to Santa Fe, either.

Backing away himself, he thought, *Whoa!* Where had that come from?

"Good night, Rebecca."

"Good night, Gary." Then, startling him, she stepped forward and pressed a kiss to his cheek before fleeing inside and closing the door.

Okay, so she didn't hate him.

A smile grew on Gary's face. Maybe she *wouldn't* mind straddling his Harley again.

Even if, sadly, he doubted she'd ever straddle him.

THE NEXT DAY, the whole family—or close to it—was to gather for a meal at Mark and Carrie's house in Seattle.

That would have been okay, except Suzanne had invited Aunt Marie and Uncle Miles as well as their sons and *their* families.

Gary didn't much want to meet the people who'd ditched him. If he hadn't hated the idea of looking gutless, he'd have refused to go.

Suzanne cooked all morning while he read the paper and stole restless, longing glances out the front window at his Harley.

I could leave now, he thought, aching to do just that. *Throw my stuff in a bag, tell her this visit has been long enough, and go.*

He knew he wouldn't do it, but didn't know why. He didn't owe anybody here a damn thing.

When he looked down, he saw that he was gripping the arm of the sofa as if it were the only thing that was keeping him here. This need to flee shocked him with its ferocity.

I've met them, okay? Done what I came for.

Why was he letting himself get enmeshed? A family gathering? Really, really not his thing.

But he kept holding on to the damn sofa, telling himself he despised cowards almost as much as social workers, and he was still sitting there when Suzanne popped into the living room.

"Can you carry some stuff out to the car?"

"Sure." He rose to his feet.

He made a couple of trips, carrying a hot ceramic casserole dish with homemade Boston beans, a grocery sack with enough chips and dip to feed forty people, and a cooler of drinks as well as a bag of his coffee roast. Then, reluctantly, he got in the passenger side of her crap car and tried not to wince when she ground the gears.

"I'm afraid the clutch is going," she worried aloud. "I know I'm hard on it, but I'm praying it holds out for a while."

He thought her foot had more to do with the unpleasant sound than did a failing clutch, but he said, "I'll take a look at it."

Her face was full of hope. "You could fix it?"

"That's what I used to do, remember?"

"I hate to ask—"

He cut her off. "You didn't ask. I offered. Might as well make myself useful while I'm here."

"That would be so nice!"

Gary tuned her out when she continued to gush. Extravagant praise and gratitude made him uncomfortable. It was easier just not to listen.

He tuned in again when he heard, "Did I tell you that Uncle Miles isn't coming? Neither is Ray and his family. Roddie's bringing Aunt Marie. And of course his wife and kids are coming."

"I didn't want to meet him, anyway," Gary said.

Suzanne stole a look at him. "Uncle Miles? I guess I can't blame you. I just thought…"

"We could be one big happy family?" He snorted. "What's Carrie think of that?"

"She still hasn't met him, either. And, um, doesn't really want to. Although she did agree I could invite him. It's so awkward for Aunt Marie if we don't."

"You mean, she doesn't want to admit that he's a jackass?"

"She's still married to him. I don't think she knows he is. Or that…" Suzanne stopped.

When she didn't continue, he prodded, "That?"

"That one of her sons is, too."

"Ah. In other words, I should be glad he isn't coming."

"I don't think you two would have hit it off. He's a bully. I can picture him wanting to be the big man there."

"You mean, demanding a pissing contest?"

She gave him a reproving look that would have been more effective if she wasn't also laughing. "Something like that."

"What about this Mark? The P.I. Is he macho?"

"Come on, you've met Carrie! Can you imagine her married to some swaggering stud?"

"People surprise me," he said.

"Well, me, too," his sister admitted. "But Mark's a really nice guy. You'll like him."

Gary wasn't so sure *he* was a nice guy, and he doubted that anyone in Mark's profession was "nice" in quite the way Suzanne meant, either. But, okay; he'd reserve judgment.

"How about this other brother?"

"Roddie—Rodney, really—is okay. He

went along with everything Ray did and said when he was a kid, which means he was a jerk, too. But since he left home and has gotten out from under his brother's thumb, he's gotten better. I like his wife, too. But, honestly, I don't see that much of them. They just had a baby, their second, and I haven't even seen him yet."

"Was that sweater with the flower on it for him?"

"It's a boy. Of course I didn't knit anything with a flower on it for him!"

He grinned at her. "How about one with a Harley on the front?"

She pursed her lips. "Actually, that might be cute. I haven't seen a pattern. Hmmm. Maybe I'll design one...." She gave herself a little shake. "I knit a crib blanket. Aunt Marie said they'd painted the nursery a pale mint-green, so I made one in bright mint-green with yellow zigzags. Somewhere I read that babies like zigzag patterns."

Trust her to know that. Suzanne, now, *was* nice. In fact, she was so quintessentially "nice" Gary kept wondering whether she ever had unworthy thoughts, whether she ever did something just because she wanted to without regard for everyone else's feelings.

He actually hoped so. In his book, someone who was too considerate was suffering from major anxiety. Why else would you want to please everyone all the time?

"You've seen Mark's house, haven't you?" she asked, oblivious to his train of thought.

"Carrie's, too, isn't it?"

"Well, I guess it is. Of course it is!" She laughed at herself. "I have trouble thinking of her as married."

"And yeah, I've picked Carrie up a couple of times. Once we just had coffee, once I took her to class."

Suzanne kept chattering, as if driving side by side in silence wasn't done in her world. Gary found a few grunts kept her satisfied. Tension was stretching tight in him. He glanced down to see that he was drumming his fingers on the armrest, and made himself stop.

Damn, he wished he'd ridden down on his own. Now he was trapped.

He almost snorted. Face it, he was trapped either way, by this inexplicable desire not to hurt the two women he still had trouble thinking of as "sisters." Especially Suzanne, with her load of guilt and her intense desire to make everything right again, as if their family hadn't been blasted into smithereens twenty-six years ago.

Someday she'd discover that Humpty couldn't be put back together again, but he kind of hoped he wasn't around when she admitted as much. Maybe, with luck, by then Rebecca Wilson would have found some cute kid for Suzanne to adopt, and she'd have a shot at a new family.

Yeah, and maybe she'd never be willing to admit that the Chauvins just plain weren't your average, back-slapping, Fourth-of-July-and-Thanksgiving-gathering family. He'd be getting invitations to her grandkids' high school graduations, if he was around that long.

She was able to park right in front of Carrie's place, pure luck on the narrow street lined with residents' cars.

Gary did like the house, he had to admit. Built in the twenties, of red brick, it was a cross between Tudor and gingerbread cottage. Most of the houses in the neighborhood were redbrick, too, from the same era, and old trees, leafless now, lined the street, buckling the sidewalks. He could tell people around here were gardeners despite their small lots. Carrie and Mark were apparently no exception; big pots exploding with color sat on every step leading up to the front porch. Chrysanthemums, he thought, yellow alternating with hot pink. Bright enough to combat the Seattle-gray overcast sky.

Carrie flung open the door before they reached the porch and bustled out to help bring in Suzanne's offerings. Her dog, Daisy, bounded out, too, tail whacking legs and excited little yips escaping her.

"Are they here?" some kid called from inside the house. Then, "Dad! Someone's here!"

He clogged the doorway just as they were all trying to go in, wide hazel eyes studying Gary with a startling lack of subterfuge. The kid wanted to stare, he stared.

"Are you Uncle Gary?" he asked.

He'd noticed a bus stop a few blocks down, on 50th. He could just walk away....

"Yeah, Carrie's my sister," he admitted.

"And Aunt Suzanne, too," the boy informed him.

"That's right. Suzanne, too."

"Mom says you ride a big motorcycle."

Mom? Appeared the kid had accepted Carrie wholeheartedly.

"That's right."

He peered past the crowd on the doorstep. "Can I see it?"

Suzanne laughed. "I made him come with me, Michael. So, no, you can't have a ride."

"Mom already said I couldn't. But she didn't say I couldn't *sit* on it." He gave Gary a hopeful look.

"I didn't bring it today. Sorry, kid."

"Michael. My name's Michael."

"Michael." Disconcerted by the correction, he realized how naturally the "kid" had slipped out. That's what Harold had called him. *Kid.* Never Gary. It was like, he'd finally realized, you didn't name farm animals, not the ones you planned to butcher someday. Too personal. He guessed he was useful, like the chickens and the few pigs Harold kept. Any softness Harold had, he'd held for his wife.

Until she left.

Gary shook off unpleasant memories and let himself be ushered in.

A man wearing a sweater and jeans was just coming down the stairs. He *looked* like a cop: tough, wary, physically fit. His scrutiny was as direct as his son's, but more reserved.

"Gary," he said, holding out his hand.

"You're Mark." They shook as the women, trailed by the boy and dog, continued toward the kitchen chattering a mile a minute.

More laconic, Mark said, "You've met Michael."

"Yeah, he already asked if he could sit on my bike."

A rueful smile tugged at his mouth. "He doesn't believe in wasting time." His eyes met Gary's. "What did you say?"

"That I didn't bring it today, so he's out of luck."

Carrie's husband nodded and muttered something Gary took as, "Just as well." More clearly, he added, "Didn't expect to meet you so soon after we talked the once."

Gary understood he was being asked why the hell he'd changed his mind so fast. He might not have much experience with men who protected their families, but he knew one when he saw one.

"I got in an accident. Pure luck I didn't die." Unless *luck* was a code word for *damn shame.* He shrugged. "Made me think."

Mark Kincaid's eyes were icy blue and perceptive. After a moment he nodded and opened his mouth as if to say something. What came out instead was a muttered, "Damn," and Gary heard the sounds of slamming car doors and voices.

Damn was right. Gary gave a hunted look

at the still open front door, then turned his head to see Mark watching him with amusement that had supplanted his own dismay.

"Not looking forward to meeting the relatives?"

"You could say that."

"Don't blame you." Mark gave him a hearty slap on the back. "But it appears you don't have any choice. And that it's up to you and me to be the welcoming party."

Gary would have known he and Aunt Marie were related if they'd come face-to-face by chance in a crowd. She was an older version of Gary's sisters and looked enough like the photos in the album of his mother to give him a shock. She hugged him and wept while he endured.

Then he had to shake hands with his cousin Rodney, a big, bluff man with light brown hair that had been buzz cut and a nose broken a time or two along the way, then with a tall, buxom woman with a sweet smile and a baby in her arms. The other kid, identifiable as a girl by the pink overalls, hid behind her dad's leg, peeking out once to take an alarmed look at Gary and Mark before retreating.

Gary didn't blame her a bit. He could have used a leg to hide behind, too.

The party moved to the kitchen, where the women heated some dishes, uncovered others, and spread the feast on the table, already set for eight. Rodney's wife Shelley disappeared for ten minutes with the baby and came back without him, announcing, "Down for a nap."

When they sat down to eat, everyone wanted to hear about Gary, his coffee empire—somehow, in Suzanne's telling, his business had grown to rival Starbucks—and whether he had a wife slash girlfriend slash kids.

"No children?" his aunt Marie exclaimed. "What a shame! Aren't you thirty this year?"

"Twenty-nine," he said, but she talked right over him.

"Plenty old enough to start a family. Goodness. You should be thinking about it, too, Carrie."

Carrie smiled at her stepson. "We *have* started a family."

Aunt Marie turned to Michael. "Wouldn't you like to have a little brother or sister?"

Not understanding his role in this conversation, he frowned thoughtfully. "I don't know. My friend Ryan? He hates his sister *and* his little brother. So maybe I wouldn't like one."

"Ryan," his father said, "is a brat. Does he like anyone?"

"Me. Most of the time."

Everyone laughed. Gary pretended to concentrate on his food.

A family. The very idea gave him a clutch of terror. He'd felt safe dipping his toe in marriage partly because he knew Holly Lynn didn't want to have children. How could he ever be a father? He didn't know jack about parenting! Abusers tended to beget abusers— or maybe more accurately, they tended to *raise* abusers. You were what you knew. How was he supposed to know how to be a father like Mark, who, with a quiet word to Michael when he started to peer under the tablecloth, straightened the boy's back but didn't leave him looking as if his daddy had scared the crap out of him.

Hell, Gary thought, look at him—he hadn't even been able to handle marriage! At least, according to Holly Lynn.

"So," Cousin Rodney said to Suzanne, across the table from him. "What's this I hear about you adopting?"

She told them her plans.

"The adoption counselor is coming Tuesday for a home visit." She laughed. "Gary doesn't know it yet, but I'm hoping he'll help me scrub tomorrow. I want the house to be perfect!"

"No problem," Gary said, without a clue how her house could be cleaned, as cluttered as it tended to be. But he'd do his best. He knew it wouldn't do any good to tell her Rebecca Wilson was genuine enough to care more about what kind of person Suzanne was than she did about soap scum in the shower.

The conversation veered to talk about her new yarn shop. Shelley wished aloud they lived closer so she could take classes.

"That afghan you knit was so beautiful! It made me want to try my hand."

"She has me knitting, too," Carrie said. "I made a couple of scarves that came out great, but I'm not so sure about the sweater I'm knitting for Mark. It seems…well, large. Even the arms are a teeny bit long."

Suzanne started talking about yarn tension. Rodney grinned at Mark and said, "Buddy, sounds like your arms had better grow a foot or two."

Carrie slipped in, "I accuse him occasionally of being he-man. Knuckles grazing the ground. Maybe that's why those damn sleeves are so long. Subconscious resentment."

Mark laughed and they exchanged a look of amusement, pure heat and tenderness, all mixed together. Gary felt a minor pang. No matter how much he'd once believed he loved Holly Lynn, the two of them had never communicated like that. She yelled, he brooded.

Funny, he couldn't imagine Rebecca yelling. Or letting him brood, for that matter. She'd been damn easy to talk to.

"So, how'd you end up down there in New Mexico?" Shelley asked.

He gave them the abbreviated version again without mentioning the last fight with his adoptive father or the things he'd stolen and pawned to pay for food. He wondered sometimes if Harold had been smart enough to check the pawnshops for his stuff. Should have been—Bakersfield still wasn't that big, and there weren't that many places he could have sold a gold pocket watch and a pearl necklace.

He didn't mention sleeping in doorways or getting the crap beaten out of him or becoming so hungry he hung around fast food restaurants to snatch people's leftovers from tables or the top of wastebins.

No, he agreed; he didn't have a good relationship with his adoptive father.

"Did your mother die?" Aunt Marie asked in innocence and concern.

He hadn't thought of Judith as his mother in a long time. As far as he was concerned, she was dead. But he gave his stock answer to that question, too.

"No, she got fed up and left."

"But…couldn't she have taken you?"

Out of the corner of his eye, he saw Carrie straighten abruptly, but Gary said evenly, "I guess I was getting to a difficult age."

"Well…" She sounded doubtful. "I suppose it would be natural to think a boy should stay with his father."

Judith hadn't thought that. She'd known that Harold resented the boy they'd adopted. Oh, yeah, she'd known the hell she would be leaving Gary to. She just hadn't cared.

But he let it ride. He didn't like talking about her, and he sure wasn't going to with a bunch of people he didn't even know, blood relatives or not.

Anyway, he thought, fanning the coals of anger that burned in his belly, who was this woman to talk? She was his mother's own sister, and she hadn't wanted to keep him, either.

Gee, maybe there was a reason he couldn't sustain a relationship with a woman. Maybe the mommy was the warm-up exercise for most boys.

He tried not to listen to the inner voice that whispered, *And maybe you're just plain not lovable. Never have been, never will be.*

Casting him another glance, Carrie said loudly, "Who wants pie?"

In the decision-making and clamor, Gary's history was forgotten, thank God for small favors.

Under cover of other conversation as everyone carried their dirty dishes to the kitchen, Mark murmured, "Well, you survived."

There were days he wished he hadn't.

"The grilling," Carrie's husband elaborated.

Oh. That. "Round one," he said.

"You should have been there the first time I met Carrie's adoptive parents. A P.I. was not what Dr. St. James had in mind for his only daughter."

As if on cue, Carrie gave Gary a one-armed squeeze in passing and said, "I wish my parents could have been here today. They want to meet you so much."

They were away. Maui, he seemed to recall.

"Why would they want to meet me?" he asked.

She gave him a peculiar look over her shoulder. "You're my brother. And…oh, I'll tell you another time."

And? But he didn't have time to wonder.

"You wanted ice cream, didn't you?" Aunt Marie said, handing him a plate with a slice of warm cherry pie à la mode.

Somewhere in the house, the baby began squalling. With a sigh, Shelley went off to get her. No, him. No flowered sweater, Gary remembered. He noticed that Rodney settled down with his particularly large slab of pie and ice cream without considering taking care of the baby. The guy had it good.

Shelley stayed gone for a while, and when she reappeared she was patting the baby against her shoulder. He gave a burp, and Aunt Marie rose.

"Oh, let me take Rory."

They did like those *R* names in that family. Gary was willing to bet Cousin Ray's two boys were something like Ronald and Randall.

The little girl in the pink overalls started getting whiny, and her mother gobbled her pie while bouncing her on one hip and whispering to her.

Gary was relieved when Rodney and company decided to pack up and go home shortly thereafter, removing Aunt Marie with them.

She hugged him again at the door. "You'll come up and see me in Bellingham before you go home, won't you? Miles was so sorry not to be able to come today. He really wants to meet you."

Gary just bet he did. He mumbled something that must have passed, because she hugged Suzanne and Carrie and let herself be swept away.

Trying to sound casual when all he wanted to do was bolt, Gary said, "You know, I think I'm going to take a walk."

"I'll come with you," Carrie said immediately.

Suzanne started to say something, but Gary shook his head at her. He had wanted to be alone, but he could tolerate Carrie. She was the easiest person in this new family for him to deal with.

She went to get a sweater, then joined him again and they started off up the street.

"You don't care which way we go, do you?" she asked.

"No."

"Were you dreading meeting Aunt Marie as much as I was the first time?"

"I don't have any problem with her. She did what she had to do."

Carrie stopped dead on the sidewalk. "Oh, come on! You don't believe that!"

He turned to face her. "Why wouldn't I?"

She demanded, "You're not mad? Deep down inside? Hurt? Confused? You weren't secretly hoping she'd be an awful woman who'd clearly been incapable of loving anyone, thus meaning it wasn't your fault she couldn't love you enough to keep you?"

He hadn't thought of that one.

"I won't believe you if you try to claim you really don't care," his little sister warned him.

"Okay. Yeah, I'm pissed." His voice emerged as gravel, painfully rough-edged. "I wanted her to say I'm sorry, I did wrong. But that's not going to happen, is it? So what's the good of talking about it?"

"Because I don't want to be all alone in this." She glared at him. "I had it good, and I'm mad. How can you not be?"

"I told you I am!" he shouted. "What more do you want?"

She blinked. "Nothing. I just wanted you to say it." She started walking again as though nothing had happened, as though he hadn't lost his cool.

Holly Lynn yelled. He didn't.

God help him, having a family was making him crazy.

CHAPTER SEVEN

REBECCA DIDN'T KNOW how she felt about seeing Gary Lindstrom again. The kiss had shaken her.

She didn't even quite know why. Because it was so violent, she thought, then shook her head. No, that wasn't right—it wasn't as if she'd been left with bruises, or that he'd forced himself on her. She'd given as good as she got. Urgent was probably a better word. Urgent, needy, passionate. Even desperate.

She'd never awakened that kind of need in a man, never felt it herself.

And maybe that was why she was so shaken.

She wanted to fall in love someday. She'd just expected the process to be gentler. Her heart would swell with tenderness and a kind of joy, the sweetness bringing tears to her eyes. She would long for the sight of him— the unknown *him* who as yet had no face. Of course she would be attracted to him, that went without saying, but their first kiss would be tentative, surprising to both, not a brutal slamming together of bodies.

Which probably meant that the kiss she was so worried about had nothing to do with love. It was just her first encounter with genuine lust. Not that she was an innocent— she'd had a couple of lovers. But in both cases sex had happened in due time, when they'd dated for a while and liked each other, when it seemed to be the normal next step. And she'd enjoyed it. But in neither case had she wanted to meld her body into the man's, as if her every cell would die if she didn't.

Lust. She relaxed a little at the idea. Powerful, sure, but safer than love.

At least, it seemed safer when the man was Gary Lindstrom, wary and emotionally scarred.

Not to mention, a man who lived out of state.

But lust… She could have a love affair. Why not? Shouldn't every woman have a breathtaking, heart-shatteringly brief affair that she would remember for the rest of her life with a bittersweet pang?

That fit with the fact that she had severely edited how much she told her mother about Gary in their regular evening phone calls.

She'd mentioned having dinner, but not the Harley-Davidson, for example. Or how weak in the knees he made her feel. Apparently she could tell Mom about nice guys, but not sinful ones.

She wondered if that's what her father had been, then shied away from the thought. As good friends as she and her mother were, she still didn't want to think about Mom in a sexual relationship. If she couldn't have a father, she'd decided when she was about twelve, she'd prefer to think she was the product of an immaculate conception.

Having satisfactorily settled in her own mind how she felt about him, she was glad when Gary called on Sunday.

"How was the family reunion?" she asked.

"I survived. Or so my brother-in-law tells me."

"You're not so sure?"

"I keep having terrifying waking nightmares of endless family dinners. Thanksgiving, Christmas, Easter, Fourth of July. Hell, President's Day and Martin Luther King's birthday. Why not?"

Love, Rebecca thought again, was *not* a good idea with a man whose idea of a nightmare was a family get-together.

"Did you like the people you hadn't already met?" she asked.

"Like?" He paused, as if the idea was foreign. After a moment, he said, "Carrie's husband seemed like a good guy. The rest of them...they were okay for the day. I won't care if I never see them again."

Well, that was understandable. Affection for family members grew from a seed planted at birth. His tiny, tentative shoot had died from neglect when he was sent to a foster home. How could he be expected to feel anything in particular for these people he didn't know and had nothing in common with? He didn't even share the memories that bound the average family together!

"My appointment with Suzanne is Tuesday."

"I know it is. So how about we have dinner tomorrow night? I have a craving for curry. Suzanne says Chutney's in Seattle is good."

Rebecca laughed. "Maybe we should have dinner *after* I talk to Suzanne, so you don't influence me."

"But then we'd both have a hard time not talking about what you thought, and you won't want to do that."

He had a point. "Okay," she said, capitulating. "I do work tomorrow."

"Six?"

They agreed and she hung up smiling.

Her heart was racing a little faster than usual, but she felt none of that fierce need that had frightened her so. Instead, she remembered how much she'd enjoyed talking with Gary, how both safe and exhilarated she'd felt on the back of his Harley-Davidson, her arms wrapped around his waist. Maybe the intensity of that kiss had all been in her imagination. She'd been nervous about it, and he'd come on a little stronger than she'd expected. When she had responded anyway…well, that was reason to have been startled.

Startled. Not scared, she decided, reassured.

Monday morning she met with a sixteen-year-old who was thinking of giving up the baby she was due to have in two months. The girl admitted she hadn't told anyone until she was five months along, succeeding at hiding her pregnancy because she was plump anyway and everyone just thought she was gaining weight.

The parents came with her, which Rebecca was glad to see. The mother said frankly, "I was nearly forty when Caitlin was born. If we were younger… But we're not. We're too old to start over with a baby."

Caitlin, eyes red, said, "You wouldn't have to. I can take care of it."

"By dropping out of school?" her father asked. "How do you plan to make a living? You're sure not getting any help from Jeremy! We'd end up taking care of the baby."

"You're too smart not to go to college," her mother argued. "This isn't the time to have a baby, Cait."

Caitlin burst into tears.

Rebecca provided a box of tissues, then talked about the agency and how they selected adoptive parents. Caitlin began to look interested when she told her she could have a voice in which couple adopted her child.

"And we do believe here in open adoption," she continued. "While you are giving up all right to your baby, we encourage adoptive parents to send you pictures, write you letters. Some couples develop quite close relationships with the birth mothers, while others choose to keep their distance, and you can certainly specify that you'd prefer a situation where you could maintain some contact."

Caitlin's mother whispered, "I thought—" She had to stop, press her lips together, regain control. "I thought we'd never know what happened to the baby."

"That's what adoption was like in the past. But we're realizing how traumatic that was for everyone concerned. Adoptive parents lived in fear the birth mother would appear and somehow be able to reclaim her child, children had to grow up in many cases not even knowing why their parents hadn't been able to keep them, and of course women like you, Caitlin, spent the rest of their lives not being able to feel at peace with their decision. It was all too secretive, which made it feel somehow shameful. Adoption is a good deal healthier option when it's open." She looked directly into Caitlin's eyes. "If you choose to surrender your baby, you'll be able to meet the couple who will raise him or her. If you'd like, they can be at the birth. Be *part* of the birth. You'll be able to see them hold the baby, fall in love like a new mom and dad should. I think you'll find letting go and getting on with your life much easier after that."

As if unconsciously, the sixteen-year-old splayed her hands protectively over her belly, but she also nodded. "That sounds okay. I mean, I didn't like the idea of him just being taken away. You know?"

Rebecca smiled at her. "I do know."

"But I still have to think about it." She turned her head to stare defiantly at her parents.

Sensitive to how harrowing this decision was for her, neither parent said anything. She took information and they left, Caitlin's dad putting an arm around her shoulders as they walked out.

Rebecca felt better about Caitlin than she did the other pregnant teenager she saw later in the day, a girl who had run away from home at thirteen and was now, barely fifteen, living in a shelter, pregnant after having prostituted herself on the notorious strip of the Pacific Highway near the airport where the Green River Killer had once stalked victims. She had no idea which of dozens, maybe hundreds, of men was the father.

Brianna's dishwater-blond hair was lank, her complexion bad, and she was too skinny, the round bump of her belly startling below stick-thin arms.

"I mostly made them use condoms," she said. "But sometimes they'd pay me extra so they didn't have to, or they just didn't and I was too scared to stop them."

Thirteen years old, and she'd been getting into cars with strange men so they could essentially rape her, all so she could buy her next meal and pay part of the cost of a cheap motel room she'd rented by the week with a bunch of other teenage runaways.

"I didn't use after I knew I was pregnant. 'Cuz I thought, well, it wouldn't be good for the kid."

"I'm glad you did that." Rebecca paused. "Did you consider an abortion?"

The girl shrugged, head bent and hair screening her face. After a minute, she mumbled, "I didn't know where to go or anything. So I kept just not thinking about it. And then, I guess it was too late."

"How do you feel about giving up your baby?"

She shrugged again, looked up and as quickly, away again. "Okay. I mean, there's, like, no way I can keep a baby. Mrs. Railey at the shelter wants me to start taking classes to get my GED, or else go back to high school. I might do that. 'Cuz then maybe I could get a real job. I don't want to go back to hooking. See, I got beat up real bad. That's when I went to the shelter."

"Brianna, I'm so sorry! I didn't know."

"The doctor said the baby was okay. See, I curled around my stomach." She demonstrated. "So he wouldn't be hurt."

Rebecca was awed that this child, hungry and needy, so desperate she'd chosen to live on the streets rather than at home, had still protected her unborn baby rather than herself.

She stood and went to the girl, giving her a quick hug. "You're very brave."

Brianna's thin cheeks flushed pink. "I'm scared most of the time," she confessed.

"I don't blame you."

"You can find good parents for my baby, can't you?" She looked up in wide-eyed appeal. "Not drunks. Okay? People with, like, good jobs. Or maybe a mom who's at home and makes cookies and can be room mother at school and stuff."

How unbearably sad that her idea of what constituted a perfect mother was so vague, taken from those women who had volunteered in their children's classrooms. Rebecca felt suddenly very, very angry at this child's parents. If they could be dignified with the title.

"We can find a mother just like that," she promised. "And you can help." She told her how she could read profiles of hopeful couples and eventually even meet with her top choices. "But you know," she said, "I met just last week with a really nice husband and wife that I think might be perfect."

Ronald and Beth Cooper were gentle, kind people. They didn't demand a child who would be a genius, and they wouldn't mind if Brianna's baby turned out to be of mixed race, which Rebecca assumed was a possibility. They didn't even care about gender. They just wanted a baby.

And she guessed, too, that they might take the baby's mother to their hearts as well. They'd seemed like that kind of people to her.

There were other couples in line ahead of them, of course, but that wasn't her first consideration.

"When you decide for sure," she began.

"I've decided," Brianna interrupted. "I don't got… I mean, I don't *have* anyone to help or anything. So I gotta give this baby up. And I trust you."

Brianna was farther along in her pregnancy than she looked, according to the doctor who had examined her. The fetus was small for gestational age, presumably because of the mother's poor nutrition. But mother and child both were gaining weight rapidly now that she was receiving care, and Rebecca tried not think about what damage might have been done when Brianna was taking drugs before she knew she was pregnant.

When she asked what Brianna had used, she said, "Mostly pot. Crack a couple of times, but we didn't really have the money for it. Maybe it was only once. Sometimes there was other stuff around, but I wasn't that into it. And I never drank."

She was proud of that, and rightly so in Rebecca's opinion. So many children of alcoholics followed in their parents' footsteps.

Rebecca gave her a warm smile. "Good for you."

"So these people. Who are they?"

She told the girl in a general way about the Coopers, and by the end she was nodding. "And you said I can meet them?"

"If they agree that your baby sounds like what they've been waiting for. I'll show you some other profiles, too…."

Brianna shook her head. Sounding stubborn, she said, "No. I like them. I want to meet them first."

"Then I'll set it up and call you."

They rarely moved this fast. The agency wanted to be sure the birth parents were committed to surrendering the child. When a birth mother changed her mind after the baby was born, it was heartbreaking for the adoptive parents who'd been so achingly close to finally having a child of their own.

But Brianna *was* committed, Rebecca believed. And she truly had no alternative, unlike Caitlin who had her parents' backing.

Tentatively, she asked, "Do you have any contact with your parents?"

Brianna shook her head hard. "My dad, when he was drunk, sometimes he'd, like, sneak into bed with me, and…you know. I told Mom and she didn't believe me. That's why I left home."

Rebecca had heard too many such stories in her time at DSHS to be shocked, but she was sickened nonetheless.

Brianna was still on Rebecca's mind that evening, long after Gary had picked her up and they'd ridden to Seattle.

On one level she was stunned again by her reaction to his mere presence. The minute she'd opened her door, her heart hammered and she remembered the feel of his mouth on hers so vividly she knew her cheeks were coloring.

His eyes were somehow knowing but also wary, as if he was having the same response and was no more crazy about it than she was.

Why him? Rebecca had no idea. He was incredibly good-looking, of course, in a Colin

Farrell sort of way, dark and rakish but without the mischief and hedonism she saw in photos of the actor. Gary Lindstrom was more like the characters the actor portrayed, men who fought back when life battered them.

Oh, God, she thought, seated on the back of his Harley, holding on to him, *I'm romanticizing him.* Lust, she told herself. Not love.

The funny thing was, even as she dwelled on her racing pulse and desire to inch closer to the man she had her arms around, her mind kept flicking to images of Brianna's face. The spark of hope in her eyes when she'd said, *Mrs. Railey at the shelter wants me to start taking classes to get my GED, or else go back to high school,* as if no one had ever believed she could do anything positive with herself. *'Cuz then maybe I could get a real job.*

Rebecca felt sympathy and liking for people such as the Coopers, who so desperately wanted a child, but it was the kids who got to her. The bewildered, abandoned, hurt and defiant ones she tried to place, and the girls— the children—who found themselves pregnant without enough of a support system to keep the babies they carried even when they wanted to.

But only occasionally did they haunt her the way Brianna was now.

Find the best home for her baby, she told herself. *That's all you can do. You know it is.*

The motorcycle zoomed off the freeway and slowed, engine throaty and sullen, to accommodate to city traffic. Only minutes later, Gary silenced it in the small lot by the restaurant.

Rebecca had never been to Chutney's, and when they walked in she looked around with interest at the traditional paintings and tapestries that decorated the restaurant. Instead of the tablecloths being white, they were all beautiful patterned fabrics that appeared to be hand-dyed.

After being seated at a table beside an interior brick wall, she and Gary considered the menu.

"*Naan* bread for sure," he said, then decisively closed the menu.

She peered over hers. "You've made up your mind already?"

"*Bhindi masala.*"

"Isn't that...okra?"

He laughed at her. "Is that bad?"

"It sounds bad!"

"I'll give you a taste."

When he grinned at her like that, she melted inside. Lust, Rebecca reminded herself. He was just so darned sexy.

Forcing herself to return her attention to the menu, she finally decided on the mango chicken, and they both ordered.

The waitress brought the wine he'd chosen and poured.

When they were alone again, Gary asked, "Well, did you crush anyone's hopes today?"

Dismayed, Rebecca said, "Is that what you think I do?"

"It was a joke." He looked surprised and a little impatient at her reaction.

Maybe, she thought, but more likely that kind of joke was either a passive-aggressive way to get in a dig, or a surfacing of some anger at her profession. The quick sight of a long, dark body gliding beneath the ocean surface.

She didn't want to get mad, though, because she understood why he might have some issues, maybe unacknowledged ones.

"Actually, I mostly did paperwork, except for seeing a couple of teenage girls thinking of giving up their babies once they're born."

His expression changed. "Is that where you get most of the babies? I mean, not, uh, like me, when parents die or courts take them away or whatever?"

Did he equate dying with court-ordered loss of parental rights, as if in both cases the mom and dad had made choices that let down their children? Rebecca supposed that would be natural.

"The vast majority of the babies we place for adoption are from unwanted pregnancies. Usually teenagers. Older children are another story, of course. They're more likely to have suffered abandonment, abuse or neglect."

"These teenagers… Why didn't they get abortions? I thought babies were getting to be a scarce commodity in this country because of birth control and abortion. Isn't that why foreign adoptions have gotten so common?"

"Yes, it is."

The waitress brought the *naan* bread, fluffy and warm. When she was gone, Rebecca continued as she took a piece, "In both these cases, I think the girls were in denial for so long, it became too late to abort. It's pretty common. They know on one level that they're pregnant, but they can't face it so they just don't think about the reality of it or the future. They hope the whole problem will somehow go away."

He nodded, tearing off a piece of bread. "I remember thinking that way when I was, oh, fourteen, fifteen. Denial is your castle wall keeping out the baying wolves. Or hell, maybe the barbarians."

She wrinkled her nose. "Or the consequences if your mother reads that note from the teacher that's in your bookbag."

"Right," he agreed, then raised a brow. "Is there a story behind that note?"

"Maybe," she said with dignity. "Another time."

"Ah. And here I pictured you as the good little girl with her hand waving in the air every time Teacher plans to call on someone."

She choked on her sip of wine. "Well, yuck! If you think I'm Miss Goody Two-Shoes, why did you ask me out?"

He leered. "Every guy fantasizes about getting under her skirt. Didn't you know?"

"Another yuck."

He laughed again. "No, I don't see you as Miss Goody Two-Shoes, not with that red hair." His gaze seemed to stroke her hair, loose tonight. "But you must have been a good student. Don't you have a master's degree on top of a B.A.?"

"Yes, and I guess I was a good student. Which doesn't mean I didn't get into trouble occasionally. I was a brat when I was twelve and thirteen."

His face momentarily closed, as if he was remembering something unpleasant. "Yeah," he said more soberly, "it's a fun age."

"One of these girls…" She stopped.

He raised his brows. "What?"

"I shouldn't talk about them."

"Do generalities hurt? It's not like I'm going to meet them."

"No, I suppose…" Rebecca trailed off again, then sighed. "She ran away from home when she was only thirteen. Her dad was an alcoholic who sexually abused her."

He swore.

"So guess what she did?"

"Not too many options. Became a hooker, I'm guessing."

Rebecca nodded. "She finally got beaten so badly she ended up hospitalized and then in a shelter. At which point she admitted she was seven months pregnant."

Gary swore again, softly but with force.

"All we can do is pray the baby is okay. Her diet was undoubtedly awful, no vitamins, no prenatal care of any kind. On the upside, she says she didn't use drugs after she realized she was pregnant."

"But the first few months are the most critical, aren't they?"

"Yep." She shrugged. "Well, it turns out she wasn't really into drugs anyway, so I'm keeping my fingers crossed."

Their dinners came then, and she did sample the *bhindi masala,* tastier than she'd expected. Her mango chicken was divine, with the curry and fruit flavors perfectly blended and ripe fruits and vegetables on the side.

Both were content to eat for a while, but at last Gary said, "It sounds like this girl got to you."

"Yeah, she did. She made me realize that I'm going to want to go back to real social work. I don't just want to place her baby, I want to help *her.*"

"If you find the right home for her baby, you are helping her."

"But she needs so much more!" Despair washed over her, but along with it came belief that the fate of children like Brianna could be changed. That she could help change it. That surprised her. She'd quit her last job because she'd lost that faith.

"And you think you can give it to her." He watched her.

"Obviously I can't without resources, but yes. Plenty of families are saved by the right intervention. Kids like Brianna have shelters to go to because of do-gooders like me. That's what you're thinking, isn't it?" she challenged.

"Not about you." The muscles in his jaw spasmed. "But in general…yeah. I think social workers blunder in, see what they want to see, and slap Band-Aids on gaping wounds. Or else they go the other way and perform surgery on skinned knees."

His bitterness shocked her a little. He'd hinted at it before, but she hadn't realized how much misplaced anger he had nursed.

"What is it you blame social workers for? The fact that you went to a foster home? That you weren't adopted right away? Or that your placement didn't turn out to be a happy one?"

He gave a bark of laughter that contained not a grain of genuine amusement. "'Placement'? Boy, that sounds sanitized! The fact is, those people were charged with my well-being. I got shuffled from foster home to foster home, until they gave me into the keeping of a son of a bitch who wanted a farm laborer and was pissed the only way he could get one was to take a little kid and raise him."

She knew it was weak, but suggested, "He might have presented himself well."

Gary snorted, his dark eyes angry. "Aren't

you supposed to dig a little? Find out what people aren't saying?"

"Yes, but that can be hard," she admitted. "It's one thing if they have other children, but if they haven't had their own or adopted before, there's no history to expose, however you dig. You ask questions, and you go with your gut feeling: will these people make good parents?"

"Nobody in their right mind could have thought Harold had it in him to be a good parent."

"What about your adoptive mother?" Rebecca asked, a little hesitantly. His anger at Harold Lindstrom was straightforward enough, but she wasn't sure how he felt about his mother.

Something flared in his eyes that she guessed was pain, but it vanished so quickly she couldn't be sure. He took a bite, ate deliberately, then drained his wine-glass before answering.

"Judith? She was the one who wanted a kid, all right." He shrugged, as if, suddenly, none of it mattered. "She's probably the one who did the talking, who convinced them that she couldn't wait to mother this four-year-old kid who'd taken to biting when he was mad."

"You?"

He inclined his head. "So I'm told."

"Did you bite Harold?"

"Once. He peeled off his belt and used it on my backside." Over the wineglass, Gary's eyes met hers. "That's my first vivid, concrete memory, you know," he said in a conversational tone. "Of screaming and trying to scrabble off a couch while this belt is whistling down onto my butt. Hurt like a—" He stopped. His mouth curled into something like a smile, but not nearly as pleasant. "Never mind."

"Oh, Gary," she whispered. "How awful!"

He shook his head. "Let's talk about something else. I shouldn't have brought it up. Apparently I harbor grudges. But I'm not idiot enough to hold you responsible. I know you do your best."

She hoped, at least, that whatever adoption counselor had placed him as a young boy into the Lindstrom home had been doing his or her best, too. That whoever it was hadn't turned a blind eye because this grieving, angry child was a problem someone was willing to take off his or her hands.

Rebecca made a vow then and there that she'd never succumb to that kind of temptation. Yes, it was frustrating to try to find a permanent placement for a kid so troubled no foster parents wanted to keep him. Or for children with fetal alcohol syndrome or cystic fibrosis, learning disabilities or AIDS. Or the siblings that should stay together, like the Chauvin children had been. When someone came along who seemed to be a solution, as a social worker she didn't *want* to find out anything bad about them.

And that was the real danger: that she would see only what she wanted to see.

On a flutter of panic, she wondered how often she willed herself to be credulous. Beth and Ronald Cooper, for example; were they really as rock solid and kind as they'd seemed? Even Brianna; had the kid conned her? Maybe Daddy never had raped her, maybe that was her automatic sympathy card, her way to play adults that insisted on sticking their noses in her business.

But Rebecca didn't believe it. Not about Brianna, and not about the Coopers. You had to take *some* people at face value. Believe what your heart told you about them.

But what about when she just didn't know?

She stole a look at the man sitting across the table from her, at ease tonight as he seemed to be every time she saw him, but far more complex than the surface suggested.

Old wounds festered. She just didn't know how deeply infected they were. Whether he was capable of normal relations.

Did it matter? she asked herself. She didn't want to marry the man. She just wanted—okay, admit it—to have sex with him. To have a wild, passionate fling.

The quiver of doubt, Rebecca ignored. Her mind shied away, too, from the picture of her saying goodbye to him when he went back to New Mexico.

"Shall we?" he said, and she realized he'd already signed the charge slip and was starting to rise.

On the drive north, darkness having folded around them, lights flashing by in her peripheral vision, Rebecca *didn't* think about Brianna. She was too preoccupied with how *this* evening was going to end.

She wasn't considering asking him in tonight, was she? This was only their second date!

Third, remember? Lunch at Olive's?

She'd paid.

Didn't make it less of a date.

Rebecca hated arguments with herself. They were unwinnable.

No, she wasn't going to ask him in. Not

yet. Right now, just, well, *thinking* about it was enough.

But what if he heads home to Santa Fe while you're still thinking?

Then he did, she told herself stubbornly. And her fling was a no-go.

But it was still too soon.

At her apartment complex, she handed him back the helmet, watched him hang it on the handlebars and then dug out her keys as he strolled beside her to her door.

She unlocked it and turned to him.

His eyes were intent on her face and his mouth had a sensual twist. "Are you going to ask me in?", he said, in the perfect echo of her inner debate.

"No." Her voice squeaked. She swallowed, bit her lip, then said, "But I was looking forward to a good-night kiss before I close the door on you."

"It's been on my mind, too." He lifted a hand, brushed it lightly over her hair, then hesitated with his palm so close to her cheek she felt his warmth. "Damn," he muttered, "I'm half-afraid to touch you."

Despite the cool night air, she was having trouble getting oxygen. But she refused to admit that she knew exactly what he meant.

"I could take offense at that."

His hand settled on her cheek and his thumb rubbed over her lower lip in a way that made heat pool low in her belly.

"I scared you the other night," he said, in a low, rough voice.

"I scared myself," she corrected him. Not entirely true, but close enough.

"Yeah." Although his eyes were shadowed when he dipped his head, she knew he was searching her face. "I scared myself, too."

The next moment, his mouth met hers, so gently her knees buckled just as they had the last time. He suckled her lower lip and let her suckle his, teased the tip of her tongue with his, and then groaned, slanted his head and deepened the kiss.

She fit against him perfectly. The unmistakable bulge of his erection felt wonderfully erotic and affirming. He wanted her. He really wanted her.

She wanted him.

Why wait?

Because he's a stranger, her cooler side cautioned.

Rebecca didn't care.

Yes, she did, but his mouth was doing amazing things to her ability to think. She was pressing against him, whimpering when his lips left hers briefly so that he could nuzzle her throat and growl something under his breath.

"What?" she whispered.

"I've got to go. Now." He let her go so abruptly she almost fell, then he backed away, just as he had last time. He looked grim, almost tormented.

And maybe, she thought, dazed, a little bit scared again.

Just like she was.

"Then…then good night," she said shakily.

"Yeah. I'll call."

She slipped inside her apartment, shut the door, then leaned on it, her forehead against the cool surface.

It *was* too soon.

But, oh, she wished it weren't.

CHAPTER EIGHT

REBECCA STOOD on the street outside Suzanne Chauvin's house the next afternoon, remembering the last time she'd been here, just over a week ago, and seen the dark-haired stranger on the Harley. The way he'd asked her, "Are you Suzanne?", wary but vulnerable at the same time. And, then, of course, the tear-filled scene she'd retreated from. At least now she understood why Suzanne had been so emotional.

Staring at the modest gray rambler, Rebecca let out a long breath. She'd never wanted so much to like a potential adopter, and that in itself was dangerous.

She should have passed the file to another caseworker. But then she'd have had to admit to having started dating Suzanne Chauvin's brother, something she knew all along was ill-advised. He *hadn't* tried to influence her. But she'd had no business putting herself in the position of having a personal stake in what should be as objective a decision as she could make. What if she decided his sister wasn't a good candidate to adopt? Would he shrug and keep calling?

Maybe, she thought, and found herself disturbed because she so easily imagined him indifferent to the pain she'd cause Suzanne.

Oh, damn, she thought in dismay. *I really, really should have asked someone else to make this visit.*

Of course, as long as she liked Suzanne Chauvin, everything would be fine. And she expected to like her.

But what if she didn't?

Last night, she'd promised herself that she would never ignore doubts because she didn't want to examine them. Boy, here was a prime example!

She saw a flash of color at the edge of the window and thought, *Double damn.* Suzanne knew she was here. No retreating now.

So, briefcase in hand, Rebecca walked up the driveway as if she had no reason in the world to hesitate.

The yard looked nice, she made herself note. Not spectacular, but then this was late October, when the ground was sodden, trees bare of leaves, flower beds dark and lumpy.

The neighbor's yard *was* spectacular, she couldn't help noticing, but in a way that might have worried her if it had been Suzanne's. It was too neat, lawn edges yardstick-straight, the hedge precisely trimmed, not a single fallen leaf left even to mulch a bed. Whoever lived there was a major perfectionist.

Suzanne didn't pretend she hadn't been hovering; the moment Rebecca rang, she opened the door. "Hi," she said. "Déjà vu."

Rebecca laughed. "All over again? I had the same thought."

The attractive brunette stood back. "Come in."

The living room was dominated by a hutch that was stuffed with yarns in colors Rebecca couldn't have even named. Beside one of the chairs sat a big basket filled with more, with what looked like a half-knit sweater lying on top. Comfortable chairs, books, a TV—all warm and homey.

At Rebecca's request, Suzanne led her on a tour of the house first, a well-laid-out rambler with three bedrooms and two bathrooms. No family room, and the dining area, part of the kitchen, would have been called a "breakfast nook" in a larger house. The kitchen was scrupulously clean and made

JANICE KAY JOHNSON 185

friendly by copper molds, bright trivets and a teakettle that was black-and-white-spotted like a cow.

Rooms were smallish but adequate. Rebecca knew perfectly well that people cleaned obsessively before home visits. But she saw nothing to make her think Suzanne's wasn't always basically clean. At the same time, there was enough clutter to suggest she'd be fine with the messes a kid makes.

Suzanne led the way down the short hall to the bedrooms, pausing briefly in front of the first open door. "I'll probably keep this as a guest room."

Gary's room, Rebecca realized, although he'd left nothing of his own in sight. The bed was covered with a red-and-white quilt, a fluffy red throw folded at the foot. An oval braided rug covered much of the slightly worn hardwood floor. Closet doors were shut, the bureau top empty.

Although what she'd expect him to leave lying around she didn't know. How much could a guy carry in a motorcycle saddle-bag? Probably not even an electric razor!

"And this," Suzanne said, going to the room across the hall, "I'll decorate for a child. It used to be my yarn room."

Rebecca glanced once more at the bed where Gary slept, imagining him stretching, sitting up in the morning, his chest bare and his jaw shadowed with stubble. Then, giving herself a mental slap, she followed the other woman.

Right now, this second bedroom was pretty much bare. It was painted an undistinguished off-white, and the only furniture was a plain wood dresser.

"When I opened my business, I moved most of my yarn and supplies there, even what I plan to use myself. I thought I'd wait to paint the room and buy furniture once I know whether I'll have a girl or boy. Which is sexist, I suppose," she gave an uncomfortable laugh, "even if I don't necessarily mean pink or blue."

"No, I understand," Rebecca said. "That makes sense."

It would make an ordinary kid's bedroom. Window looking onto the front yard, closet, plenty of room for a twin or even double bed, dresser and desk or toy chest, depending on the child's age. If a room could be said to have a good feel, this one did.

"It'll be perfect." She smiled at Suzanne, who noticeably relaxed.

Rebecca peeked at the bathrooms and at

Suzanne's bedroom, the largest with double closets, a rocking chair upholstered in a floral chintz, and notes and keepsakes tucked around the frame of the mirror over the low, white-painted dresser. Several rugs warmed the hardwood floor, floral patterns that didn't seem to clash with each other or with the rocker. Like the rest of the house, the master bedroom was comfortable, in the nicest possible way. Rebecca always tried to imagine whether a child running in to leap onto the bed to wake adoptive parents in the morning would be welcome.

Here, she had no doubt.

The backyard, small as it was, was perfect for a child, big enough for a swing set and completely fenced with a secure gate. A mature apple tree even looked climbable for the adventurous.

"I don't know what kind of apples they are," Suzanne said. "They're not great for eating, but they make fabulous pies."

She poured them coffee, and they went into the living room to talk.

Rebecca had begun to relax and get over her earlier anxiety. Of course she could be objective! She just wouldn't think about Gary, that was all.

Fortunately, she found herself liking Suzanne as much as she'd expected to from reading the file. She was an unpretentious, restful woman who seemed to be lacking in vanity and was ready to laugh at herself.

They talked about discipline, holiday traditions, children in the neighborhood, Suzanne's dreams about what a child of hers could or should turn out to be like.

Conversation kept wandering, as if they were two friends instead of interviewer and interviewee. Laughing after a funny story about a knitting class, Rebecca had to recall herself to her few concerns about Suzannes's ability to handle a child as well as a fledgling business.

"I wanted to find out more about your family. I know your relationships with your sister and brother are new. Do you expect them to take active roles in raising any child you adopt?"

You'd have asked that anyway, she told herself. *You're not asking so you can find out if Gary is likely to be in Edmonds often.*

Suzanne took a sip of now cooling coffee. "Probably not Gary. As I'm sure you're aware, he lives so far away. I don't know how often he'll be able to visit."

In her pause, Rebecca heard an addendum: *Or want to visit.*

Or perhaps she was imagining things. He seemed to be making this stay an extended one.

"But Carrie is almost as excited as I am. We talk a couple of times a week, see each other almost weekly. She recently married and has a six-year-old stepson, so any child of mine will have a ready-made cousin."

Rebecca made a note on her pad. "You mentioned being raised by an aunt and uncle. Are they in the area?"

"Bellingham. I see them a couple of times a year."

"And did they have children?"

Suzanne talked about her two cousins and their wives and children, but with a level of restraint that made Rebecca suspect they weren't in and out of the house and likely to be babysitting, offering sleepovers or serving as father figures.

"Have you considered how to handle child care? Either in terms of practical arrangements or cost?"

"That was one of the first things I worried about, when I decided I wanted to adopt. But I think my budget can handle it. Depending on how old a child I adopt, I've gotten to know a couple of really nice older women who take knitting classes at my shop who say they'd be interested in after-school care. And if I end up with a two- or three-year-old…well, I'll pay for day care, just like every other working parent does."

They talked about boys versus girls, and Suzanne admitted that she'd been concerned about whether she could serve as the role model a boy needed.

"I know Mark—Carrie's husband—would be around some. We've gotten to be good friends. But, honestly, most of my friends are women. I hope someday to remarry, but I'm not dating anyone at all seriously right now, so I don't know when—or if—that might happen."

"Plenty of single women have raised boys successfully," Rebecca remarked.

"Yes, they have. In fact, some men could have used a little more feminine influence."

They both laughed.

"Have you considered a teenager?"

Suzanne hesitated. "I won't rule out anything, but I suppose my preference would be for younger, for a child who could still come to think of me as Mom. You know? Maybe, I don't know, five to ten or eleven?"

"You do realize that even a five-year-old

who has been abused or abandoned can have significant behavioral issues."

"Oh, sure. That's not what I meant. Just the level of attachment that's likely for us to develop. And also… Well, from a selfish standpoint, I'd like to look forward to more than three or four years before I have an empty nest again."

Rebecca closed her notebook. "I always ask this, and it's not that I have any kids in mind right now. But would you consider taking on siblings who need to stay together?"

Suzanne's eyes widened. "Oh, wow. I should have expected you to ask since…" She waved a hand. "You know what happened to my sister and brother. But… Gosh. I suppose I would if I thought I could handle it financially."

Rebecca smiled. "Don't get too scared! Like I said, it's not as if I have specific children in mind."

Suzanne laughed. "I had this sudden image of bunk beds and a minivan!"

Rebecca closed her briefcase. "I need to write up a report and do some thinking about what kind of child I see as the best match for you, but I should give you fair warning. There are long waits for healthy babies, but older children are another story. Plenty of them are waiting for adoptive homes, so you're not going to have a year to plan."

Suzanne pressed her hand to her chest. "You mean...that's it? You're going to approve me?"

"Yep!" Rebecca chuckled at the other woman's expression. "We've started a background check, gotten a credit report, and spoken to the people you gave as references. And you're right. Carrie is excited."

"I'd forgotten you talked to her." Suzanne gave her head a shake as she rose to her feet with Rebecca. "I'm stunned."

"Why? Did you think being a single woman was a problem?"

"That, and I'm not exactly loaded with money."

"My mother wasn't loaded with money, either. In fact, most parents aren't."

"And if they were, they aren't anymore by the time they put their kids through college. Yeah, I know." She accompanied Rebecca to the door. "It's just that having to beg for a child like this makes you start wondering how you look to other people. I was terrified you'd see nothing but the dandelions in the lawn, the fact that the floors need refinishing and that I'm thirty-two and trying to adopt because my marriage failed and I have no prospects for marriage or family." She puffed out a breath of air. "Wow, that sounded pathetic!"

Opening the door, Rebecca laughed again. "And here I hadn't even noticed the dandelions!"

Suzanne made a face at her own front yard. "How could you miss them? I'm sure the neighbors don't."

"Especially that neighbor." Rebecca nodded toward the razor-edged green sward next door.

"Yeah, he gives me a major inferiority complex. On the other hand, he's been really nice. He's actually mowed my lawn the last month to save me having to get my mower fixed before spring. And I think he fertilized with a weed-and-feed. I noticed some granules clinging to the grass, so I peeked in his garbage can. Which I know is awful of me," she added hastily. "But there were a couple of empty bags."

"He's probably been dying to get his hands on your lawn. So to speak."

Suzanne rolled her eyes. "Which makes me feel guilty and inadequate, but thankful."

"I don't actually have a lawn to take care of, and I'm starting to be glad."

"Oh, but gardening is such fun! Well." She

held out a hand. "Rebecca, thank you. Both for today, and for being understanding about our last appointment."

"How could I help it? Having your long-lost brother show up was pretty amazing."

Her face softened. "It was. I'd lost hope… A couple of times when he and Carrie and I were hanging out, I've had this wave of disbelief. All those years of wondering, of missing them, and here we are together." She shook her head. "This has been the most incredible year."

"And it may get more incredible yet," Rebecca warned.

She left Suzanne standing on her doorstep with a dazed expression, probably imagining school lunches and Christmas morning and a small hand in hers.

Rebecca got into her car and started down the street, glancing in the rearview mirror when she reached the end of the block.

Had she missed anything in her desire to approve Suzanne? She really, truly, didn't think so. Which meant she'd been unbelievably lucky.

Way luckier than she deserved.

GARY SAUNTERED UP to the house at four o'clock, from the porch able to see his sister sitting in her favorite chair in the living room staring straight ahead as if she were watching TV. He craned his neck. Nope. The television wasn't on. What in hell *was* she doing? So far as he could tell from here, even her hands were idle. She never sat without knitting.

Then it hit him. *Oh, crap.* The interview hadn't gone well.

He was surprised by the rage that filled his chest. Damn it, how could Rebecca have failed to see how just plain *nice* Suzanne was? Was she blind? Or had she decided, in some labyrinthine way, that she couldn't approve Suzanne because she'd been prejudiced by dating him?

He took a deep breath and opened the door. "Hey."

She looked up, her eyes glassy.

"Are you okay?" Stupid-ass question; of course she wasn't okay!

But she was nodding. "Yes. I'm fine. Oh, Gary." Her eyes abruptly filled with tears. "I'm going to have a child of my own. Soon!" She hugged herself. "Maybe even before Christmas. I'm...what's that old-fashioned term? Pole-axed. That's it." Her voice was gaining speed, animation. "I don't know why a pole is being axed, but that's me. I think I'm in shock." She swiped at her tears, but she was smiling, too.

His rage fled, leaving him weak and—hell, kind of shaky. He sank onto the couch and said stupidly, "She approved you? Just like that?"

"Yes! Oh, Gary!" Suzanne said again. "You were right. She's really nice. It felt like we were good friends. Once we got talking, I forgot how nervous I was."

"She liked the house?"

"She said the bedroom would be perfect! And that she hadn't noticed the dandelions. But I guess she doesn't have a yard, so maybe she wouldn't."

"She lives in an apartment."

"I even admitted I'd peeked in Tom Stefanic's garbage can. Which could have been awful. What if he'd been throwing away some pornography, or…or…" Her imagination apparently failed her.

"You discovered that he washes all his trash before he discards it."

She laughed. "That's mean, but…"

"Possible?"

"Oh, dear." She wiped her eyes again. "Oh, Gary, I feel so fabulous!"

"Let me take you out to dinner," he said on impulse. "To celebrate."

"That sounds lovely. If it won't leave you short."

He grinned. "I thought I was a business mogul to rival Bill Gates?"

"You haven't really said, you know."

"Over dinner, I'll tell you. Have you called Carrie?"

"Yes. She wasn't home. You're the first person I've been able to tell."

At his suggestion, she tried Carrie again and still got no answer. She shook her head and said, "I'll get my purse. Wait. Maybe I won't. I should ride your motorcycle once at least, shouldn't I? Why not tonight?"

Amused by her expression, which implied that she thought she was being truly daring, Gary laughed. "Why not?"

She put on the helmet, tested it with her hands to be sure it was snug, then climbed on gingerly behind him. He could feel how tightly she was holding on even though he started down the road as slowly as a new driver merging onto the freeway. But when he kept the speed down, Suzanne gradually relaxed her grip. When she got off the Harley in front of the restaurant and took off the helmet, her cheeks were pink.

"That was fun!"

"I told you it is."

Her brow crinkled. "Just driving in Edmonds is tame, isn't it?"

Hilly, residential streets, parked cars on each side, frequent stop signs… You could say so. "Yeah. It is."

"It was still fun."

She'd suggested Anthony's Home Port. He gathered from her pleasure at perusing the menu that she couldn't afford to eat here often. Vegetarian choices were few and far between, so he settled on char grilled halibut, and she chose prawns.

The place had a hell of a view, big windows overlooking the water and the green-and-white Washington state ferry that tooted its horn and steamed away from the dock just as they closed their menus.

Over dinner Suzanne talked excitedly about redoing the bedroom, buying furniture, a bike or tricycle, toys. "Even clothes. Although I suppose most kids who've been in the foster system have some stuff of their own."

He didn't remember. "Probably not a lot."

"I wish I knew whether it would be a girl or boy so I could start! And how old, and…"

Gary laughed at her. "She said it wouldn't be long, right?"

"Yes, but what if it's really sudden, and I don't have time to paint and decorate?"

"People who have kids paint their rooms," he pointed out.

She looked at him as if he didn't understand. "Yes, but I want it to be perfect when she comes!"

"Suzanne." There'd been something that had been bothering him, but he'd figured none of it was any of his business. He wasn't big on concerning himself with other people's motivations or decisions unless they directly impacted him, but he'd done a lot of things lately that weren't usual for him, so why not one more? "You deciding to adopt. This isn't all about what happened to us, is it?"

"You mean, not being able to keep us all together?"

"Yeah." Okay, lay it out: "You're not acting out some fantasy of being able to step into Mom and Dad's role the way it sounds like you wanted to do with us?"

"I'm thirty-two—"

"I know you are," he interrupted. "Most women these days don't seem to start families until they're in their thirties anyway. They don't give up at thirty-two and assume they'll never have kids of their own."

She hadn't yet taken offense, but she was getting there. "I haven't given up."

"Then this is some kind of atonement."

"I suppose it is, in part."

He shifted uncomfortably. "What I'm trying to say is, don't take a kid home because it gives you a glow right now. Make sure you're in it for the long haul."

She still didn't get mad the way he'd expected her to. Instead, she got this gooey look of pity and reached for his hand.

"You think I might be like your adoptive mother."

"This isn't about me."

"Isn't it?" his big sister asked softly.

"I'm saying people have all kinds of reasons for adopting. Just be sure yours is more than redressing some cosmic balance. Because, if the kid's more than three or four, he's already going to be worried that you won't want him if he screws up. If he thinks his job is to make you feel good because you gave him a home, what happens when he decides to find out if that's all he means to you?"

Her eyes had gotten wide. "Is that what happened with you?"

"Goddamn it!" he almost roared, before stealing a look at other diners and lowering his voice. "I keep saying, it doesn't matter what happened to me. Did I test Judith? Shit, yeah. Did she fail? Hell, I don't know. Maybe I failed. The point is, I know this won't be a cakewalk, Suzanne. Don't do it if you don't mean it."

She was silent for a moment, her big brown eyes taking him in as if she'd never seen him before. Finally, she said in a quiet, tremulous voice, "I mean it, Gary. I suppose I was quicker than most people would have been to think of adoption, because of what happened. But mostly, I want to be a mom. I don't need a perfect little angel. If I had a baby, he or she sure wouldn't be. I just want to have somebody who needs me, and who I need…" She had to stop when her voice got shaky. After a moment, she said more steadily, "Is that reason enough?"

"Yeah. That's good. I, uh, had to ask."

"I'm glad you did."

"You're glad?" he said incredulously.

"Sometimes…" She bit her lip. "I don't know how to say this. You seem so…apart from everyone. You're with other people, but not really. And I wonder if you actually care what any of us do or think."

She'd finished in a rush, then sat with her mouth open as if appalled at what she'd said.

She was obviously afraid she'd wounded him. If he showed that she had—and he hadn't made up his mind about that yet—she was the one who would feel bad.

Feeling awkward as hell, he said, "This is all new to me, you know."

Expression perplexed, his sister said, "Well, it's new to us, too."

"No. Not the same way. See, you and Carrie, you're used to having people you're supposed to care about. I'm not."

It was a fact, not something he'd ever regretted, but he could tell that from her point of view he'd just made himself sound pitiful.

"Oh, Gary," she breathed.

Damn, he hated it when her eyes got misty and she looked at him as if he were a puppy with a broken leg lying in the ditch beside the road.

He shook his head. "Suzanne, most people I know don't even like their families. Come on, you don't like yours except for Carrie!"

"And you," she said automatically.

"Ha. You gave yourself away. You *don't* like them."

Her gaze shied from his. "I—"

"You're going to lie."

Her shoulders slumped. "Okay, I guess I

don't like them that well. I love Aunt Marie, but…"

"She lets herself be bulldozed."

Suzanne gave a tiny nod.

"Plenty of us are used to being on our own. I'm not the only one. All I know is, this family thing… I'm probably not very good at it."

"Oh, Gary." This time she said it differently. "Actually, you're pretty amazing at it, considering. I can see sometimes that you're uncomfortable…"

Read: *Wish you could leap on your motorcycle and get the hell out of there.*

"But you stick it out. And you've been… thoughtful. Like tonight." She gestured at the table, the restaurant. "So, thank you."

She was thanking him, because he'd questioned her commitment to taking on a kid.

He shook his head. "How you find a good take on everything, I don't know. You're too damn nice, Suzanne."

She sighed. "Maybe *that's* what scares men off."

Maybe it was. Maybe they were afraid they wouldn't measure up. Gary knew he sure as hell was afraid that sooner or later, he'd disappoint her.

Afraid? Who was he kidding? Sooner or later, he *would* disappoint her.

Funny thing, though. He was beginning to think it wouldn't matter, that she'd still— well, *love* was a strong word, but care about him. Not give up on him.

He had this weird flash, remembering his adoptive mother tucking him in, the hall light creating a halo around her, her voice tender. "I love you, Gary."

So long as you're little and cute and grateful. Because she hadn't loved him anymore when puberty made him clumsy and sullen and needing to be a man and not always mama's little boy.

He almost laughed out loud, harshly. Sure. This sister who'd known him—what—two weeks? was with him through thick and thin. You betcha.

But she was a nice woman who meant well, so he said, "The men you've known are idiots," and she smiled at him as if he was the nicest guy in the whole damn world.

Sooner or later, he thought, and was actually sorry.

CHAPTER NINE

"YEAH, I really like him," Rebecca told her mother. Telephone tucked between shoulder and ear, she set the iron on the stove to cool and folded the ironing board to put it away. Usually she had her week's wardrobe ready Sunday night, but this past weekend she'd never gotten around to ironing. Thus the late-evening realization that she had nothing to wear tomorrow.

"What a shame he lives so far away."

"I don't know if he's the kind to settle down, anyway," Rebecca admitted. "He's really not my type."

"Because you can't picture him mowing the lawn and changing diapers?"

Something in her mother's tone surprised Rebecca. "Shouldn't I be able to picture a guy I'm serious about doing those things?"

"Maybe, but you tend not to give men a chance."

Closet door open, she stopped with the blouses still not hung up. "What do you mean?"

"Even when you were in high school, you were only interested in boys you thought would be the perfect fathers and husbands someday." Her mother laughed. "Of course, not many qualified."

"I had boyfriends."

"Until they disappointed you. Did any of them last more than a few weeks?"

Not in high school. Later, she'd stuck with Guthrie for a year and Aaron for eight months or so. She'd felt guilty about breaking up with both, because they were nice guys. Perfect candidates for husband and father, she realized ruefully. Unfortunately, she'd gotten bored in each relationship.

"Teenage romances aren't supposed to last," she tried to argue.

"I'm not complaining." Her mother's voice was gentle. "Just saying that you seem to be looking for the kind of man you wish your father had been. And maybe that ideal man seen through a child's eyes isn't really who you want to spend your life with."

Her mother changed the subject then, and they chatted about her work and the symphony tickets she'd bought with friends.

Rebecca, a little dazed, was brushing her teeth when the phone rang again.

She spit and rinsed quickly, then padded back into the bedroom to pick up the telephone.

"Hello?"

"Hey," Gary said. "You made Suzanne a happy woman today."

"Which is much closer to my goal in life than crushing hopes is."

"I don't know where that came from."

"Don't you?"

He was silent for a moment. Then said the magic words. "I'm sorry, Rebecca."

Phone to her ear, she sat down on the edge of the bed and said, "It really is okay, Gary. Since you're repenting."

"I missed you today," he said, voice husky.

Her heart squeezed. "I kept thinking about you, too."

"I didn't wake you, did I?"

She glanced at the clock. 9:45. "No, I was getting ready for bed, but I probably won't fall asleep for another hour."

"You want to go for a ride and dinner tomorrow night? I've been looking at the map. We could head up to the Salish Lodge."

"Are you kidding?" she exclaimed. "Do you know how much dinner there costs?"

She could hear the smile in his voice. "You and Suzanne both worry more about my finances than I do."

"I think it would give me indigestion."

"Is that a no?"

"Don't be silly. It's a yes, with bells on."

Gary laughed. "Five-thirty?"

"I'll hurry home."

His voice lowered again, to a sensual burr. "Sleep tight."

"You, too," she all but whispered, before hanging up.

Well, damn. She'd already worried about being able to sleep for wondering if her mother was right about her taste in men. Now she *knew* she wouldn't be able to, not feeling restive, just a little turned on and giddy. Plus, since she'd seen his bedroom at Suzanne's house, she could picture him in it. Turning down the cover, stripping off his shirt and tossing it on the chair, unzipping his jeans. She saw him stretch, muscles elongating, jeans slipping down his lean hips…

She gave a tiny moan that startled her.

Jeez, sleep with the guy and get it over with! Chances were, it wouldn't be anywhere near good enough to get so hot about. It would be fun, she'd later embroider it a little in her memory, because he was sexy and he did wear black leather and ride a Harley, but it wouldn't be life-altering or leave her in a panic because, ohmygod, he's heading back to New Mexico.

Okay, then: tomorrow.

A decision that didn't make falling asleep one whit easier.

NOT MUCH OF a morning person at the best of times, Rebecca slapped the alarm off when it screamed at her, dragged herself into the shower, then got dressed. She ate her bowl of cereal in the kitchen, half perched on a stool at the counter and drank her coffee back in the bathroom while putting on makeup and drying her hair. She didn't once look out the window. Not until she slipped on her suit jacket, grabbed her purse and started out the door did she see the downpour.

Mumbling words her mother didn't know she said, Rebecca scuttled back inside to get her raincoat and umbrella. She glanced down at her panty-hose-clad legs and high-heeled pumps, wished she had time to change to slacks, sighed and went back out the door.

When the rain hadn't let up by lunchtime,

she ordered in a sandwich and called Su-
zánne's house.

Gary answered.

"Somehow," she said, "that ride on the back
of your motorcycle doesn't sound like nearly
as much fun today as it did last night. Besides,
I'd be embarrassed to stroll dripping like a wet
dog into a place as luxe as the Salish Lodge."

"Got to admit, this is one of those days
that I'd take the pickup if I had it. Shall we
can our plans?"

"I was thinking." She took a deep breath,
ignoring the butterflies in her stomach. "I could
drive, but… Why don't I just make dinner?"

"That would be a heck of a lot cheaper."

She laughed. Okay, giggled. "Yes, it
would. For you, anyway."

"That sounds good. I'd invite you here, but
I'd kind of like to have you by yourself."

She sneaked a peek around to be sure no one
was within earshot, then still lowered her voice
as if she were conveying a state secret. "Me,
too. I mean, I'd like to be alone with you."

"I'm glad to hear that. Listen, do you want
me to pick up any groceries?"

"Would you?" she said gratefully. She gave
him a short list and said, "Then I'll see you
at five-thirty, six o'clock?"

"With bells on."

Rebecca was smiling when she hung up.

HE'D HAD women since he and Holly Lynn parted ways, but only a couple, and even then he'd been a little ashamed of himself because he knew he just wanted female companionship and sex. He guessed he'd been attracted, but he could hardly remember either woman's face.

This was supposed to be the same. A little release from the stress of letting himself get enfolded in the bosom of his family.

Yeah, well. Relief wasn't what he felt.

Nope, he was fluctuating between desire that kept him tossing and turning at night and the uneasy knowledge that he liked Rebecca Wilson more than he'd ever liked a woman before.

Like wasn't a word he used for many people, and most of those were buddies. Guys. Bob, who worked for him, and Jagger who'd bought into ownership of Chimayo Coffee Company a couple of years ago. McGinnis, who'd taken him on trust and set him back on his feet when he was a scared, desperate kid. McGinnis's wife, Martha, yeah, he'd liked her, too. From the beginning, she'd treated him as if he were her son. He didn't think he'd ever told her what that meant to him.

But even Holly Lynn. Gary couldn't remember ever thinking he *liked* her. He'd had the hots for her, sure. She'd been sharp and funny, but, thinking back, he doubted she had Rebecca's need to do good. To heal. And maybe that's what he found himself craving.

Crap, Gary thought in dismay. He wasn't deluding himself that she could heal *him,* was he? With the balm of her love, and all that hokum?

If so, it was past time he headed home. This little vacation had already stretched into almost two weeks, counting travel time, and just today, after discussing a potential new account with Jagger, he'd said, "You know, I'm going to hang around another week or two. Since you don't seem to need me."

"Nah, we're good," his friend and VP said, promptly enough to bring a reluctant grin to Gary's face.

"It's nice to be missed."

"Man, you've had a dark cloud around you this last year. You needed to get away. When's the last time you took a vacation that lasted more than two days?"

Never.

"This isn't what I'd call a vacation. No sun," he cast a sardonic glance at the slanting rain outside the window, "no babes in bikinis…"

"No babes at all?" Jagger asked.

"Uh…"

"Yeah. Thought so." His burly friend had a deep, rolling laugh. "Go get some, buddy. No hurry coming home."

Remembering Jagger's parting shot, Gary hoped like hell he would be getting some tonight.

Maybe even more, he hoped it wasn't nearly as good as he thought it would be.

That good could be dangerous.

Suzanne knew he wouldn't be home for dinner, so he donned rain gear and headed out to the store. He was dripping when he rang Rebecca's doorbell.

She opened the door and reached immediately for the grocery bags. "Oh, no! Look at you! Come in." She stepped back. "Um… why don't you take those off right here? I'll get you a towel."

He was down to jeans and a sweater by the time she left the groceries in the kitchen and returned with a towel for him to dry his face and hair.

"Does it rain all winter like this?" he asked, giving his head a shake.

"Not usually this hard. But, sure. Seattle's the Rainy City, you know."

"It could get really old."

"But that's how Washington stays so green."

"Uh-huh. Desert plants are pretty, too."

She laughed at him, leading the way to the kitchen. "Wimp."

"That's me." He watched her delve into a grocery bag. "What are we having for dinner?"

Enjoying just looking at her, he didn't much care what they were eating.

She'd hit him hard the first time they met, but that had just been the beginning. Somehow she got prettier every time he saw her. Which was not theoretically possible, but was happening anyway.

She'd obviously changed clothes since she got home from work, because instead of a suit and heels, she wore a pair of black, wide-legged pants that were probably meant to be comfortable but also outlined her butt and thighs in a way that made lifting his gaze to her face a challenge. A V-necked, three-quarter sleeve sweater in a rust red that reminded him of the Southwest mesas made her pale skin even creamier and her freckles more pronounced. Didn't hurt that it hugged her breasts and bared a glimpse of cleavage.

Freckled cleavage.

She was fine-boned, her cheekbones delicate, her lashes and brows a deep auburn. Her hair was curlier than usual today, maybe because of the humidity.

He was surprised she hadn't quelled it in a braid, rather than leaving it wild.

Turning away, she answered his question without having noticed his scrutiny. "A shiitake-ginger pasta with radicchio. Rolled up in a pita." She glanced over her shoulder at him where he lounged, one hip against the counter. "Unless you hate mushrooms? Or it just plain sounds awful?"

"No, could be interesting." Nice, he reflected, that she'd chosen not to serve meat, knowing he didn't eat much of it. "What can I do?"

She set him to chopping both common mushrooms and the shiitake she'd had him buy into small chunks while she put water on to boil for the farfalle pasta he'd also picked up at the store.

Good thing; he needed distracting.

They talked while she got the wok hot and he went on to mincing ginger and garlic.

"One of those girls I told you about the other day has changed her mind. She's decided to keep her baby."

"The one who'd been a hooker?"

"No, thank goodness. That would be a disaster in the making." Rebecca shook her head at the thought. "The other one. Her parents are in their mid-fifties and weren't enthusiastic about starting all over with a baby, but when it got down to it, they didn't want to let their grandchild go, either. The three of them have come up with a plan."

"Do you feel like a fisherman when a big one got away? Or like they made a good choice?"

"Oh, a little of both," she admitted. "We have so many nice couples waiting for babies, and my favorite part of the job is calling and saying, 'You have a baby daughter.' But I also don't want anyone to feel regret down the line. In this case, they were an unusually stable family to be exploring the option of surrendering the baby for adoption. No, I think they'll manage fine. She'll grow up faster than she should have, but that's life."

Yeah, it was. You lived with your decisions, in Gary's book. You didn't farm 'em out to other people.

The other girl, the one who'd never gotten a break, she was another story. She deserved a childhood of her own, if someone could figure out a way to give her one.

"You ever tempted to adopt a kid yourself?" he asked her. "Seeing what you do every day?"

"Constantly. I actually did take in a foster child for six months back when I was still with DSHS. It was a good experience. But she needed a real family, not to come home to an empty apartment after school every day, and we found her one. I've stayed in touch with her. In fact, we've made tentative plans to go shopping this weekend."

Why wasn't he surprised? Of course she'd taken in a kid who needed her. That's who she was.

Unease rippled through him. Was that what she was doing with him? Had they slapped together like peanut butter and jelly because he so obviously needed rescuing and she was so obviously good at it?

God, he hoped not.

He hadn't liked the notion that he wanted her to heal him, and he liked even less the idea that she was attracted to him because he was as pathetic in his own way as the kids she spent her life saving.

He realized suddenly that she was looking at him funny, apparently waiting for an answer to some comment he hadn't heard. Hiding his disquiet, he said, "Sorry. Mind wandered for a minute."

"Work?"

"Hm? Oh. Yeah. I talked to my second in charge today. Guy named Jagger DeLong." At her expression, he grinned. "In a drunk moment, he admitted to me that his real name is Horace."

"Wow. Not much you can do with that. Poor guy."

"His brother is Delmore. I met him once."

She wrinkled her nose. "He hasn't acquired a nickname?"

"Actually, I think he takes pride in being a nerd, and the name fits. He's some kind of computer geek with Google."

"The name doomed him to being a computer geek."

He laughed. "Yeah, probably. Of course, he's rich, so there are worse things."

Conversation briefly lapsed while the pitas were warming in the oven and she was stir-frying. Over her shoulder, she said casually, "You haven't talked much about growing up. I've never been to Bakersfield. Is it nice?"

He shrugged. "Small town. Hot, dry. Irrigation is all that makes farming possible."

"What kind of farming did your dad do?"

"He isn't my dad."

The harsh words hung in the air. She turned, obviously startled.

Gary swore. "Sorry. You took me by surprise."

"No, I'm sorry. I knew you didn't like him, but I assumed you still thought of him as your father."

"I never thought of him as my father." The edge had crept back into his voice, and he rotated his shoulders to ease the tension he felt every time he thought of Harold. "Even when I was little. I remember Judith saying things like, 'Go tell your daddy dinner is ready,' and me thinking, He isn't my daddy. So I just didn't call him anything. You'd be surprised how easy that is. Later, I took to using his name." On a note of wry humor, he added, "I could inject a heck of a lot of snottiness into 'Harold.'"

Taking the pitas from the oven, she smiled over her shoulder. "Oh, I can imagine."

"Here, I'll take those."

They carried the warm ingredients and a fruit salad she'd made earlier to the table, along with a Washington State white wine and glasses.

Woodward Canyon, he noted, after pouring and sipping. Not bad. He'd heard eastern Washington had turned into wine country, but hadn't sampled any of the region's product.

Ladling the mushroom and pasta mix into a pita, Rebecca said, "So what about your adoptive mother? You called her by name, too?"

He didn't know why she cared, but shrugged. "No, she was Mommy when I was little. Took awhile. The word stuck in my throat, I guess because I still remembered my real mom. I doubt I understood the concept of death. Maybe if I had, I'd have adjusted better in the foster homes. I don't know."

Rebecca was watching him with eyes that were soft with compassion, but she didn't say anything.

"Eventually I spit it out. When I got to eight or nine, she became Mom."

"Why isn't she still Mom?"

He hated talking about this stuff, but didn't

see a way out. So he put it as succinctly as possible. "Moms don't ditch their kids."

"Did you know she was going?"

"Harold had hit her a couple of times, and she'd scream, 'You do that again and I'm gone.' I don't think either of us believed her."

"You mean," her expression was appalled, "she didn't even say goodbye?"

He sipped wine and pretended none of this bothered him anymore. "Yeah, she did. She drove me to school that morning. Turned out, her suitcases were in the trunk. She waited until I was opening the car door to say she'd had all she could take and was leaving."

Gary remembered the moment as if it had happened yesterday. He could still hear kids yelling, the buzz of conversation, the squeal of school bus brakes. Feel the heat of the day leaking in, even with the car door only six inches open. His own shock as he froze, hand on the door and his bookbag lifted to sling over his shoulder.

"What about me?" he'd asked, and knew the minute he saw her face. She'd looked uncomfortable. Ashamed.

"You're going to have to stay with your dad for now. Once I've settled and have figured out how to make a living, I'll call. Then we can talk about it. Okay?"

"Sure," he'd said with a shrug, as if he didn't give a rat's ass. But he'd scrambled out of the car and slammed the door so fast, he didn't hear whatever it was she was still trying to say.

In his dreams, it was, *I love you. Please try to understand, Gary.* Maybe that's what she'd said. Maybe not. He didn't suppose it mattered.

Voice soft, Rebecca asked, "Did she ever call?"

He shook his head and took a bite, eating as if he tasted what was in his mouth.

"Maybe she did, and got your…Harold."

That's what he'd told himself, back when delusions helped keep him going.

He didn't play those games anymore. "Then she could have tried again."

"Battered women—"

"Usually don't leave their kids behind." He met her gaze, his own demanding truth. "Do they?"

After a moment, she bit her lip and shook her head.

"I don't think she would have when I was younger," he said. "Maybe I'm why she stayed as long as she did. I don't know. But when I hit about twelve, I started getting lippy with her, too, not just Harold. I remember feeling mad that she didn't do anything to rein him in. That she didn't leave him and take me with her." His mouth tilted into a humorless smile. "Never occurred to me that if I wasn't nice, she'd go and not take me."

"Oh, Gary! It wasn't your fault!"

"Fault?" he echoed in surprise. "That she didn't love me the way…" he had to clear his throat. "The way my own mother might have? Maybe not. But I sure as hell did forget which side my bread was buttered on."

He was flat-out horrifying her. "You were a child!"

"Kids can calculate, too." He lifted his glass. "Good wine."

"What?"

"Good wine," he repeated.

"I heard you. It's…" She shook her head. "Who cares? Gary…"

"It's done," he said. "She went. I never heard from her again. But that was, what, fifteen, sixteen years ago?"

"Have you ever considered trying to find her?"

"One of my sisters asked that, too. Why would I?"

Rebecca looked like she wanted to shake him. "Curiosity?"

"I'm not curious."

"I don't believe you!"

"What are we talking about here? Idle curiosity? Sure, it might be interesting to know what happened to her. Did she remarry? Have kids? End up happy? Then I start wondering whether she ever thinks about me, and I'm not so sure I want her to have ended up happy. Which makes me feel like a self-centered SOB. But back to your question. Are you really asking whether I want to find her? As in, touching reunion? No. She sent her message loud and clear. She was done with me."

"You don't know…"

"Yeah, I do. I don't know *why*. But does that matter anymore?"

Saint Rebecca said, "What if something awful happened to her? What if she ended up living in a shelter, or got sick? What if she left partly because she knew she was dying of breast cancer?"

He had to laugh, and about a subject that rarely amused him. "Skipping all treatment, she nobly set out into the world so that her snotty teenage adopted son wouldn't have to see her go through the rigors of chemotherapy? Is that what you're suggesting?"

She glared at him. "You don't have to make it sound so...so..."

"Ridiculous? Unlikely?"

Gary laughed again, watching her struggle to think of a more palatable word.

"Get real," he said. "Judith left because her husband was beating her. And, hey, he'd been a jackass all along. Her sweet little boy had metamorphosed into a sullen teenager who bewildered her as much as the jackass did. She had no idea what to say to him, how to deal with his moods, whether Harold wasn't right in believing that the belt was the answer to all problems. So she threw up her hands and saved herself. End of story."

Rebecca's mouth was still opening and closing.

Gary pushed back his chair, circled the table and kissed her. When he straightened again, grinning at her, she pressed her fingers to her lips.

"What was that for?"

"To save you from the necessity of talking." He sauntered back to his seat. "And because I wanted to kiss you."

Of course, she fixated on the first. "Save me from talking?" Her voice rose. "What an insufferable thing to say!"

"You didn't want me to kiss you?"

"Not to shut me up!"

He was beginning to realize that she was seriously ticked off.

"Rebecca, I'm kidding. Half kidding. You can say anything you want. What I'm trying to tell you is not to bother peering through those rose-colored glasses and coming up with excuses for Judith. You think I didn't dream up every one of them myself back then?" Heat had entered his voice. He didn't like it, clamped down on the renewed anger at someone who'd been gone from his life for a long, long time. "Here's news: I did. But finally I grew up and faced facts. Sad facts, maybe, but I don't want to live in a damned dream. Finding Judith now would be asking for a sucker punch to the gut."

Rebecca thought that through, her face expressive. "Point taken," she finally conceded. "I guess I do tend to want to be hopeful."

He smiled at her. "That's one way to put it." Maybe, he thought, nobody could have her passionate belief in the ability to change people's lives without first possessing a warehouse full of hope. Most people's stingy gunny sackful would be expended in weeks, working at a place like that government agency.

It hit him with a shock that he didn't just like her, he admired her for her convictions and for her ability to deal in hope. A man who'd spent a lifetime despising the kind of do-gooders who thought they could rearrange lives as if they were cooks playing with ingredients, free to mix 'em any way they damn well pleased. And now he *admired* a woman for doing just that?

Think about it later, he ordered himself. *Not now. Now, to quote Jagger, you're going to get some.*

"Would you like some dessert?" Rebecca asked, starting to rise to her feet. "I have mango sorbet...."

"Maybe later," he interrupted. "Right now, I think I'd like to kiss you again."

"Oh." Her redhead's skin flushed rosy pink. "That does sound nicer than mango sorbet."

"Nicer?" His voice had lowered by the time they met at the foot of the table. "'Nice' wasn't what I had in mind."

She melted into his arms and lifted her

face. He kissed her with pure erotic intent, and she answered the same way. Just like that, they were both hot—tongues tangled, hips rocking, her moans playing counterpoint to the rough sounds that escaped him when he left her mouth long enough to taste her throat and suck her earlobe.

Seemed dinner had been enough foreplay. Maybe arguing had been. All he knew was, this wasn't going to be leisurely.

He got a grip on the hem of her sweater and peeled it up until he had to quit kissing her, then pulled it off, giving him a glimpse of creamy skin, pale freckles and a lavender satin bra. But her mouth was swollen and damp and he had to kiss it again, even as he reached for the bra catch.

He fumbled and swore against her mouth, making her laugh in a shaky way.

"I can—"

"No, I've got it. Damn." He licked the hollow at the base of her throat. "Yes!"

The bra fell loose, and he slipped it from her shoulders. It dropped between them. Gary didn't notice. He was too captivated by the sight of her breasts and dusky, peaked nipples.

Groaning, he gripped her buttocks and

hoisted her so he could take as much of her breast into his mouth as he could get. She squeaked and wrapped her legs around his waist, gripping his shoulders. He lifted his head with the intention of trying the other breast and paused just to drink in the sight of her. Head thrown back, bare from the waist up, hair tumbling loose, she looked like a Valkyrie, some glorious fantasy heroine.

At some point, he staggered into the living room and dumped her on the couch, then followed her down. It wasn't really long enough for them to stretch out, but he didn't give a damn. He was too busy yanking her pants off, tiny lavender panties and all.

Oh, yeah. She was the genuine package, all right. Deep auburn curls at the juncture of white thighs. Gary shuddered and closed his eyes. *Not too fast.*

But Rebecca's fingers fumbled at his waist, and he wrenched off his shirt while she was dealing with his pants in an intensely pleasurable if inefficient way. She wrapped her hand around him, sliding up and down, then kissed him even before she'd gotten his jeans below his hips.

"Wait," he said in a strangled voice, as they finally dropped. "I brought…"

"I'm on the pill." Her gaze flashed to his. "You're not…"

"No, but I'll wear a condom anyway." Although, God, he was tempted. To slide into her, nothing between them…

He found the damned packet in his back pocket, stepped out of the jeans and kicked them aside, then ripped the top off the metallic package.

"Afraid of where I've been?"

He didn't have to ask to know she hadn't been all that many places. "Just don't want you sorry tomorrow."

"Oh! Can I?" She held out her hand for the condom.

He let her take it and, with agonizing slowness, roll it onto him. By the time she was done, he was sweating. He bore her down, his hand between her thighs, stroking, taunting, testing.

Her hips rose; she let out a little cry. "Gary…"

"Now?" he whispered.

"Yes." Her legs wrapped his, pulled him toward her. "Now."

He braced one foot on the floor and entered her, hard and fast, beyond finesse. Her back arched and he squeezed one breast as he pulled out, pumped. His vision had narrowed until he saw nothing but her flushed face and big moss-green eyes that didn't look away from his, her wild red hair clinging damply to her forehead and his shoulders.

She was the whole damn world. His whole world. He was nothing but sensation and her, hanging on to a thread of sanity.

"Come," he said hoarsely, as he rotated his hips and pushed deep.

She keened and her body shivered, gripping his in a tight, long squeeze.

Gary let himself fall. Incredible, deep, ripples of pleasure and release like nothing he'd ever felt seemed to pull the marrow out of his bones. Emptied him, weakened him, left him collapsed atop her.

Only, she didn't seem to mind. Her arms and legs both clasped him still, as though she wasn't going to let him move away.

They lay there for the longest time, their heartbeats gradually slowing, their skin cooling, their cheeks pressed against each other, his face buried in her glorious hair.

Awareness crept back in. He didn't welcome it.

Because—shit!—making love with this woman hadn't just been as good as he'd feared.

It had been better. Mind-blowingly, never-match-this-with-another-woman better.

Scary better.

His eyes opened wide and his muscles began to tighten with a panicky desire to run.

Time to figure out what to say to get him out of here without hurting her feelings.

CHAPTER TEN

LAST NIGHT, Rebecca hadn't minded that Gary had left somewhat abruptly. He'd probably had no idea what to say. Heaven knows she didn't! They had known each other such a short time. And then, to make love like that. Right there in her living room, not even making it to her bed...

She'd never gotten aroused so fast, or lost her inhibitions like that. Just remembering, she felt color mount in her cheeks and sneaked a look to be sure no one was passing in the hall outside her office to see her. She'd practically stripped him! And...and nuzzled him. She'd never done anything like that before!

In fact, she could see now how tame her previous sexual experiences had been. How unsatisfactory. No wonder she hadn't particularly cared when the relationships fizzled. The sex already had.

But this...this was amazing. Somehow

he'd made her feel beautiful and wanton and *free*. It wasn't until afterward, when they lay there and he didn't say anything and then she felt him begin to withdraw into himself even before he'd moved a muscle that she became self-conscious.

When he sat up, said casually, "Well, this couch isn't quite comfortable enough to stay on," and began pulling on his pants, that self-consciousness had encouraged her to grab for her own clothes, too.

She'd chattered. About how she'd considered a bigger couch, but the apartment was really pretty small and she'd been afraid they wouldn't be able to get it in the door and similar inane subjects he couldn't possibly have cared less about.

She didn't say, *Maybe we should move to the bedroom, then.* Because he already knew she had a bedroom, and *he* hadn't suggested it.

He'd offered to help clear the table and wash dishes, and she'd tugged her top over her head to avoid meeting his eyes and said, "Oh, no. It won't take me long at all. You already helped make dinner. *And* you grocery shopped, don't forget."

"Hard labor," he'd said, looking amused but also…something else. Something she couldn't put her finger on. Mostly, he just wanted to be gone. Out of her apartment. She could *feel* it, even though outwardly he was relaxed and friendly.

She'd let him go gracefully. What else could she do?

"I've got an early morning tomorrow," she'd said, as if hinting, and he didn't point out that it was only eight-thirty and she had told him herself that she rarely fell asleep before eleven.

At the door he kissed her on the cheek— the cheek! A quick peck, a casual, "I'll call," and he was gone. She closed her door and stood just inside, hearing the rumbling when he started his motorcycle, then drove away.

The weird part was, instead of being hurt Rebecca had been almost relieved. She'd needed to process what she had felt, what it meant. She wanted to be alone to remember every moment, every touch, every sensation.

It wasn't until now that the chill set in and she wondered whether he would call.

No, she knew him better than that! Of course he'd call, if only to say goodbye.

He hadn't mentioned departure plans, but he'd been here… Rebecca had lost track. Was it even two weeks yet? He had a business.

Friends. Maybe even a girlfriend, although she hated to think that. A life.

This had been an interlude, nothing more. She'd known she'd be heartsore when he left.

She just hadn't known quite how much it would hurt. She'd romanticized the idea of a passionate fling. Imagined herself many years from now taking out a photo of him—which she didn't actually have—and smiling in remembrance.

Now, staring at the computer screen but not seeing a word on it, Rebecca became conscious of dismay welling from her midsection, spreading to paralyze her heart.

Oh, God. He would go back to New Mexico, and she'd never see him again.

And she was falling in love with him.

Shivering, she wondered how she could have been so stupid. Stupid to fall in love with a man who had so many issues, stupid not to have realized what was happening to her before she'd done the stupidest thing of all.

Given herself to him, heart, body and soul.

GARY HAD LAIN awake most of the night. He'd made some excuse to Suzanne when she commented on how early he was home, using the fact that he was drenched as an escape to retreat to a hot shower and then his bedroom.

The rain had hammered on the roof all night long, a loud accompaniment to his unrest. About the time the sky outside his window grudgingly faded from black to gray, he decided he was going home as soon as the weather cleared. He finally fell asleep and didn't wake until long after Suzanne had left for the shop.

The downpour hadn't abated when he made himself coffee and went to stand in front of the window in the living room. Water rushed into a culvert by Suzanne's driveway and overflowed her gutters. They were probably filled with leaves and fir needles; he suspected that cleaning out gutters was the kind of task she put off.

Well, he couldn't leave today anyway. He wasn't that big a bastard, although he felt like scum right now. Sure, screw a good woman and then run. What was it he'd thought last night? That he'd "get some"?

Crap. He'd known all along that Rebecca wasn't the easy type. Did she think they had something long-term going? He guessed she did, or she wouldn't have given herself to him so willingly.

But long-term… The very idea made him twitchy. He didn't even know why. He'd been okay when Holly Lynn wanted to get married, even when they'd said "I do" in front of the magistrate. He hadn't felt any of this terror that was gnawing at him like the mother of all ulcers.

So why now? Why Rebecca?

His mind kept jumping around. He didn't want to confront the answers to his own questions.

He could wait until the rain let up, see if Suzanne had a ladder, clean her gutters. Find out if there were any similar tasks he could do for her before he went back to New Mexico.

He'd offer to help her out financially, too. Despite the government's best efforts to take every cent he made, he was doing more than okay. Not spending anywhere near what he brought home. He didn't like knowing he had plenty and Suzanne was struggling. She'd been nice to him.

And then there was that way of looking at him she had, the one where her eyes grew moist and he knew she was still flooded with guilt because, as a six-year-old kid, she hadn't managed to keep her little brother and sister with her.

Yeah, he'd stay a few more days, at least, he decided, ignoring the way tension in his chest and belly eased. See Rebecca a few more times, not leave her thinking all he'd wanted was to get down her pants. She knew he'd have to head home soon, that wasn't news to her. He just didn't like the idea of her feeling ashamed of their brief relationship. Hey, he didn't want to carry shame in his baggage, either.

He spent a good part of the day cleaning and reorganizing Suzanne's garage. He could tell she'd made some effort, probably because of Rebecca's home visit, but about all she'd managed was to sweep and toss a new tarp over the pile of broken furniture. Sometime in the past, she'd bought shelving and then never gotten around to hanging it.

Gary put the shelving up, took a trip despite the rain to a hardware store for hooks and hangers of various kinds to make use of rafters and a dusty peg board above an unused workbench. The only possessions—*things*—that Gary valued were tools. He'd been sorry about that vintage Harley he'd totalled. But he'd been able to shrug. He could restore another one. His everyday working tools, though, each had a place in his garage and he kept them in mint condition. They were useful. Maybe, he reflected, that was one of the few valuable lessons he'd learned from Harold.

He shook his head at the neglect out here. Shovels and hoes were rusty, the lawn mower was dirty, the blade caked with dirt and dried wads of grass. Pruning shears, dull and rusting, lay atop the hot water tank; worn, worthless furniture cluttered the middle of the garage under that shiny blue tarp; and a corner was occupied by flowerpots, still filled with dirt, that Suzanne had brought in for the winter. There were heaps of boxes filled with God knew what—it wasn't likely Suzanne did. Gary shook his head. Did the woman ever throw anything away?

Tools first. He used steel wool and a rasp and oil, doing the best he could to restore them to a functional condition, then hung them. Long-handled tools in a neat row by the garage door, hand tools on the peg board. She had a compost bin out back. He dumped soil from the pots, then stacked them. Miscellaneous crap and smaller cardboard boxes went on the shelves. Larger ones he put beneath the workbench. The furniture...

Gary shook his head. Some of it might sell at a garage sale. Maybe.

Midafternoon he took out his cell phone and sat on a rickety kitchen chair to call Rebecca.

"Hey," he said when she answered. "I've spent the day wishing I hadn't gone home so soon."

She laughed. "And here I thought you'd be a tiny speck on the horizon, running as fast as you were."

With a grimace, he said, "That obvious?"

"Afraid so." At least she sounded cheerful. "That's okay. I was a little shaken myself. I, uh, don't do things like that very often."

"I figured." A smile tugged at his mouth. "Things? Now, let me think. What things did we do?"

"You don't want me blushing at work, do you?"

"But you blush so well."

"Oh, yeah. That's one thing redheads really can do. We fire up like a hot stove."

"You are hot," he murmured, grinning at the choked sound she made.

"Damn it, Gary! Now I am blushing!"

"Couldn't help myself. You hung yourself out for that one."

They bantered for a few more minutes.

Finally, he said, "Carrie's coming up for dinner tonight, so I'm tied up. You free tomorrow?"

"It's still supposed to be raining."

"I noticed. We could stay in again. I'll even volunteer to cook."

"That sounds nice, Gary. Oh, just a minute." She must have covered the phone, because all he heard was muffled voices. Then she came back. "I've got to go. I'll see you tomorrow? Same time, same place?"

"Yep. Question. Do you have Italian spices? Oregano, basil, thyme?"

"Sure."

"I make a prize-winning marinara sauce."

"Um. Sounds good." Somebody started talking to her in the background, and they signed off.

So, a little voice in his head asked, *you planning to get some again before you go? That what you're going to her place for?*

He told it to shut the hell up.

The voice fell silent, but smugly, having made its point.

"So what do you want me to say?" He glared around the garage, as if his alter ego stood there shaking his head over him like a disappointed schoolteacher. "I'm in love with her? Sorry. Ain't happening."

Yeah? But you just said it.

How did you punch yourself out? Gary snorted, stood and went back to work.

SUZANNE STOOD in the doorway and gaped at her garage. "Gary! You did all that in one day?"

"I should have started doing something useful sooner." He shook his head at the days he'd wasted. "If you're going to have a kid around the house, you'll need to keep a bike out here, maybe a sled for winter—you do get snow, don't you? Basketball, soccer ball, baseball. Who knows."

Her eyes filled with tears, as was her habit whenever she got emotional. "It's beautiful!"

He hated to be the one to give her the news, but felt obligated. "Not yet. I didn't, uh, feel like I could go through your stuff…"

Her saving grace was her sense of humor. She laughed, if in a watery way. "Tempted though you were?"

"You've got to admit, there's not much worth salvaging in that pile." He nodded toward the furniture.

"No, I suppose not…" She walked over to it. "I just hate to discard furniture that could be mended or refinished. That dresser, for example…"

"Wood's swelled," he informed her. "Drawers don't want to open."

"Oh. Maybe it *isn't* worth refinishing."

"It might be for someone. You don't have time. You'll have less time once you have a kid."

"I don't have a pickup to haul it to the dump."

"Why not have a garage sale? You might have stuff in some of those boxes to get rid of, too."

"Well, of course I do! I've been embarrassed to have one because it was such a mess out here. Hmmm." She looked around. "But now... I could use the money."

"There you go."

She turned her head. "Oh! I hear the doorbell. It must be Carrie. Wait here, I'll get her." Starting to turn away, she spun back and gave him a quick hug. "Thank you, Gary."

He stood there in the middle of the garage, chagrined to realize he had been moved by something so minor. But he couldn't remember the last time anyone had hugged him out of simple affection.

Suzanne reappeared with Carrie, who oohed and aahed some more. "Gosh, you can visit me anytime," she told him with a grin.

It seemed tidiness didn't run in this family.

Maybe something else Gary should thank Harold for. Not words he'd ever expected to even *think*.

Carrie had brought the makings for burritos, and they cooked together more companionably than he would have imagined when he arrived—was it only ten days ago? She talked about her classes and her excitement to begin practice teaching the next year.

"Michael thinks I should apply to his school." She laughed, spooning black beans onto the tortillas. "I told him I'll wait until he's in middle school, *then* get a job where I can keep an eye on him. He wasn't convinced that I'll ever embarrass him."

Suzanne laughed. "Aunt Marie agreed to chaperone an eighth-grade dance when I was at the middle school. It was the most humiliating evening of my life. She talked to everybody, teachers, kids, other parents. She kept pointing me out! She wasn't supposed to be friendly, she was supposed to lurk out of sight."

"She was there," Gary said, stopping the conversation dead.

They both looked quickly at him, then Suzanne said, "Of course you're right."

Way to dampen spirits, he congratulated himself. She *knew* she'd been lucky that her aunt had been there. God! She remembered losing their parents. Even then, she hadn't been an idiot, just a typical teenager.

Eighth grade, that was the year Judith dropped him in front of the school and said her not-so-tender goodbyes. In seventh grade, he might have been embarrassed if she'd chaperoned a school dance, too— assuming he'd ever been able to go to them.

Eighth grade, he'd have given anything to have had her around. She could have walked him to class every morning and he wouldn't have minded.

Instead, he'd spent the rest of that year waiting for her call. Knowing in his heart it wouldn't come, but still clinging to a shred of hope anyway.

He looked at his sisters, both concentrating on assembling the burritos, and wished he could take back the words. *At least she was there.*

They'd both had someone there, and now they felt bad for him because he hadn't. He was lucky Suzanne wasn't getting weepy again at his tragic childhood.

"Did you ever dance at those things?" he asked.

"Me?" Suzanne glanced at him. Probably

relieved to be thrown a line, she began chattering again. "Oh, a few times. I only slow-danced once in middle school, and I lived in a dream for about two weeks afterward. I secretly tried out my married name a few thousand times instead of taking notes during class. The next thing I knew, he was 'going' with this girl I hated even before she stole him from me. What about you?" She cocked her head. "Did you have a girlfriend when you were that young?"

A girlfriend implied something more romantic than he remembered, but he shrugged. "Deborah Wyatt. Her dad's farm was maybe a mile down the road. She was an older woman." He grinned at his sisters. "Two years older."

They made noises to indicate how impressed they were, and he resumed, "I was fourteen the first time we had sex. I used to sneak out at night to walk to her dad's farm. She'd climb out her bedroom window and we'd go up in the loft in the barn."

"Were your friends impressed?" Carrie asked.

He'd had guys he hung out with at school, but no one he called friend. Anyway, he'd been closemouthed even then.

"No one would have believed me. Deborah and I had a torrid secret affair. Hey, I was a little kid by the standards of her friends. We sat together on the bus sometimes, pretending we hardly knew each other. Otherwise, we were never seen in public together."

"But I'll bet you were dark and brooding and sexy even then," his little sister said. "She was crazy! Her friends would have been jealous."

"Skinny, pimply and sulky is closer to the mark." Although he did brood.

"Were you seeing her 'til you ran away from home?" Suzanne asked.

Gary shook his head. "She'd started dating a guy who went to our community college. I'd hear her on the bus talking about him. Her voice would rise so she could be sure *everyone* heard. 'Ian called me so-o late last night,'" he mimicked. "'He had a midterm in psych today. At BC, you know.'"

Carrie rolled her eyes. "Like anyone cared."

Gary imagined having had her around all those years, growing up. Maybe it wouldn't have been so bad, not if the two of them had stayed together. Harold might have had a soft spot for her, the spunky little girl. Judith might not have left.

"I can just hear you, if you'd been on that bus. This snotty kid announcing, 'Does anyone care what classes dumb Ian is taking?'"

She didn't laugh, the way he'd expected. Instead, he'd somehow killed the conversation yet again. His two sisters exchanged a look he couldn't read.

"Um, there's something I've been meaning to tell you," Carrie said.

Suzanne put the burritos in the oven and set the timer.

"Yeah?" he said, wary.

"Let's sit down. Suzanne, do you mind if I pour a glass of wine? Anyone else?"

He shook his head. Both women came to the table with glasses.

Carrie, being Carrie, got to the point. "You know I was adopted first."

He nodded.

"My parents thought about taking both of us."

He should have realized that any potential adoptive parents would have been encouraged to take both siblings.

"I was…really angry when I found out about you. Well, you and Suzanne both." She gestured broadly. "Because they'd lied to me, and I didn't know I was adopted at all."

She'd told him that before. He nodded again, waiting.

"But especially about you. Mom cried when she told me about meeting you. You were scared, and mad, and had taken to biting, she was told. She felt…rejected when she and Dad met you and you ignored them. She didn't have very much confidence in how good a mother she'd be because she'd been trying to get pregnant forever, and miscarrying."

She looked at him as if she expected comment, so he nodded. He felt like one of those bobble-head dolls, unable to speak, head nodding away, unable to stop once it started.

But she was apparently satisfied, because she continued, "They told Mom and Dad you wouldn't miss me."

He had. Memories weren't clear, but he had the ghost of one that was bewilderment and loss. Loss upon loss, and he hadn't understood any of it.

"Mom says she never forgot you. She's wished a thousand times she could go back and do it again. She'd have brought you home, too."

Why was she telling him this? Gary

wondered. Did she think he'd feel *better,* knowing he'd come a centimeter from having been adopted by a doctor and his wife and being loved and spoiled?

"I know she and Dad would like to meet you." Carrie eyed him uncertainly. "I mean, someday. They're away right now. Mom talked Dad into a real vacation, and they're in Maui for three weeks. But another visit."

He might still be nodding for all he knew. But inwardly he was recoiling. *Meet them?* He'd felt obligated to suffer through the reunion with the aunt who couldn't possibly keep her niece and nephew after her sister's death and who'd agreed to give the two little kids up to some social service agency. Now he was supposed to meet the couple who'd decided his cute baby sister was good enough for them but he wasn't?

"No." He stood and shoved back his chair. "No, I don't want to meet your parents."

They both stared up at him in shock. He didn't know what his face showed and didn't care.

"Why would you think I'd want to?" he asked, voice hoarse.

"I...didn't think. I hoped..." She started to stand, too.

"Don't." He turned and walked out of the kitchen.

Her chair clattered. Carrie ran after him. "Gary, come back. I didn't mean to upset you."

He said a word that wasn't very nice and, halfway down the hall, turned to face her. "You just thought it would be fun to reminisce? We could all get a chuckle out of the fact that I was this little shit when I was a kid and nobody wanted me?"

Her face paled. "Don't you know me better than that?"

"No. I don't."

He started to turn away again, but she grabbed him and held on. "I told you because I thought you should know. I don't like secrets."

"Fine. Now I know."

"Would you rather I'd left you imagining why my mother broke into tears at the sight of you?"

Would he have been okay with meeting her parents, if she hadn't opened her big mouth? He didn't know. He'd wondered, back when he wasted his time wondering about crap like that, why he and the baby sister he vaguely remembered had been separated.

Well, good. Now he knew.

"Will you come back and eat?" She looked uncertain, but gripped his arm tightly.

"God." He hadn't felt grief tear at him like that in years. "Yeah. Okay. I'm sorry."

"*You're* sorry?" She gazed at him as if he was crazy.

Which maybe he was.

"I'm the one who was tactless!" Carrie exclaimed. "Here I was trying to... I don't know. Prepare you. And instead I hurt you. Gary, I am so sorry!"

For the first time he noticed that Suzanne had followed her and now hovered at the end of the hall.

Awkwardly, he said, "I try not to think about those days. It's done. I guess I'd rather leave it that way."

Now they were both nodding fervently as if they'd agree to anything he said. Aching to walk out the front door and go for a ride, rain or no rain, he instead went back to the kitchen with them.

Although they stayed skittish, somehow all of them patched together the rest of the evening. Gary couldn't remember a time he'd tried so damn hard for someone else. Two someone elses, in this case.

Thinking it, he knew what a selfish bastard

he was. Because usually, when he got pissed, he left. Jagger and Bob, they let him. Later, the three of them would hash it out.

With Holly Lynn, he'd walked out, too. If she yelled when he came back, he walked out again. When she left for good, one of the things she said was, "Just a good argument now and then. If we could have screamed and thrown things at each other and made up later... But no. You never cared enough to bother screaming, did you? You'd just get irritated and take off. Boy, you sure let me know where I stood."

He hadn't meant to do that. He just knew he had a low threshold for anger. He'd feel pressure building inside him until he felt as if he'd explode. The walls were suddenly dangerously close, confining. He had to be outside. Alone.

Apparently Holly Lynn was right. He didn't care enough to try to ignore that boiler pressure inside for her sake. It had never even occurred to him that he should.

But these sisters... He wanted them to like him.

Simple as that. He'd known them less than two weeks, and their opinion—*they*—mattered to him in a way that perplexed him.

But by the time Carrie left and he retreated to his bedroom since it was raining too hard for a walk, Gary thought he'd figured it out. He hadn't known them for just two weeks; he'd been three years old when their parents died, so they were part of his earliest experiences, his earliest sense of who he identified with. All he had to do was remember the photos in the album—Suzanne in most of them, directing him, hovering over him, teaching him, making him laugh. Then Carrie joined them, big-eyed and eager to crawl wherever they went, to learn from him in turn.

He had ties to these two women that went back to before his earliest memories. But his subconscious *hadn't* forgotten.

Simple again. Weird as hell, but logical.

Okay, he could live with it. Hey, maybe trying to please and impress them would have the effect of making him a more decent human being.

Lying on his bed, hands clasped behind his head as he stared up at the ceiling, Gary made a derisive sound.

He could struggle for a few weeks, but his basic nature wasn't likely to change.

If it had, he'd go to Rebecca's tomorrow night and say, "I'll be heading back to New

Mexico soon. Maybe in a few days. I want to screw you again, but because I'm a decent guy, I gotta say this. That's all that's happening here." Pause. "You still want to have some fun?"

Nope. He wasn't that decent. Because, damn, he wanted her with a clawing need he didn't understand any more than he did all these complicated feelings for his sisters.

But he told himself it, too, was simple. He had the hots for Rebecca. End of story.

And, yeah, he was going to get some. *So there,* he told his conscience.

CHAPTER ELEVEN

"OH, THAT *is* good." Rebecca closed her eyes in pleasure when she took the first bite of spaghetti. "Maybe you're in the wrong business."

"I did make my own muffins to sell when I opened my first coffee shop," Gary said. "Everyone else had those ones that come in plastic and are kind of…"

Twirling the next bite, she supplied, "Sticky."

"Yeah. Sticky. I make the best coffee, but I bake damn good apple-walnut muffins, too. Didn't hurt business."

"Did your mom teach—" She stopped. "Judith. Did she teach you to cook?"

"'Mom' is okay." He sprinkled parmesan on his spaghetti. "Yeah, she did. She was a good cook. Basics—pork loin roasts, pot roasts, cobbler. She didn't experiment." Gary's mouth twisted. "Harold would have dumped his plate and told her to get her butt back in the kitchen and bring him some real food if she'd presented him with *gang gai*."

"He sounds like a real charmer."

"Oh, yeah." He took a bite.

"It would be interesting," Rebecca said thoughtfully, "to read the notes the adoption counselor made. See what she thought of him, of them together, of the way they interacted with you during the first visit."

His head came up and his nostrils flared. "Is it possible to get them?"

"I don't know. Probably not. But maybe." She hesitated. "Would you really want to know?"

He brooded about it for a minute. "There's no sense in getting madder, is there?"

"What if the counselor did a thorough job? If Harold seemed to genuinely want you? Or faked it real well? Would that make you feel better, or worse?"

His brows drew together. "I don't know." Still frowning, he stared at some point past her, and she guessed he was replaying long-ago scenes. Abruptly, his focus returned to her. "Maybe neither. It doesn't matter, does it?"

Gently, she shook her head. "I said it would be interesting, not…" she groped for the right word and settled for, "meaningful."

"Was there a point here?"

"Nope. My professional curiosity ran away with me."

"Ah." He nodded at her. "You're always poking about my parents. What about yours?"

"Singular," she reminded him. "Mom was quiet but supportive. She'd listen to me, say a few words and I'd feel better, no matter what was wrong. It's a gift."

Straight-faced, he said, "So you figure if a few words worked, more would be better."

She threw her napkin at him. "Are you calling me a loudmouth?"

Laughing, he tossed her napkin back and she caught it just before it landed in her spaghetti. "Never said loud."

Rebecca narrowed her eyes. "What, then?"

"You have plenty to say, that's all."

She couldn't tell if he was just teasing or was issuing a rebuke of some kind. But she felt tentative enough with him tonight, she wasn't going to ask.

"Well!" she puffed. "I think I'm going to sulk!"

"Quietly?" he asked, with apparent hope.

She threw the napkin again. He caught it deftly in midair, shook it out and tucked one corner in the neck of his shirt to form a bib.

Rebecca waggled her fingers in demand. He gazed blandly back.

"Hmmph!" She started to stand to go get another napkin.

Grinning, he wadded hers up and lobbed it back across the table.

He was still smiling, but his voice was serious. "I like the way you talk. Wouldn't be sitting here if I didn't."

She pretended to simper. "Well, you do know how to flatter."

"Holly Lynn didn't think so." He frowned again, as if he hadn't meant to say that.

"Holly Lynn?"

"My ex."

Okeydoke. A new can of worms.

"Your only ex?" Rebecca inquired carefully.

"Huh? Oh. Yeah. Don't make a habit of standing in front of a judge and swearing 'I do.'"

"Well, good," Rebecca said with irony. "Do you have kids?"

If he did, and hadn't mentioned them, she'd have to write this relationship off. If what they had could be dignified as a relationship.

"God, no," he said in surprise.

"Married couples do tend to have babies."

He shook his head. "Not us. Holly Lynn

asked me once if I especially wanted kids. I said no, she nodded and said, 'Good,' and that was the end of the subject."

Her heart sank a little, telling her she'd been fool enough to harbor hope despite what she'd believed was clear-eyed realism about this man.

"You don't intend to ever have children?"

He looked back at her without expression. "Not likely to come up now."

Rebecca hid her reaction. At least, she hoped she had. She felt as if she'd been slapped.

No, just warned. He might as well have come right out and said, *Don't get ideas.*

And what had she been doing but getting them. Stupid, stupid, stupid!

She looked straight back at him and said, "So, when do you intend to go home?"

It might have been her imagination, but she thought his tension lessened.

"Maybe next week. I wish I hadn't wasted so much time since I got here."

"Wasted time?"

"Suzanne's place needs work. She doesn't know how to do it and doesn't have time anyway. Right now, her shop is open six days a week, which means she spends the seventh doing the books and orders."

Rebecca frowned. That didn't sound like someone who had room in her life for a child. They'd talked about the stresses of opening a new business, but Suzanne had downplayed the time investment.

"What do you mean, 'right now'?" she asked.

"She's planning to stay closed on Mondays, too. Doesn't do much business, and she's getting worn out. She thinks she can do more of her bookwork during the days, too, now that she's getting the hang of things. She was real slow with her accounting program," Gary said. "I've been tutoring her."

"Really."

"I do run a business."

"I know you do." Reassured about Suzanne, she turned the subject back to its beginning. "What kind of work?"

"Gutters need cleaning, if it would ever quit raining." He glanced with disfavor toward her window.

"It's the Northwest."

"Yeah, yeah. Rain's why it's green here. I remember."

"We have nice summers," she said defensively. "It's coming on winter."

He ignored her promotional spot and continued, "I spent yesterday and today cleaning out her garage. I'm trying to get it ready for her to have a garage sale in a couple of weeks. If it ever…"

Rebecca rolled her eyes. "Quits raining. Uh-huh."

His mouth relaxed into the first smile in a while. "You've got to admit, one hell of a lot of water has fallen from the sky this week."

Thinking of the soaking wet heels she'd positioned beside the heating vent in her bedroom, the panty hose she'd peeled from her wet legs when she got home, and the way her hair was frizzing, Rebecca sighed. "It's getting a little old."

"Now, in Santa Fe right now…"

"Don't tell me it's eighty degrees."

"No, but our streets aren't flooding, either."

Exasperated, she said, "Can we forget the weather?"

"If all that rain's making you grumpy." He gave her a kind smile. "Sure we can."

Rebecca had to laugh. "All right, already! So, you spent the day sweeping your sister's garage?" Mr. Big Businessman? Mr. Black Leather Biker?

"Oiling her tools, hanging shelves." He shrugged. "Installed a new showerhead in her bathroom. Old one was dripping. Sharpened the blades on her lawn mower, replaced the spark plug and drained the gas and oil for the winter." He was obviously ticking off a list. "Glued the rung on one of her kitchen chairs."

"Aren't you handy." She sounded snide but was secretly impressed. She loved the idea of being a home owner but was terrified of how much she didn't know how to do.

"Grow up on a farm, you learn to be handy," he said succinctly.

And they were back to Harold. *All roads,* she thought.

"Do you have pictures of them?" she asked. "Harold and Judith?"

He looked surprised. "No. I didn't take anything like that when I left."

"What did you take?" she asked out of curiosity.

"Things I could sell. Harold had some jewelry that had been his parents'. A string of pearls, her engagement ring, a gold pocket watch…"

"You took his mother's jewelry?" She couldn't help it if she sounded shocked. "Was she still alive?"

"Why would he have had the jewelry if she was alive?"

"I just thought… If that's all he had to remember her by…"

With apparent surprise, Gary said, "They were *things*. He never looked at them."

"But they were heirlooms!"

He studied her in perplexity. "Do you really think crap like that is important?"

"Yes. Yes, I do. Things, as you put it, give us a way of literally touching previous generations. They place us in context."

He shrugged. "I don't see it that way. Even if I had… Honestly, I hated his guts."

"So you wanted to hurt him."

"Damn straight I did! He beat me the night before. I had a broken rib and one eye was swollen shut when I took off. Wouldn't you have wanted to hit him where it hurt, too?" he challenged.

"So that is why you took his mom's jewelry."

"Actually…no." He shrugged again. "It was the only thing I could find that looked valuable and easy to sell."

Rebecca couldn't even have said why she was so disturbed. Not, she knew, because he'd wanted to lash out at his horrible adoptive father. That was natural.

No, it was something else—the indifference with which he'd said "things." And "crap like that." As if he had no sense of the ties between generations, of roots.

She blinked. Of course he didn't! Why would he? He hadn't felt he had any.

"Do you have anything *you* treasure?" she asked. "That you'd be devastated to lose?"

He shook his head. "Devastated is a strong word. Stuff can be replaced."

"What about the photo album Suzanne gave you?"

"She's got the originals."

"But what if she didn't? If you couldn't replace those pictures?"

Gary set down his wineglass. "You're riding this hard. Why does it matter?"

"I don't know. It just…does."

"Then…yeah. I'd hate to lose it. Okay?"

Rebecca nodded. "It bothered me to think you were completely lacking in sentiment."

He laughed. "Sentiment? If you mean what I think you do, I am. What have I ever had to get sentimental over?"

And there it was, in a nutshell: he hadn't grown up with normal bonds. Normal ties of family, of—as she'd put it earlier—context. And now, it appeared, he was incapable of forming those kinds of bonds.

And *that* was what disturbed her.

No, she was exaggerating, Rebecca thought. After all, he wanted to help Suzanne out. That suggested he was forming ties, didn't it?

"I suppose that's true," she said. "Anyway, I guess men tend to be less interested in *things,* as you so rudely put it."

He grinned. "I take it you are sentimental over every chipped vase and ragged quilt your great-grandparents left?"

She was careful not to shift her gaze toward the glass-fronted hutch of the buffet, where she kept a set of amber goblets that had a few chips, sure, but were still beautiful and had belonged to her great-grandmother. But she did admit, "Guilty."

"You'll end up with a cluttered house and junk piled up in the garage, just like Suzanne. You won't be able to get rid of anything."

She lifted her chin. "There are worse sins."

"Yeah, there are," he agreed, a flash of dark remembrance in his eyes momentarily. Then he nodded at the tabletop. "Can I help clean up tonight?"

"But you cooked!"

"You know, at home I cook every night. But, funny thing, I still have to clean the kitchen."

Weakening, she said, "Well, that's true. Oh, fine. We'll be companionable."

He might not be sentimental, she reflected, watching him efficiently stack dirty dishes from the table, but he was domesticated.

And very, very sexy, she added, following him to the kitchen. Even when he was rinsing dishes.

Conversation stayed trivial while they loaded the dishwasher and stowed leftovers in the refrigerator. Was he intending to leave when they were done? she started wondering. Was he waiting for a signal of some kind from her? Or did he just *assume...?*

She hung up the dishcloth and turned, only to bump right into him. He wrapped his hands around her hips and pulled her snugly up against him.

"Watching you dry pans got me excited."

"You were kind of cute yourself, running the disposal," she countered, although she sounded breathless.

She expected a riposte. Instead, his expression sobered, and he searched her face with odd intensity.

"I don't know what it is about you," he said, almost as if he wished she *didn't* get to him.

Trying to keep it light for reasons she

didn't understand, Rebecca suggested, "Maybe it's the freckles."

For a moment his face relaxed. "Maybe it is." Then, he frowned, shook his head and kissed her.

She didn't know what it was about him, either. All she *did* know was that when he touched her like this, she responded like she never had to another man.

Maybe never would.

Kissing him back, she shut her mind to that idea. Of course there'd be other men! There'd be… Abruptly, she lost the ability to think. Gary was crowding her back against the refrigerator, his hand on her breast, his mouth hot and insistent. She hooked one of her legs around his to pull him closer, if that was possible.

They started shedding clothes right there in the kitchen. With her shirt gone, the refrigerator was cold against her back, but his bare chest was warm, the thud of his heartbeat seeming to drive her own.

She hardly knew when her jeans went the way of her shirt, only that Gary's hand was between her legs, stroking, driving her crazy. Moaning, hips rocking, she managed the button and zipper on his jeans and began to work them down.

"Fair's fair," she said, voice unrecognizable, as she wrapped her fingers around him and his body jerked.

Somehow he found a condom again, then lifted her right there, against the refrigerator. Magnets clattered to the floor. She squeaked and wrapped her legs around him just as he entered her and her back arched in a spasm of pleasure.

Their faces were inches apart, his strained, his lips drawn back from his teeth. Muscles bunched in his shoulders from the strain of carrying her weight. His gaze never left hers as he thrust, as she whimpered and held on, as tension coiled.

When relief washed over her and she let out a cry, he growled something. He thrust a few more times, hard, then made a guttural sound and she felt the force of his orgasm deep inside her.

She was shivering in reaction. Gary let his head fall forward until their foreheads rested against each other. They stood there for the longest time, Rebecca braced against the refrigerator, her legs starting to tremble from gripping him so tightly. Then, finally, he straightened up and gently let her down.

"Well, we never seem to make it to your bedroom."

Feeling unusually timid—tentative, just as she'd been conscious of earlier—Rebecca still said, "You could stay for a while, you know. I do have a bed. Or isn't Act Two likely?"

They were still close enough that she felt him tense. Because he was insulted, or because he felt pressured? She had no idea. But after a moment, he smiled.

"Oh, yeah. Give me a brief intermission." He stroked the curve of her waist. "Very brief," he added, voice low and rough. "Act Two is a good one."

More confident now, she kissed his jaw and murmured, "Tell me about it."

He did.

And he was right: it was a good one.

THE RAIN LET UP the next day. Prepared to knock on every door in the neighborhood, Gary started next door and found the guy home.

He came to the door wearing nothing but sweatpants, swaying as if he was on a binge.

Or was sick. When he saw the puffy, watery eyes and red nose, Gary retreated a step. He looked like hell. Gary didn't want whatever he had.

Unable to remember the neighbor's name, he said, "Uh…sorry to bother you. I'm, uh, Suzanne Chauvin's brother."

The guy nodded and croaked. "Seen you around."

"Just wondered if you had a tall ladder. I was hoping to clean her gutters out today."

"Been tempted." He could barely whisper. He swallowed, mumbled something that was probably a profanity. "Thought she'd be insulted. I'll open the garage door. Help yourself."

"Great." Gary kept backing away, with the result that he almost fell off the first step. "Thanks. I'll bring it back—"

"Just lean it against the house. Don't worry about putting it away."

"Good. Thanks."

Even as he started across the wet lawn, the garage door glided up. Gary liked the look inside. The black GMC pickup gleamed, the painted concrete floor didn't have a mar, and tools were spotless and hung in places meant for them. No clutter here. The Honda mower was cleaner than Suzanne's blender.

The extension ladder hung on hooks along

the far wall. Gary carried it out. By the time he got to the front of Suzanne's house, the garage door behind him hummed and closed itself.

He'd earlier found gloves in her garage. Now, armed with black plastic garbage bags, he climbed the ladder and began scooping the soggy fir needles and rotting leaves out of the gutter. He'd lean a ways, then have to get down and move the ladder. As he filled them, Gary tied the bags closed and heaped them at the foot of her driveway for pickup.

He'd started out chilled. It might not be raining today, but it was still a raw, cold day with a gray sky that looked ready to open up again any minute. He warmed up as he worked, though, enjoying some real labor.

Tonight he'd try talking to her about money. Seemed like every time he edged that way, she deflected the conversation. Not deliberately, he thought; she seemed genuinely innocent about where he was taking it.

Midmorning his cell phone rang and he had to climb carefully down and pull off the gloves before he could take it from its holster on his belt and answer.

"Hey," Jagger said. "Thought you should know we had some shit go down at the Church Street shop in Albuquerque."

"What kind of shit?"

"Got held up. Can you believe it?"

"Who was working?"

"Consuela."

Gary swore. Consuela Santillan had to be seven, eight months pregnant. She'd worked for them since she was in high school, and now, in her midtwenties and the mother of a three-year-old, managed their busiest coffee shop.

"Was she hurt?"

"No, she's fine. A little shaken. The son of a bitch stuck a gun in her face. She handed over everything that was in the cash register. I guess it got a little dicey for a while, because he was mad that there wasn't more."

"She didn't tell him about the safe? Damn it, she knows better than to risk her life to hold on to a few bucks!"

"Yeah, I chewed her out. She wasn't impressed. She said she wasn't going to let that… Well, I'll spare you her description of the punk. I didn't know Spanish could be that expressive. Anyway, she wasn't going to let him have any more money than she could help. Even if he did shoot her. I quote."

"She called the cops?"

"Yeah, and they think they might know

who did it. She gave them a good description. Less obscene than the one I heard."

Gary gave a grunt of laughter. Consuela was an amazing woman. Her parents were illegals, but she was born in the U.S., and they'd made sure she stayed in school until she graduated. Poor as the family was, she'd insisted on going straight to work out of high school, but she'd taken classes part-time at the University of New Mexico and would get her degree, she'd told Gary, about the time her three-year-old started kindergarten.

Jagger and Gary had talked before about promoting Consuela as soon as they expanded some more. Right now, the whole corporate office was the two of them, Bob and a secretary. They were getting stretched thin.

"Let me know when an arrest is made. If you need me I'll start home—"

"Don't need you," his friend interrupted. "Just keeping you informed."

"Am I going to have a job left when I get back?" Gary asked, only half kidding.

"You mean, am I planning a coup?"

"Something like that."

"Nope. Just want you to take as much time as you need. Okay?"

"I don't *need* any time at all—"

His buddy told him succinctly and obscenely that yes, he did.

Nice to be transparent, he thought ruefully.

"How's it going with the lady?" Jagger asked.

"Uh…good."

"Real good? Or just potentially good?"

On a flash of irritation, he said, "None of your goddamn business."

There was a moment of stunned silence during which he thought, *What in the hell is wrong with me?*

Then Jagger laughed, a hearty sound that made Gary grit his teeth.

"Hot damn! Lindstrom has a soft spot for a woman! We going to meet her?"

"No, you're not." Funny that he had a fist of pain in his belly. "I didn't know you were a closet romantic."

"I'm only in the closet because I haven't found a woman to match Consuela."

"You're kidding."

The pause was a hair too long. "Don't be an idiot."

Gary gave his head a bemused shake. Jagger was carrying a torch for Consuela? Why hadn't he acted on his feelings back when she was single?

Wait. Hadn't there been a time when the two of them seemed awkward together? Gary had vaguely wondered what their problem was without pursuing the thought.

Big, brusque *Jagger,* in love with a feisty, then teenage, Consuela? And still in love with her, now that she'd been married for three and a half years?

Stunned, Gary signed off. It appeared that he was oblivious to human emotions. Holly Lynn had thought so, but he'd shrugged off her opinion. He could see, though, that he shocked Rebecca and his sisters sometimes, too, even if he didn't always get why.

Shaking his head again, he stowed his cell phone and climbed back up the ladder.

Poor bastard, he thought about his friend. Maybe they *shouldn't* promote Consuela, putting her in the office where Jagger would have to work with her all day.

But that wasn't fair to her, and they'd end up losing her if they didn't soon take advantage of her drive and ability.

This was why he'd just as soon not deal with all this emotional crap! People made stupid decisions.

He respected the fact that Jagger had kept his mouth shut all these years and apparently intended to keep it shut where Consuela was concerned. That being so, whatever the hell it was that he felt shouldn't be part of the equation.

Should it?

Gary swore aloud, then again when he saw the banana slug atop black sodden leaves in the gutter. Call him a wimp, but he didn't like slugs any more than he liked rain.

Flicking it off the gutter with one gloved hand, he grabbed the leaves. The wet had long since penetrated the gloves, which squished as he scooped handfuls into the bag.

As if to confirm his mood, he felt a drop on his face, then another one. The sky had opened.

Determined to finish, he ducked his head and kept working.

Lousy damn climate. Why was he hanging around? Why didn't he go home?

Good questions. He just couldn't answer them.

CHAPTER TWELVE

"YOU'VE WORKED SO hard," Suzanne marveled. Despite the rain, she'd admired the gutters. They hadn't lingered outside, however, since the droplets had progressed to a full-fledged downpour. "You didn't have to rent a ladder, did you?"

Gary could just see himself carting a ladder through the streets of Edmonds on his motorcycle.

"Borrowed one from your next-door neighbor," he said.

Heading in the direction of the kitchen, she turned her head, her eyes widening slightly. "Which one?"

He jerked his head in the appropriate direction. "Guy with the buff GMC truck and the perfect lawn?"

"I'm terrified of setting a foot on his lawn," his sister confessed. "It'd be like walking on a twenty-thousand-dollar Persian rug."

"Poor guy was sick. I tried not to breathe his air."

"Oh, dear." She looked befuddled. "I didn't know he ever…" She caught herself. "I mean…"

"You didn't know he ever got sick? Is that what you were going to say?" Gary threw back his head and laughed. "You think nothing, including germs, dares touch him?"

She glared at him, but spoiled the effect by laughing, too. "Well, you have to admit, it would take nerve to, say, toss a beer can onto his parking strip."

"Germs don't have nerves." He dropped into a kitchen chair and mulled that over. "Do they?"

"I don't think so." She peered into the refrigerator, then shut the door as if not finding what she sought. "But really, that isn't what I meant. It's that… Well, his yard isn't the only thing he maintains to a state of perfection. He jogs practically every morning. Haven't you seen him?"

"In case you haven't noticed, I'm not much for mornings."

"Well, he does. And he probably eats nothing but whole grains and broccoli and…tofu."

"More likely rare steak." The guy had looked too crew-cut to be into tofu.

"Maybe lean cuts," she conceded. "Still, I imagine he's as intolerant of flaws in himself as he is in his yard. Anyway, a cold just seems so *ordinary.*"

Curious, he asked, "What is it with this guy? Does he try to intimidate you?"

She seemed to sag. "No. Tom's been really nice. It's not that. I just can't picture him sick."

"Maybe you should take him some chicken noodle soup," he suggested.

"He can warm up a can of Campbell's himself, which is all I'm capable of doing." She shook her head. "Forget Tom Stefanic, okay? What are we going to have for dinner?" Reversing herself, she said, "*He* wouldn't forget to defrost something!"

"I already called for a pizza," Gary said. "I hope veggie is okay."

"Pizza sounds wonderful. I've eaten out more since you came than I have in years, but tonight it's worth every penny."

"*My* pennies," he said firmly. "I ordered, I pay."

"Gary, you shouldn't have to pay for everything! For goodness sakes…"

Perfect opening. He'd started to talk to her when the doorbell rang. "No," he said, standing and holding up a hand to stop her from racing for the front door. "I meant it. I'm buying."

She gave him a sunny smile. "Thank you."

He came back with the pizza to find she'd already poured lemonade for them both and gotten out plates and napkins. They sat at the kitchen table, pizza box in the middle of it, and put slices on their plates.

"Oh, this is so good," she sighed a minute later.

He'd had better, but didn't say so. He'd picked the place out of the phone book, and the pizza was edible.

"I've been meaning to talk to you," he said.

She took another bite. "Mm?"

"I can tell your money is tight. I make more than I spend. I'd like to help you out."

His sister stopped chewing, her mouth unattractively open. "What?"

"I could set up a way to deposit some income in your account every month, or give you a lump sum now."

She gaped at him, then seemed to recollect herself enough to hastily swallow the bite. "Gary…I don't want your money!"

"Why not?"

"I didn't find you because I needed bailing out financially!"

"But you spent money to track me down," he reminded her.

"Because I wanted to."

"The first year or two after starting a new business is tight. Do you have enough to cushion you if Boeing has major layoffs and the economy goes tits up?" He knew that the Puget Sound region's major employer was Boeing, and that the economy rose and fell on the basis of airplane sales.

He could see Suzanne's answer on her face.

"Even assuming all goes well with the store, kids cost bucks."

"I know that," she said with dignity. "Like every other parent, I'll cope. Children don't have to have luxuries to thrive."

"But wouldn't you like to be able to buy a few of them?"

A new struggle showed on her face, but pride won. "Not if I have to beg for it."

"Goddamn it, Suzanne! I'm offering. You're not begging."

"I just wouldn't feel right," she said stubbornly.

Frustrated, he asked, "Why?"

She lifted her chin. "Why are you offering?"

"Because…" Because she was his sister, along with Carrie the only bona fide family connection he'd ever had or felt. He didn't know how to say that without sounding pathetic. He wasn't sure that, to someone like her who'd always had family, it was an adequate reason anyway. "I owe you for looking for me," he said instead.

But she shook her head, an expression of finality on her face. "You don't owe me for anything, Gary. I wanted to find you for my own reasons. If anything, I'm the one who owes you. I know you didn't want anything to do with us, but you came for this visit anyway. You've really helped me lay a lot of anguish to rest."

She owed *him?* After he'd been a jackass when Kincaid contacted him originally and then when Carrie made that follow-up call? Owed him, because he'd grudgingly come to say hey and stayed for a couple of weeks? Cleaned her damned gutters?

"And you've worked so hard," she said, as if reading his mind. "I really appreciate everything you've done."

Incredulous, he said, "I was supposed to watch the soaps all day?"

"But you didn't have to—"

"Yeah, I did. Isn't that what family does?" Her face went still, and he saw in shock that, for all her talk about finding her baby brother, she didn't really see him that way. He was a guest.

"It's just—" She faltered. "I haven't known you that long…"

"And you don't take money from acquaintances." Even as something inside him froze, Gary picked up a new slice of pizza as if nothing they'd said really mattered. "Okay. I get it."

"Gary…even if Carrie offered, I wouldn't—"

He cut her off with a, "Don't worry." Then, so he didn't sound hurt, he added, "The offer is open, Suzanne. If you ever do need help."

Her voice was small. "That's really nice of you, Gary. Thank you."

He nodded. What else was there to say?

Pretty much in silence, they finished eating their pizza.

Alone in his room later, Gary realized he'd outstayed his welcome. It was time he got back to his real life and quit pretending he'd found a home.

Not tomorrow morning; he didn't want Suzanne beating herself up because she'd chased him away. Monday or Tuesday, then.

He lay on his bed and stared at the ceiling,

reflecting that the hard part was going to be telling Rebecca.

He grunted. Who was he kidding? Face it: the hard part was going to be leaving her.

REBECCA DIDN'T ANSWER her phone the couple of times he tried on Sunday. He worked outside, raking wet leaves and picking up fallen branches while Suzanne did her paperwork. Monday morning he called Rebecca at the office and asked her to lunch. She sounded pleased, and they were throwing around ideas of where to meet when she got interrupted. After covering the phone for a moment, she came back on.

"Why don't you just stop by my office, and we'll decide then?"

"Works for me," he agreed. He hung up, feeling like scum. Why hadn't he just said, *I've got to go, but I wanted to see you one more time?*

At noon as agreed, he arrived at the adoption agency. As he entered, a couple who might have been in their forties walked out, the woman red-eyed and the man's arm protective around her. Disappointed? Or just emotional because they'd finally applied to adopt?

In the waiting room, two teenage girls sat

beside each other, heads together, talk intense. Gary couldn't tell if either were pregnant, but presumed one was. Or, God, both.

The receptionist smiled and waved him down a hall to Rebecca's office. The place wasn't big. He guessed it didn't have to be. It wasn't as if they kept babies in storage to place on demand. He saw a meeting room big enough for maybe thirty people, a couple of small conference rooms, a closed door marked Records, and half a dozen open-door offices where friendly looking women were on the phone or, in one case, opening a brown paper bag and taking out a sandwich.

It was the records room that made him queasy. In there were files. Probably thousands of them, within each secrets that could shatter people's lives.

Of course that was ridiculous, he told himself impatiently; most modern adoptions were open. But Rebecca had said this agency had been in existence for almost fifty years, which meant that rigid, closed adoptions were part of its history, too.

The very idea of what went on here made him twitchy. Commerce in kids. Relieved teenagers able to jettison a problem, ecstatic couples able to take home a child.

All good for the adults, but what about the kids?

What about 'em? he asked himself. They should stay with mothers like the one Rebecca had told him about? The girl living in a shelter after being sexually abused by her father and then selling herself to all comers when she was only thirteen? Hell of a mother she'd make.

You got a better solution? he asked himself, and he didn't.

Still, the fact that he was *in* an adoption agency at all, the kind of place where his life had been decided, was downright weird.

The kind of place? Gary felt the hair on the back of his neck prickle. What if this *was* the adoption agency that had found homes for him and Carrie? He'd never thought to ask anyone. What if his file was in that records room? Did Rebecca know?

He almost wheeled around and went back. Maybe it wasn't locked.

But a woman appeared in an office door and said, "May I help you?"

Gary realized he'd probably been standing there for a suspicious length of time. "No, thanks," he said. "I'm here to see Rebecca. Just waiting until she gets off the phone."

"Oh, fine." The woman retreated.

But now he had to keep going. Rebecca's door was open, and she smiled when she saw him. "Gary! One sec. Let me answer this e-mail—"

"Was I adopted from here?" he asked.

Sitting behind her desk, she blinked at him. "What?"

"You heard me."

"You don't know what agency handled your adoption?"

"Why would I?" Anger bubbled in him. "Answer me."

"No, it wasn't this agency."

"And you know that because…?"

Face defiant, pale enough to make the freckles stand out, she said, "I looked! Okay?"

"God." He collapsed onto a chair facing her desk. "I'm sorry. It was seeing the records room. I suddenly thought…"

"What if I'm in there?" She understood, all right. "But it wouldn't be you there anyway. Just a small slice of your history. Like…like your elementary school transcripts."

"A little more life-altering than that." He felt as if he'd just survived a tense altercation with someone who wanted to beat the crap out of him. Adrenaline, no longer needed, left him shaky.

"Maybe, but…" She bit her lip, betraying hesitation. "Gary, you've had almost half your life since you ran away from your adoptive home. That means who you are now has been formed by a lot more than Harold."

Half his life? He calculated quickly and realized she was right. It had been thirteen and a half years since he'd hitched out of Bakersfield at sixteen years old. Maybe it was time to let his anger go. Maybe he had, mostly, until this visit to his sisters reawakened memories of what had been and taunted him with a vision of what could have been.

"You're right," he admitted. "I'm sorry. Write your e-mail. Then I've got to tell you something."

He hadn't paid attention to the footsteps in the hall, but turned at the sound of a light rap on the door.

"Rebecca, I thought I'd pop in and— Oh! I'm interrupting."

He knew the minute he saw her that this woman was Rebecca's mother. Not because she had freckles and red hair; those must have come from Dad. But her carriage, the shape of her face, the nose, the cheekbones, the smile in her eyes replaced by surprise… those were Rebecca.

"Mom!" Rebecca stood. "How nice to see you! Um…did I know you were coming?"

Her mother laughed. "No, you didn't. I was in Edmonds for a knitting class, and thought I'd see if you had time for lunch."

Knitting class? Good Lord, she'd probably taken it from Suzanne. It's a small, small world, Gary thought.

Rebecca's gaze flitted to his face, then back to her mother's. "Oh. Um. Mom, I told you about Gary, didn't I? Gary, my mother. Mom, Gary Lindstrom."

Her mother flashed an amused glance at her daughter and held out her hand to him. "Mary Wilson."

He forced a smile. "Not just Mom?"

She laughed merrily. "It seemed like it when she was younger, but no."

"Oh, gosh! I'm sorry." Rebecca had blushed. "My manners are a little lacking, aren't they?"

Mom had a good handshake and a shrewd way of assessing him. "I'm glad to have the chance to meet you. I was afraid when I saw someone was here that you were a client."

He cocked his head. "I'm not pregnant."

"You could be trying to adopt."

Not so likely. With his history, who in their right mind would give him a kid?

"Are you in town for much longer?" she asked, in that polite "I'm just making conversation" tone that didn't fool him for a second.

He couldn't say, *I'm leaving tomorrow.* Not this way, in front of an audience. After her mother was gone...

"Probably not long." Out of the corner of his eye, he tried to assess Rebecca's reaction, but her face gave nothing away.

"Oh, what a shame. I hope you'll be back for another visit soon."

Doublespeak, but he wasn't sure whether Mary Wilson was trying to convey a steely, *You* will *be back to see my daughter, won't you?* or a, *Please tell me you won't be back for ten years.*

"Hard to say at this point," he murmured.

"Well, I assume you two had plans," Mary Wilson said. "So I'll get out of your hair. Rebecca, we can do something another day."

Rebecca cast him a helpless look. "Mom, I'm sorry..."

Cursing himself, Gary still did the nice thing. "Why don't you join us? Or Rebecca and I can get together later."

"Don't be silly!" Mrs. Wilson told him. Then, "Would you mind if I joined you?"

She sounded so damn hopeful, all he could say was, "Of course not."

Rebecca's mother. He was going to get to know her mother. In his two years of marriage, he'd never even met Holly Lynn's. They didn't speak. He was here to say, *So long, nice to know you,* to Rebecca, and instead he was having lunch with both her and her mother.

"If you're sure…?" It was him Rebecca looked at.

"Yeah. I'm sure." That he was crazy.

So he and Mom chatted while Rebecca sent her e-mail, after which the three of them walked out to Rebecca's car. They went to the Red Robin, where they were seated in a generous-sized booth. All three ordered the soup, salad and bread sticks option.

Then he braced himself for the inquisition.

"Rebecca tells me you own coffee shops?"

"That's right."

"In the Southwest, she said?"

"Just in New Mexico so far. I live in Santa Fe, but we're spread from Farmington up in the north to Las Cruces in the south. We're talking about opening our first shop in Arizona."

"Really?"

She looked politely interested, and he kept

talking because they had to talk about something.

"That's right. We're considering Mesa or Scottsdale, both on the outskirts of Phoenix."

"Is there much competition there?"

"There is everywhere now, but not like up here. Looks like Seattleites can't walk a block without buying a latte."

"A block?" Rebecca rolled her eyes. "Downtown, it's half a block. Between Starbucks and Tully's and Caffe Ladro, the city is blanketed. Never mind the independents."

"Yeah, I think I'll stick to the Southwest," he said, before realizing that could be taken two ways. As in, *Don't expect me to move up here and court you.*

"And you sell your roast in stores, too?" Mom continued.

"That's right. Locally, of course, but now we have several major nationwide accounts."

"It's in both Trader Joe's and Whole Foods," Rebecca told her mother, a note of pride in her voice.

"Really? That's impressive," Mrs. Wilson said.

The waiter brought their salads and bread sticks, and while they dished up Gary asked about her work.

She told him about her job as a nurse in intensive care at Overlake Hospital in Bellevue. She smiled fondly at her daughter. "I hoped Rebecca would become a doctor. I'm sorry I didn't have the opportunity to try for medical school myself. But, of course, she took a different direction."

Rebecca smiled back with equal affection. "You just wanted to be able to say loudly, 'My daughter, the doctor...'"

Her mother laughed. "A lot of those doctors *are* awful snobs."

"My sister's adoptive father is a doctor," he heard himself say.

"Oh? Where does he work?"

"I'm not sure. He's a cardiac surgeon. St. James. Dr. St. James."

She shook her head. "I don't know him."

He nodded, unsure why he'd even mentioned the guy. He preferred not to think about the St. Jameses.

"How odd, just getting to know your sisters now."

"Yes, it is." *You don't know the half.*

"I was always sorry Rebecca didn't have a sister or brother. Not so much for myself," she said, giving her daughter another one of those gentle, extraordinarily loving smiles, "as for her sake. Did you have adoptive brothers or sisters?"

He shook his head.

"What a shame."

Not really, he wanted to say. *Harold would have just beaten the other kid, too.*

Except he himself had wondered if Harold might have softened for a little girl.

Uh-huh. And how much would you have resented that?

Their soup came, and he was surprised at how good the minestrone was, considering Red Robin was a chain.

Hell, his coffee was good, and Chimayo Coffee Company was a chain, too. Who was he to sneer?

The lunch seemed interminable, Rebecca mostly silent, her mother relentlessly pleasant and determined to find out everything she could about him. He didn't even blame her, he *liked* the woman, but a headache grew from a band of tightness to a dull throb. He kept watching Rebecca and thinking, *I'll never see her again.* It was killing him.

Gary's relief was intense when Rebecca glanced at her watch and said, "Oh, gosh. I'd better be getting back. I have an appointment at one-thirty."

"Oh, dear, and here I've dominated conversation!" Rebecca's mother smiled at Gary. "Thank you for including me."

"I was glad to have a chance to get to know you."

Live and learn. He hadn't known he was capable of such civil insincerity.

But no lightning struck him down for the lie. And, hey, at least his intentions were good. That counted, didn't it?

In the parking lot back at the agency, Mrs. Wilson said her goodbyes, hugged her daughter and went to her own car.

The minute she was out of earshot, Rebecca said, "I'm sorry, Gary! I know getting grilled by my mom wasn't exactly what you had in mind today."

"No, it's okay," he assured her. "She's nice."

Her face softened. "Yeah. She is. I'm lucky. None of my friends have as good relationships with their mothers."

"Because it comes from the fact that it was just the two of you."

"Maybe. Well. I need to get back to work. Do you want to come over later?"

He should say goodbye now. It would be

easier here in the parking lot, not so pro-
longed. More casual.

But what came out of his mouth was, "Do
you have dinner plans?"

"I do, but I should be home by eight."

He felt like a desperate refugee informed
that there was one more spot on the boat.
"You sure?" he asked.

She kissed him. "I'm sure."

He watched her walk back in, her stride
confident and feminine both, and thought
again, *Why her?*

He had no more answers than he'd had the
last time he wondered.

Or maybe he did. Maybe it was that confidence coupled with the softness inside.
Thinking about the smile she'd exchanged
with her mother, the love unashamedly dis-
played on both faces, Gary thought maybe
that was it, too. Her capacity for love. She
didn't shy away from it.

Highly illogical, considering he wasn't
looking for love. But he had a very bad
feeling that he was attracted to her partly
because he knew Rebecca would give her
love generously and be steadfast in it.

His being attracted to that quality, he reflected, was about like an atheist drawn to the

Catholic Church. He could admire and envy it, but he wasn't likely to join.

Tonight was probably a bad idea. But he couldn't stay away.

CHAPTER THIRTEEN

REBECCA LOVED HER MOTHER dearly, but today her timing had really stunk. Gary had been nice about inviting her to join them, but Rebecca knew he didn't have the slightest bit of interest in meeting her mother or friends. And after his explosion, his wild-eyed fear that a file with his name on it was locked in the records room, she'd really needed to clear the air.

She'd been well aware that he had issues about his adoption, but his crackling anger because she might have known his file was here and not told him had still come out of the blue. Did he really think she'd keep that kind of secret from him?

And then, just before her mother had knocked, he'd started to say something about wanting to talk to her. All during lunch, Rebecca's stomach cramped every time she looked at him.

Please, please, don't let him say he's leaving.

But what else could it be?

Nobody else had seemed to notice that she didn't eat much. Somehow she'd kept chattering, laughing in response to her mother's gentle teasing, pretending the only awkwardness was the fact that the man she was dating was meeting her mother for the first time.

Her friend Jeanette would have understood if she'd begged off their dinner, but Rebecca knew that a big downtown gallery had just agreed to hang Jeanette's artwork and she was understandably excited and dying to talk about the glorious, incredible possibilities. Anyway, Rebecca didn't approve of blowing off friends just because a man crooked his finger.

Thank goodness Jeanette was excited enough to free Rebecca from any conversational burden except an occasional question and murmured expression of shared delight. And she *was* happy for her friend! They'd been housemates in graduate school, where she'd been awed at Jeanette's talent—not to mention her ability to drink lots and lots of beer and *still* skewer someone with a caricature sketched on a napkin.

She did have to admit why she couldn't linger. "I told him eight...."

Her statuesque blond friend said, "You've

let me blather on and never said a word about a new guy in your life?"

"I'll let you know if it gets serious."

"Rebecca, how many dates have you been on in the last year?"

She had to think. "I don't know. A couple, maybe?"

"If you bothered to see this guy twice, it's serious." She signaled the waitress. "Why *isn't* it serious?"

Before she could think better of it, Rebecca blurted, "Because he lives in Santa Fe."

Jeanette's eyes narrowed. "If he lived in Seattle…?"

"I guess I would be serious," she admitted.

Jeanette asked the waitress for the check, waiting until she was out of earshot to say, "Ha! You're in love, and you didn't tell me?"

"Did I say love? I've only known Gary for two weeks." Was it really that short a time? "And sometimes he scares me a little."

"Scares you? Whoa, girl…!"

"No, no." Rebecca waved off her friend's alarm. "Not that way. He's a perfect gentleman. It's just…he had a really crummy childhood. He was adopted…."

"Don't tell me you're trying to save him," her friend moaned.

Rebecca scowled at her. "I never try to save men. *You're* the one—"

"You'll never let me forget Joel, will you?"

"Not when there's the slightest chance of you repeating the mistake."

Joel was a profoundly depressed man ten years Jeanette's senior, also a gifted artist who created astonishing, large-scale metal sculptures. Moving in with him right out of graduate school, Jeanette had been positive that love would heal him. Instead, he'd gotten moodier and moodier, with occasional outbreaks of violence. When she had shown up on Rebecca's doorstep one night with a black eye and a purple bruise on her cheek, Rebecca persuaded her to stay. Joel destroyed some of Jeanette's canvases, much to her grief, then up and moved to San Francisco, taking his talent and his moods with him.

"Gary isn't like Joel," Rebecca said. "But he is emotionally damaged. Sometimes he just doesn't seem to feel the same things normal people do. He'll look surprised when I comment that oh, gosh, so-and-so must be upset about that, as if he wouldn't have felt anything. It's like he became so self-reliant, I wonder if he's capable of any real connection with other people."

"If he's capable of loving you, you mean."

She gave a wry smile. "Okay. Yeah. And if he is, whether he'd want a family." She shook her head. "Never mind. It doesn't matter. He lives in Santa Fe, and I suspect that the reason he's stopping by tonight is to say goodbye."

They figured out who owed how much, calculated the tip and left bills on the table. Outside, Rebecca paused at Jeanette's car to say good-night.

Her friend said, "Call me if you're sad, okay? You know I'm a night owl. I'll be up whenever."

"Thanks."

They hugged and Rebecca hurried to her car.

Gary was waiting outside her apartment, leaning casually against his motorcycle as he had the first time they'd met. He reminded her of James Dean, who, in old photos, always looked as if he was resigned to being alone. Rebecca remembered walking up Suzanne's driveway and glancing back to see Gary leaning, just like that, arms crossed, as if he had all the time in the world and it didn't matter when, or even if, he met this sister he'd come so far to find.

That was the thing with him—she couldn't tell if his occasional, strange indifference was real or a facade to hide vulnerability he didn't want to admit.

Jumping out of her car and locking it, she said, "Gosh, I cut this close. I hope you haven't been waiting long."

"Nope. Just got here." He straightened and ambled toward her as she opened her door. "Did you do something fun?"

Dropping her purse in its usual spot on the small table beside the door, she shed her coat and hung it in the closet. "I had dinner with a friend. Jeanette and I knew each other in high school, and then along with two other women we rented a house together while we were in graduate school. She's this amazing artist."

"Yeah?"

He probably wasn't at all interested, but Rebecca kept chattering as they went to the kitchen, where she ground coffee—from Chimayo Coffee Company, of course—and started it brewing.

"Our other two housemates have scattered. Gail went into the Peace Corps, in Malaysia. When she came back, she got a job in Baltimore. Lisa stayed on for her doctorate and is teaching at the University of California at Davis."

He nodded, and she realized Davis wasn't

that terribly far from Bakersfield, where he'd grown up. At least, it was close enough that he'd know where it was.

"So anyway, that just leaves Jeanette and me. We try to get together every few weeks. She's excited because a really major gallery, by Seattle standards, anyway, wants to put on a show of her work." She waved toward the living room. "That painting over the couch is hers."

"Really." Suddenly he did sound interested. Even though he'd seen it before, he wandered over to study the oil painting of two women sitting on a couch talking. The colors were warm, vivid, the body language and expressions somehow conveying both affection and tension, as if something stood between them despite their intimacy.

"I wouldn't mind owning one of her paintings. Does she have a Web site?"

"Yes, I have some of her cards in my purse." Rebecca got him one. "If you buy one, hang it in your corporate offices. It would be great advertising for her."

He laughed. "Have I mentioned that our corporate offices are crudely partitioned out of a warehouse space in a crummy part of town? Jagger, Bob and I and a secretary are the only people in the offices proper. We've got others who roast the coffee, package, pick up the beans and deliver to the stores."

"Don't you have people coming there to, I don't know, sample your coffee before they start selling it?"

"Occasionally, but we're more likely to send out samples and travel to see the customers."

Deflated, she sat down on the couch. "Oh. Phooey. Well, forget the great plan to dazzle the world with Jeanette's remarkable talent."

"You're loyal, aren't you?" Settling in the easy chair facing the couch, Gary watched her as if she were some kind of curiosity.

"To my friends, you mean?"

"To people you love."

"Well, of course I am! Aren't you?"

"Haven't had reason to test myself."

"You're not claiming you don't love anyone, are you?" she demanded. "What about this Jagger you keep mentioning? Isn't he a friend?"

"Yeah. He's a friend."

"And the guy who gave you a break when you got to New Mexico. Did you drop him when you didn't need him anymore?"

"No," Gary said, sounding amused by her vehemence. "I kept working for him longer than I should have. Your point?"

"That yes, I'm loyal to friends. But most people are. Including you."

"I suspect not with your passion, though."

"I'm pretty ordinary."

His face and tone both became dead serious. "No. You're not."

It would be silly to keep arguing. As lightly as possible, Rebecca said, "Well, I'm glad you think I'm wonderful and fabulous."

He leaned forward, elbows on his thighs and his hands dangling. "I'm leaving tomorrow."

Her heart plummeted. For a minute she could only stare at him. "Oh," she said finally, weakly.

"I think I've worn out my welcome at Suzanne's."

"You could, um, stay here for a few days if you wanted." A few weeks. Or forever.

That thought shocked her, but told her what she hadn't yet wanted to admit: despite every good reason not to, despite the short time since they'd met, she'd fallen in love with this man.

He shook his head. "I've been gone too long. Businesses don't run themselves."

"No, I suppose they don't." She'd *known* that's why he wanted to talk to her tonight. So why was she stunned? Why did she feel as if he'd tossed her heart on the floor? But her pride would not let her cry. He'd never led her to think their affair was anything but a fling. Fun. If she'd started hoping for more, well, she'd been an idiot. And it wasn't his fault.

"I was going to tell you at lunch…."

"But Mom showed up. I didn't set that up, you know."

"I didn't think you had."

"I'm going to miss you," she said, almost steadily. "It's been…" Not fun. Not just fun. But she couldn't tell him what it had been for her. Because then he'd feel sorry for her, and she didn't want that.

"Yeah. I'll miss you, too." For a moment, his voice became almost ragged, giving her hope. But then he straightened. "I suppose I should go."

"You must have to pack and…" What?

His grunt might have been a laugh. "Packing will take five minutes. I figured I'd better call Carrie, though."

"Suzanne knows you're leaving?"

He hesitated, and Rebecca realized that he hadn't yet told his sister.

But, "Sure," he said with a shrug.

What was he going to do, leave her a note? None of her business, Rebecca thought.

She should be grateful he'd come to say goodbye to *her* in person. Think how insulting it would have been if he'd just left a phone message.

"Will you e-mail and let me know when you get there safely?" she asked.

"Sure. What's your address?"

"I'll write it down." Somehow they were on their feet and walking toward the front door. She detoured to scribble her e-mail address on a slip of paper.

When she handed it to him, he took out his wallet and carefully put the slip in it, then restored the wallet to his hip pocket.

They were almost to the door. Panic clogged Rebecca's throat.

"Do you really have to go?"

He half turned. "Home?"

"No, I mean now. To Suzanne's. Can you stay for a little while?"

His voice had become hoarse. "I thought you'd want me to go."

I never, ever want you to go.

"You could…you could even spend the night. Or, well, awhile."

If that didn't sound desperate! But she didn't care. She just wanted to put off the inevitable.

"God." Now the voice wasn't even his, so

desperate and hungry did it sound. Half a stride, and he snatched her into his arms and kissed her.

Rebecca had a moment of triumph, of relief. He still wanted her, at least.

Then she responded fiercely, all coherent thought gone.

They tangled, fought, nipped, tore at each other's clothes. She didn't know when he groaned, when she cried out. He lifted her and carried her as far as the couch, although she hardly noticed. He could have had her on the floor next to the front door for all she'd have cared.

They'd barely fallen backward onto the couch when he entered her. She came, just like that; no preamble, no waiting.

"Rebecca," he whispered, gaze fierce on hers, one hand gripping her buttock to lift her higher for his next thrust. "You can do it again. For me."

She could. Need built as quickly the second time, as sharply. He would be leaving, and she couldn't bear it. But now, *now,* she had him.

She saw his climax in his eyes before she felt the shudder in her body, a quaking that set off her own. She keened, and he kissed her, as if he wanted to take the sound of her pleasure and grief into himself.

Then he collapsed on her, shoulders sweat-slick, his mouth against her cheek. Rebecca squeezed her eyes shut, as if she could stop the tears.

"God!" He reared up from her, face tight with alarm. "I didn't use a condom. Damn it, how could I forget?"

"It's okay…"

"It's not okay! What if you were to get pregnant?" He looked toward her belly and swore again. "What if you *are?*"

She felt a cramp of longing but ignored it. Her dismay at his expression was too great.

"Gary, I take birth control pills. Remember?"

He stared at her for a long moment, then abruptly sagged. "Thank God. I've never forgotten before."

"I suppose I should be flattered." It was all she could think to say, to hide her hurt.

"What an idiot!" He sat up, put his feet on the carpeted floor and ran his fingers through his hair, messing it.

Rebecca grabbed for the only item of clothing she could reach—his shirt—and clutched it to her as she, too, sat up. A minute ago, she hadn't been self-conscious about her nudity. Suddenly she was. "Would becoming a father be the worse thing in the world?"

He looked at her, expression scathing. "What do I know about being a father? Yank the belt out of the loops when the little brat irritates me? Come on, you hold godlike powers. Would *you* give me a kid?"

She was horrified by her answer, instinctive and so certain. At work—no. But if the baby was also hers—yes. Oh, yes. She wanted to have children with him.

With a man who by his own admission neither knew how to parent nor wanted to. A man she would professionally consider unfit.

He saw the response on her face, or, at least, the part of it he expected to see.

"Didn't think so." He stood and grabbed his jeans, discarded halfway into the living room, and hopped until he had both legs on and could yank them up.

Rebecca swallowed. The pain she saw on his face was so terrible, she knew she had to strip herself bare if need be to salve it.

"If you and I had a baby together, I'd trust you to be a good father."

His laugh was unpleasant. "Are you nuts?"

"I've seen nothing to make me think you're

anything but a good man." She pressed her lips together. "Am I wrong, Gary?"

He let his head fall forward and scrubbed his hand across his face. After a moment, during which she wasn't sure he'd heard her, Gary turned and came back to the couch. He sat next to her, elbows on his thighs as he had earlier, shoulders slumped. "You must think I'm an SOB."

"No. No."

"What I am is a coward." He swallowed. "Rebecca, I'm not father material. Your rational side knows that."

She was terribly afraid it did, but she refused to believe it.

But he read her thoughts, and his expression closed, becoming the one of indifference that had so often baffled her. "I thought so."

So it *was* a veneer, she saw, a way of hiding hurt and confusion. The hurt she had just dealt.

"No…"

"Rebecca." He sat up, as if conscious of his body language revealing too much. Or perhaps he wasn't just pretending indifference; perhaps he was able to shut down his own emotions. He sounded kind. Determined to show her the error of her absurd infatuation. "What do you want, long term? Husband? Family?"

After an instant, she nodded.

"Children are important to you, aren't they?"

She'd always dreamed of a kind man who'd swing his toddler in a circle until they were both dizzy, who'd play stupid games and carry kids on his shoulders at the zoo, galloping when ordered. She'd seen their family complete with two or three kids. And with laughter. Lots of laughter.

And tenderness. He had to be tender.

"Yes," she whispered.

"I'm not your guy. You didn't think I was, did you?"

She bit her lip and shook her head, though it was a lie.

"Good. I don't like to think I misled you."

"No." Her voice came out small, strained. "You never did. Don't worry, Gary."

"Hey." He wrapped an arm around her. "You cold?"

No. Just nude.

"I guess so." She forced a smile. "Let me grab my clothes. In fact, I think I'll change quick."

She had to give him his shirt, then fled to her bedroom. For a moment there, she leaned her forehead against the cool, slightly rough-textured wall and thought,

How can I go back out there and act as if my heart isn't broken?

But what defense did she have if it wasn't pride? So, mechanically, she opened drawers and got dressed, pulling on underwear, jeans, a turtleneck sweater, even socks and shoes, as if she were donning armor. She glanced in the mirror and thought about brushing her hair, but didn't want to look at herself that long. Her face was too white, her freckles too shockingly vivid in contrast, her eyes too wide and staring. Instead, she gave her head a shake and made herself walk back into the living room.

Gary had found the rest of his clothes while she was gone and was dressed, too. He'd also, considerately, picked up her discarded garments and laid them on the back of the sofa. He looked much as usual. Only the dishevelment of his hair, like hers, suggested that they hadn't been sipping wine and chatting.

He gave her a quick, thorough look, his expression wary.

He was afraid she'd weep all over him, Rebecca diagnosed. Well, if it killed her, she wouldn't.

"You know, Gary," she said, as if this didn't

matter so much, "I think you're shorting yourself. You weren't raised to be a business-man, but you've succeeded. Great athletes sometimes are lousy coaches, and great coaches never actually played the sport. You know what kind of father you *don't* want to be. You could be a good one if you wanted to."

But, of course, he didn't, which was the point.

When he didn't say anything immediately, she continued, "I wasn't proposing, you know. I was just disputing your determination to think of yourself as some kind of monster."

He raised his eyebrows at her comment. "I think of it as taking preventative measures."

"Are you like Harold in other ways?"

"Hell, no!" Gary said explosively.

"Then what makes you think you would be as a father?"

He stared at her.

"Never mind. I'm not trying to grill you. Just… think about it."

The lines that deepened between his brows weren't precisely a frown. Instead, he looked disturbed. Troubled.

"Maybe you should go now," Rebecca said. Before she broke down.

"Yeah. You're right." But he didn't move

until she started toward the front door, then he followed her.

When she handed him his leather jacket, he shrugged into it.

"I'll walk you out." She opened the front door.

She was glad he didn't argue. She wanted to see him as long as she could, so she could hold on to a last glimpse of his motorcycle turning the corner.

She left her apartment door open, the light falling onto the concrete walkway in front. Gary had parked virtually in front of her door.

It wasn't raining, but the night was chill and damp, the air scented with decaying leaves and storms to come. She felt cold and sorrowful and achy, as if she'd been ill.

He hesitated, gave her a quick, awkward hug and a kiss that missed her mouth and landed on her cheek instead, and climbed onto his Harley, pulling it upright and toeing the kickstand up.

Their eyes met one last time, his too shadowed for her to see what he felt, if anything. Then the engine roared to life, he backed out and drove away.

Going, he looked as sexy and dangerous as she'd thought him at first, when she'd imagined this parting as bittersweet instead of wrenchingly painful.

But what she hadn't seen then was the loneliness in a man who preferred a motorcycle because he didn't have to share the front seat with someone who expected conversation. A man who clearly expected to be alone for the rest of his life.

He was out of sight, but the throaty growl of the Harley was still audible when she turned and went back into her apartment, locking and putting on the chain before she sank to the floor.

Back to the door, Rebecca drew up her knees, wrapped her arms around them, and cried, as she'd never cried before.

GARY WALKED INTO his sister's house, right past her where she sat knitting in the living room.

Her head came up and she half rose, her eyes widening. "Gary…?"

"Not now." It didn't sound like him. He didn't care.

He went on to his bedroom—no, the *guest* bedroom—and closed the door behind him.

Inside, he looked around with as little comprehension as if he were suddenly discovering himself to be in a strange motel room. He'd come here without thought, by instinct, but now that he'd made it, he didn't know why.

Finally, he threw his jacket over the chair and went back out to the bathroom, where he splashed water on his face and then stared at himself in the mirror. His face hadn't changed, which surprised him on some level. Shouldn't the night have marked him in some way? His inner landscape had been devastated. It felt like one of those aerial photos of a third-world city flattened after an earthquake or mudslide. Just…gone. Unrecognizable.

Uninhabitable. Except he was stuck.

He swore aloud, the sound shocking in the small bathroom. He dried his face and returned to his bedroom, glad Suzanne wasn't lurking in the hall to find out what was wrong.

Gary took off his boots and lay down on the bed. With a groan, he pulled the extra pillow over his face.

What had happened? Why, *why,* did he feel so destroyed? What had Rebecca said? Done? Or was it all him?

He couldn't believe that he'd forgotten to put on a condom. He hadn't been lying. Never, not once in his life, had he failed to protect the girl or woman he was having sex with—and protect himself, too. But tonight, when she said, *Can you stay for a while?*, he'd lost it. All he'd known was that he had to have her. Be in her. Join with her, in the most primitive, satisfying way possible.

There'd been no conscious thought. He'd become an animal, but not one that was rutting, no, one that was burrowing frantically into sanctuary to escape some horror outside.

Leaving. Never seeing her again.

In those few words, she'd offered a reprieve, and he'd seized it with desperate relief.

And then, when he realized he'd forgotten, when he thought, *I could have just gotten her pregnant,* he'd felt… He couldn't believe it. A wave of some powerful exhilaration. Triumph. An alien kind of joy.

Followed by unadulterated terror. He couldn't be what she needed, what a baby would need. So he'd said… He didn't even know what he'd said. Only that he'd thrashed about, not caring what—or whom—he crashed into. In his panic, he'd probably hurt her, the last thing he wanted to do.

Not because the subject of children had come up. He and Holly Lynn had discussed the possibility, too. No, he'd reacted with violent, mindless fear because he wanted a baby with Rebecca. And wanting something you shouldn't have was the most dangerous thing in the world.

He groaned and shoved the pillow harder into his face, all but smothering himself.

He'd be Harold, the only example of a father he'd ever known.

Are you like Harold in other ways? she'd whispered.

Maybe not, but if he became like Harold in this one way, he'd destroy them all: her, their kid, himself.

Swearing, he flung the pillow across the room. It smacked into the closet door, which rocked on its track.

With dry, burning eyes, Gary stared at the ceiling. Why in God's name was he even thinking about this? He'd made the decision by the time he was fifteen years old never to become a father. He'd known the minute he met Rebecca that, unlike Holly Lynn, she was a woman who'd want it all: a home, a man's wholehearted love, babies.

She wanted the life he'd seen in the photo album that lay on the bureau top. The life he'd had, before uncaring fate tore the parents from the children and scattered them to random fates.

The life he'd hoped, somehow, to recapture on this trip, and now knew was gone forever.

He'd found what he could reasonably have expected to find when he came out here: two sisters, for whom he'd developed a degree of fondness. But some deeper meaning to live his life by?

Wasn't happening.

Feeling no better than he had when he'd woken up in the hospital and realized that he'd lived after all, Gary got up.

Time to tell Suzanne he was going in the morning. Let her think something had happened with Rebecca. Better all around.

As he walked out to the living room, he relived his last sight of Rebecca, in his rearview mirror. Standing so alone on the curb in front of her apartment, hugging herself, even the sodium lights failing to leach the color from her hair.

So damn beautiful, so vulnerable, so deserving of someone better than him.

CHAPTER FOURTEEN

GARY LEFT EARLY the next morning, before Suzanne had even gotten up. He wasn't sure he could handle another goodbye, and he wanted to get as far as possible this first day. It seemed important to open distance between him and Edmonds, put it behind him. He wanted to think it would be that easy.

With the weather turning cold in mountainous regions now as November set in, Gary chose to head straight south on I-5 through Oregon and California before turning east into Arizona. He was slowed by light snowfall in southern Oregon, but wouldn't let himself get a hotel room even though his hands became numb. He rode until exhaustion forced him to stop, the first night in Red Bluff in Northern California, the second in Needles on the Arizona border.

Each morning, he awakened early and was on the road again with dawn's breaking. The third day, he roared into Santa Fe, and went straight home.

With the sun setting, the temperature was plummeting. Snow dusted the Sangre de Cristo Mountains. But the cold was different than the Puget Sound area's because it was dry. To him, the air felt good to breathe in, crisp instead of damp. As the sun settled behind the mountains, they glowed with the blood-red color that had given them their name, literally the "blood of Christ", said to be the last words of a dying padre who'd asked for a sign from heaven.

The first time Gary saw Santa Fe, the mountains had been this color. He'd been drawn to their fire. Sometimes he thought that was why he'd stopped here. He'd been fascinated by the Spanish and Pueblo architecture, the vividness of flowers and strings of drying red chiles against the cream and terra-cotta adobe walls. The mixture of Spanish and English he heard was familiar to him from Bakersfield, where most of the farm workers were Mexicans, legal and illegal.

His own house was clearly modern and yet borrowed from the Pueblo tradition, with thick adobe walls, rounded parapets and *canales* to drain the flat roof. Inside, the stuccoed walls were painted creamy white contrasting with the raw wood exposed beams and the terra-cotta tile floors that held the cool of the night when days grew hot. He'd had no reason to get a house sitter, so when he walked in the front door, the air smelled musty and the house was freezing. He went to the thermostat first, then the kitchen. Crap. He should have stopped at the grocery store. He'd thrown out everything perishable before he left, and now the refrigerator held a few cans of beer, mustard, mayonnaise and not a hell of a lot else.

He found a frozen pizza in the freezer, took it out and turned the oven on to preheat, then popped open a beer even though he was still cold. While the oven warmed up, Gary carried his bag into his bedroom and dumped the contents on the bed. The photo album Suzanne had given him he carefully set on the dresser. Clothes into the hamper, toiletries into his bathroom. Chore done.

Back to the kitchen. Pizza in the oven. He had no vegetables, fresh or frozen, so pizza was going to be it. He'd shop in the morning.

He thought about calling Jagger to let him know he was home, then decided against it. Tomorrow was soon enough. His cell phone had been on, and he hadn't been needed. He wasn't in the mood for conversation, especially his buddy's direct form of it.

So, did you bring the babe home on the back of your Harley?

He didn't want to think about Rebecca, not now. He chose a CD and put it in, then went back to the kitchen when the oven beeped, while the mournful sound of Miles Davis followed him. Real cheerful choice, he congratulated himself.

Will you e-mail and let me know when you get there safely?

He'd promised. Would she care now? He didn't know, but a promise was a promise.

He ate standing up in the kitchen, his plate on the dark wood island. After three days of travel, his butt was sore. Besides, he felt restless.

The dishwasher was empty, as he'd left it. His single plate looked lonely as hell sitting in it. It seemed too cruel to leave it there. After a minute, he took it back out, washed and dried it, and put it away in the cupboard. Which was a stupid-ass thing to do; he'd never have a full load to run if he kept feeling sorry for single dishes that might have to sit for a couple of days.

Finally, he went to his office and turned on the computer. His house was mainly open, since he didn't like feeling hemmed in. The kitchen connected with the dining room via a large arch, and the dining room to the living room. Only his bedroom, the bathroom and the home office had doors. He didn't know why he'd even bothered with those; he almost never closed them. Why would he bother, when he lived alone and rarely entertained?

Of course, after a three-week absence, nine hundred and forty-nine e-mails had piled up. Most were spam and quickly disposed of, although the necessity irritated him. A few were business related, and he hoped the inquiries had eventually been redirected to the company e-mail. A scattering were from friends, including McGinnis's wife Martha, who regularly e-mailed in a newsy sort of way.

This time, she sounded unhappy and said she was thinking about returning to Santa Fe.

I enjoy being closer to Brett, but he's busy with work and family and I feel as if he and Linda are including me more often than they should be. The climate is awful! I miss the slower pace down there, the warmth of strangers, my friends. And you, Gary, of course. Have I ever said that I think of you as my youngest son? I haven't told Brett yet what I'm considering. Thank goodness I didn't buy a house here in Bangor! I suppose real estate listings are online, but I don't know if my "surfing" skills are up to that. Would you mail me the Sunday listings from the paper? Perhaps consider looking around yourself? I'll want just a small place. Maybe a condo, but one with a small garden.

That e-mail he read a couple of times, surprised by how much it moved him. She'd always been good to him, made him feel as if he belonged in her home, but to have her say she thought of him as a son… Yeah, that felt good. He'd missed her, too, even though he understood her desire to be closer to her son. Her real son.

He remembered Rebecca asking one time about family—the kind you made. He guessed he'd had more of a family here than he'd realized. Maybe he would again.

He e-mailed back, apologized for the delay and told her about his trip to Washington state and the reason for it. She'd be glad to know he'd decided to meet his sisters. He didn't mention Rebecca. He said he'd send her that Sunday's real estate listings, and check out what was available within the next day or two.

I'll call if I find anything good, he promised, which reminded him of the other promise.

He carefully took the slip of paper from his wallet and laid it on the desk. There it was, in her handwriting: her name and e-mail address. After a moment, he called up an outgoing message box and typed in her address, then Hello from Santa Fe on the subject line.

Hey, he typed, I said I'd let you know when I got here safe and sound, and here I am.

Okay, that sounded stupid. He erased it and started over.

Got here safe and sound. Hit one snow-storm, nothing major. Hope you're good.

After a minute, he backspaced over the hope you're good part.

Refrigerator is empty.

The house felt empty, too, but he wasn't going to say that.

He continued to type.

It's cold here, but no rain. I'll miss you, Suzanne and Carrie, but not the rain.

Gary liked the tone of that, lumping her in with his sisters. He didn't actually miss *them*, yet, except it occurred to him that he wouldn't mind wandering into the living room and finding Suzanne sitting there knitting. She'd smile at him, say something undemanding, then keep knitting, the click of the needles a homey sound. Sometimes her need to get to know him had made him feel cornered, but mostly she was easy to talk to.

Yeah, okay; maybe he did miss her.

But mainly, it was Rebecca. Except *miss* was way too mild a word for the tearing pain he felt every time he thought of her. He'd hoped all the way that distance would diminish it, but so far that hadn't happened. And so far being home wasn't helping, either. What he'd forgotten when he fled was that he hadn't been all that happy here, or he wouldn't have been speeding on that canyon road with the dark beyond the guardrail summoning him.

Still, he left the last sentence. He couldn't say, I'd give up the rest of my life just to have you here tonight. He'd left because he wasn't good for her and couldn't give her the life she wanted. And maybe, he recognized now, belatedly, because he was afraid to try.

But the truth was, he had no idea how much he meant to her. He couldn't figure out himself how a woman he'd known only two weeks had changed him the way she had. To her, he might be a blip on the screen. She hadn't argued when he told her he was leaving. She'd said, *I wasn't proposing, you know,* and looked like she meant it. She must have known from the get-go that he wasn't that family man she needed for the long haul. He'd probably been nothing but a fling to her.

Profoundly depressed now, he added, It would be good to hear from you sometimes, and hit Send before he could change his mind.

Rocking back in his chair, he skimmed the rest of his e-mails without interest, then went off-line. Now what? he asked himself.

He was almost grateful to realize how tired he was. He could hit the sack. The oblivion of sleep gave him some respite from the mass of regret and loneliness he'd carried home from Washington.

Turning out lights, he went to the bedroom, stripped and fell into bed. The last thing he saw behind closed eyelids before he fell asleep was Rebecca, standing there in the parking lot watching him leave, hair vivid, face bleached of color, looking so alone it killed him.

REBECCA READ the brief e-mail a hundred times, but didn't let herself answer it for two days. That was the right length of time to allow to pass for the casual acquaintances they were apparently going to be.

Glad you got there safely, she typed. I worried, with the weather getting nasty. I'm sure a motorcycle isn't made for snowy roads.

She told him she and her mother had had lunch, and her mother had conducted an inquisition on whether she and that nice young man were going to see each other anymore. Did you know you're a nice young man? she asked. If Mom had seen us that night in the kitchen, she might not have said that.

Maybe she shouldn't mention sex. She deleted that last line, substituting, Turns out Mom's knitting class is at Knit One, Drop In. Small world, huh? She was amazed to find out that Suzanne is your sister. She says the class is full, and the line to buy yarn before and after is long. So I guess her business is going well.

Talking about Suzanne seemed safe. Rebecca ended with, Did the coffee business survive your absence?

She didn't know why she'd worked so hard on this e-mail, why she was trying to keep

even this tenuous connection with Gary. He'd
made it crystal-clear that he wasn't interested
in any kind of future with her. She knew she'd
be better off *not* hearing from him.

But right now, even a pathetic crumb
sounded better than nothing. She missed him
so terribly. How could you miss someone so
much, when you'd known him such a short
time? she wondered. It was ridiculous!

She'd admitted to her mother that she was
in love with Gary, but told her they'd ended
their relationship.

Mom had said, "The way he looked at you,
I'd have sworn he was in love with you, too.
I thought, 'So this is the one.'"

Unfortunately, all Mom had seen in his
eyes was lust. Not something you could tell
your mother.

She had wept on Jeanette's shoulder a couple
of nights after he'd gone, but mostly went
straight home from work every day, turned on
the TV for the illusion of companionship and
pretended to watch while she thought, *What if
I'd asked…? Said…? Done…?*

What if he'd left because he *didn't* know
how she felt?

Uh-uh. What was it he'd said? *I'm not your
guy. You didn't think I was, did you?*

Not a man who wanted to hear that she was pining for him.

Occasionally she remembered his odd lapses in appropriate emotion, and wondered again if he was even capable of the genuine, forever kind of love.

But then she'd hear him again.

What do I know about being a father? Yank the belt out of the loops when the brat irritates me? Come on, you hold godlike powers. Would you give me a kid?

What if he was holding back because he was afraid and not because he didn't love her? He'd called himself a coward. And sometimes...sometimes she'd have sworn he felt more for her than desire. Sometimes, his eyes had held such naked longing, it had hurt to see.

But then she bounced back to hear him.

Rebecca, I'm not father material. Your rational side knows that.

Was he right? What *would* she think, if she were evaluating him objectively to decide whether to place a child with him?

His background was a problem. There was a reason that child abuse tended to perpetuate itself. Parenting skills were learned, not in a one-semester class but over a lifetime. Someone like Gary would have to

work a whole lot harder at keeping his
patience, at knowing when to say yes and
when to say no, at the everyday dance of authority and accommodation.

Men and women who'd grown up in atro-
cious circumstances were often capable of
becoming good parents themselves, but they
were less likely to have the skills, the instinctive knowledge of how to react when they got
stressed. On the other hand, there were
people who'd grown up in loving homes but
ended up being lousy parents. So it was complicated. Individual.

But he didn't want to try, so what difference did it make what he might be capable
of? she thought, depressed anew.

Maybe he did want to try, and was just
afraid to?

What if she told him she could live without
having children, if only she could have him?
Would she mean it, or would she end up
bitterly regretful? And if she did mean it, was
she brave enough to say it to him? She
imagined a look of surprise, of distant apology.

*I'm not your guy. You didn't think I was,
did you?*

Yes! Yes, she had!

I don't like to think I misled you.

But he had! she cried inside. Because he let her fall in love with him. Why had he done that? Why had he made love to her as if he needed her more than food, or water, or air? Why?

He wasn't here to answer. He might never be here again. He'd said nothing about coming to have Christmas with his sisters, and giving her a call. Nothing about ever giving her a call again.

And she didn't think she could bear it.

"So let me get this straight." Gary glowered at the young man. "You decided to experiment, and now we have to throw away this entire batch of beans."

"I thought...darker..." the employee faltered.

"Darker? Burned, you mean. Clean up and start over." He stalked through the vast building past the hot roasters and mounds of coffee beans in gunny sacks to the offices at the front of the building. In his own office, he slammed the door and sank into his chair behind his desk.

He left for a few weeks, and they hired some sixteen-year-old idiot who thought he could roast better coffee? He hadn't noticed that Chimayo Coffee Company was expanding at breakneck speed because it was known for the best?

Still simmering, Gary went back to composing a letter to the buyer from a grocery chain back east who'd expressed interest in their coffee. An employee, he'd said in his e-mail, had visited Santa Fe on vacation and come back to work raving. This was a major chain that would be a real coup, and if they decided to start carrying Chimayo beans, it might mean expansion here—more roasters, more employees.

More idiots.

"Damn," he said aloud. He'd been hard on the kid.

With no forewarning knock, Jagger opened the door and walked in. He closed it behind him, grabbed a chair and spun it around so he could sit astride, arms crossed on the back.

"You've gotten to be a surly bastard."

"Thanks."

"What was that about out there?"

"It was about some teenager…"

"Jose is twenty-three."

"…deciding he can roast better coffee than we can and ruining hundreds of dollars' worth of beans."

"You used to encourage initiative," his bulky, bearded partner said mildly.

"We don't need initiative any more. We need production."

"That the kind of place you want to run?"

The question stung, because it wasn't. Gary was already bothered by the factory they were running out there. Not so long ago, all the employees had done everything from roasting to packaging to serving as baristas. Now, he had roasters, and half a dozen women who did nothing but package the roasted beans that were going to retail outlets.

"If the idiot had just asked! Said, 'I think I can bring out the flavor in the dark roast a little.' I might have been okay with it. But he knows better than we do? Bah!"

Jagger laughed, his teeth a flash of white. "Weren't you a young idiot once?"

Gary glared at his friend. "No. I couldn't afford to be."

"A minor mistake out there isn't the problem, is it?"

"What are you talking about?"

"You came back from your trip with the personality of a bear coming out of hibernation. What happened, Gary?"

Gary tried to hold the glare, but his depression was deeper than his anger. "Nothing. I told you."

Jagger shook his shaggy head. "'Nothing' doesn't turn an even-tempered guy into a jackass."

Gary swore and pinched the bridge of his nose. "You want me to go apologize to the kid? Is that it?"

"No, I want you to tell me what's wrong."

"What's wrong is..." He didn't even know. How did he say, *I didn't find what I was looking for?* Or maybe, *I found it and threw it away.* "I don't know. I'm just not settling back into the routine well."

His friend eyed him shrewdly. "It's the babe, isn't it?"

"She's not a babe, goddamn it!" he fired back. "Her name's Rebecca!"

A ghost of a smile showed in Jagger's eyes. "Okay. Rebecca. What happened? She didn't want you?"

"She wanted me. For fun and games." He let out an explosive breath. "That's not fair to her. I don't know what she wants. I didn't ask. I'm not husband and daddy material. It was time I came home."

"And you're so glad to be here."

JANICE KAY JOHNSON 341

Gary said something succinct and rude that made his buddy grin.

"You think I ought to go back and walk her down the aisle? Get her pregnant? Come on! Hell of a father I'd make!"

"Hmmm." Jagger contemplated him. "Why wouldn't you?"

"The only parenting technique I know is to whip my kid with a belt!"

"Your adoptive mom sounds like a pretty nice lady from what you've told me."

"Until she walked out, you mean? She a better example than Harold and his belt?"

"You know Marcie's husband?"

Impatient, Gary said, "Tony? Sure I know him. What's your point?"

"You know those burns on his face?"

"Yeah, from a house fire."

"Set by his father, who knew his kid was in the bedroom. Tony's got cigarette burns on his back, too. I saw them one day."

Silenced, Gary stared at him.

"You ever seen him with his own kids?"

He gave a brusque nod. Of course he had. Employees of Chimayo Coffee Company were one big happy family. They had barbecues, they attended each other's weddings and christenings, they turned out for grand openings of new shops. Tony Rodriguez owned a house painting business and was a good guy. He and Marcie, the front office manager slash secretary, had two boys, five and seven. Gary had felt a pang a few times, seeing how patient the guy was with them.

"He was tortured by his own father. But it seems to me he's doing okay himself."

"I don't know what to say."

"Well, I do." Jagger rose to his feet, spun the chair and set it precisely back where it had been. "You're afraid to have kids, fine. But don't make excuses. In the meantime, let Bob supervise the floor."

Temper rising again, Gary said, "I own the goddamn company!"

"We own it."

"I let you buy in. I'm still majority owner."

Jagger laughed. "Which means if you want to be a son of a bitch, you can be?"

He sagged. "Seems that way, doesn't it?"

After a moment, his friend sat back down. "What *are* you afraid of?"

The words rose as quick and acidic as bile. "Being like Harold."

"How would you describe him?"

"Stupid, self-centered and violent."

"You're not stupid."

Gary managed a wry smile. "Good to hear."

"I've seen you seriously pissed, what, a dozen times since we've known each other?"

Gary said nothing.

"You raised your voice today." Jagger said it as if surprised. "Usually you get quiet. You smoulder. One thing I've never seen is you getting violent. Have you ever slammed a fist into a wall?"

Gary contained his rage, shoved it down to eat at his gut. No, he didn't punch walls. Self-control was too important to him. One of the worst things about his current mood was his bewilderment about emotions he couldn't seem to make go away.

"Ever hit a woman?" Seeing the answer on his face, Jagger added, "Ever *thought* of hitting one?"

"Hell, no!"

"So here's news: you're not Harold. Never have been, never will be."

Okay, he wouldn't beat his children. Gary guessed he knew that much about himself. It didn't mean he'd be a good parent. That some day he wouldn't decide he'd had enough and just walk, the way Judith had.

Walk out on Rebecca, leaving her alone to raise their children? No. He wouldn't do that.

Couldn't imagine even considering doing that. Right now, he'd do anything to have her in his life. Even reexamine his lifetime conviction that fatherhood wasn't for him.

"So this is why you didn't bring the babe... Rebecca," Jagger corrected himself, "why you didn't bring Rebecca back with you."

"No, it's more complicated than that. She's got a life there. A job. She's close to her mother. I can't ask her to move."

"People do, you know. They get new jobs."

"I'm—" the words clogged in his throat. "I'm not much to take that kind of chance on."

Jagger swore and leaned forward, his gaze fierce. "You're not much? Do you know how many people count on you? Admire you? I don't go for touchy-feely crap like this, but you're the best friend I've ever had. If this babe thinks you're not much, she ain't worth pining over!"

Stunned, Gary said, "Uh, I didn't know you felt that way." Then, "Nobody admires me!"

"That idiot kid did. Why do you think he screwed up? He was trying to impress you."

"Damn."

"Gary, you're as good as the next man, and a hell of a lot better than most. Once you get your head out of your ass."

He gave a choked laugh.

"Think about it," Jagger advised, standing again. "I say we go get a drink after work."

"Yeah, okay," Gary agreed, dazed.

Left alone in the office, he didn't move for a long time.

Was there any chance it was that simple? That he wasn't quite what he'd seen when he'd looked in the mirror all these years? That if he could push through the fear, maybe he could have it all?

That he could have Rebecca?

New fear rushed in. Maybe she didn't want him. Maybe he had just been a nice distraction. He remembered the look on her face when he'd asked for her professional opinion.

Come on, would you *give me a kid?*

He'd seen a great big "no" before she hedged it. Because, he'd assumed, she was being nice.

But what if he'd seen what he expected to see, not what she really thought? Maybe she'd hedged because she knew people like Tony who had overcome their pasts. Maybe she thought *he* could.

Gary had decided a long time ago not to let himself get hurt again. Marrying Holly Lynn had been an anomaly. Or maybe not. Maybe he'd married her because he knew he wouldn't be that hurt when she left someday. He sure hadn't cared enough to try to change to keep her.

But now, he was desperate. Desperate enough to take the chance Rebecca would leave someday. At least he'd have some happiness first.

How would he persuade her to take a chance on him? What would he have to give up? He wished he could just send an e-mail and say, I miss you. How would you feel about moving down here?

He might not be a romantic, but even he knew that didn't cut it. He'd have to do better than that. Court her. Get her a ring. Propose. He could do that.

The possibility was real that she'd say no. That she'd say, "Gee, we only dated for two weeks." Or, "I really care about you, Gary, but you were right. I need to hold out for a man who wants what I do out of life. I'm sorry."

He could beg. Say, "I can be that man, if you'll give me a chance."

The worse thing would be if he knew she was just being nice when she said, "I really care about you." If he could tell she didn't feel a fraction of what he did.

So, what if he tested the waters before he laid himself bare? Say, sent an e-mail that said, I miss you. Then waited to see what she said. Because he really didn't look forward to being cut off at the knees.

But maybe, he thought, that was the only way he could prove to her that he meant what he said. Maybe laying yourself out there *was* the proof. If she'd take him, he had to give her whatever she wanted. *Become* what she wanted.

He kept thinking about it, not emerging from his office until quitting time, when Jagger stuck his head in. "You want to go get that drink?"

"Sure." He snagged his jacket from the coat rack that stood behind the door and followed his friend out. "Enrica's?"

Neither of them were big drinkers, but when they wanted to talk away from work, Enrica's was often where they went. It was quiet, shadowy, lacking pool tables and strutting young studs.

"Where else?" Jagger asked.

On the edge of the old town, the bar was in a plain concrete building. Any character it had was on the inside, where the owner— Enrica herself—had tried hard to recreate the interior of a pueblo, with curved stucco walls that mimicked adobe. Dark wood tables and bar and pierced iron lamps made for a nice atmosphere.

The two men found a booth in the back. The owner herself brought their pitcher, exchanged a few pleasantries, then left them to themselves.

"I've been thinking," Gary began.

"I hope to hell you have."

"You want to hear this or not?"

Rocking back in his chair, Jagger grinned. "Yeah, yeah. Just don't want to make it too easy for you."

"Thanks."

"So, you've seen the error of your ways, and you're going to ride back to—where was it? somewhere it rains all the time—and snatch up your babe."

Gary recognized deliberate needling when he heard it. "I need to offer to move there."

All four legs of Jagger's chair hit the tile floor. "What?"

"I'm not asking you to buy me out. Here's what I've been thinking."

He made it businesslike. The wholesale of their roast was growing and would soon surpass the take from the retail side of their business. "It makes sense to keep expanding both. I've been spending more time on cultivating new accounts anyway. But I don't have to be here to do that. I could spend maybe a week a month here. Fly down when I have to. Otherwise, I can conduct business from up there."

"You think this is what you need to do?"

He nodded.

"You hate the rain."

The words were easier to say than he'd expected. "I love Rebecca."

Jagger's face was engulfed by a huge grin and he half stood to reach across the table and whack Gary on the back. "About damn time!"

"You think it'll be enough? That she'll go for it?"

His friend sobered. "Gary, I don't know her. Loving someone else doesn't always mean they love you."

They were both silent for a moment, the near admission Jagger had made on the phone that day there between them. Consuela *didn't* love him, plainly.

Rebecca, Gary thought with sickening fear, might not love him. Might not think she could.

But he had to find out. He couldn't let himself be crippled by the decision Judith

had made to leave, to sever all connection
with him. He still didn't know if it was his
fault. Even partly his fault. He did know that
maybe he had another chance.

If he had the guts to take it.

Jagger wrapped his beefy hand around his
glass but didn't hoist it. "The thing is, usually
you know if she doesn't love you. You may
kid yourself, but deep inside, you know. If
you knew, really knew, you wouldn't be
letting yourself hope. 'Cuz hope doesn't
come easy for you, does it?"

Gary's fear subsided a little, became mere
anxiety, intense but something he could tamp
down for now.

"I didn't know it when I went up there, but
I had hopes of what would come from
meeting my sisters."

"You get what you hoped for?"

"I don't know. I'm not sure." He'd been
certain he hadn't when he left, but now he
wondered if he'd jumped to conclusions about
what Suzanne thought. He seemed to be good
at that. Reverting to their earlier conversation,
he said, "What do you think? Can you manage
the day-to-day operations on your own?"

"Can I manage?" Jagger huffed. "Can I
manage? What do you think?"

"I think I haven't been needed for a long time."

"Yeah, you are. If it were up to me, we wouldn't be selling to these high falutin grocery chains. Me, I wouldn't know how to talk to those guys. You've got the knack." He gave a decisive nod. "We've been heading this way, anyway. Whether you stay or go, maybe it's time we make the division of labor official."

Gary nodded. "Then let's do it." He lifted his glass. "Here's to Chimayo."

"To Chimayo." They clicked glasses and drank. Jagger held his out again, waiting until Gary did the same. "And to taking chances."

Gary could, and did, drink to that.

Jagger held up his glass one more time. "Oh, yeah. And to the rain."

Gary grimaced, but drank. "To the rain."

CHAPTER FIFTEEN

GARY HAD BEEN GONE ten days when Rebecca made her decision. She had to talk to him. And it had to be in person, not on the phone. But she'd already checked, and found out he wasn't in the phone book. Unless she wanted to take a chance of having what was left of her heart ground under his heel in front of whatever employees of Chimayo Coffee Company happened to be around and were interested, she had to find out where he lived.

She stopped by Knit One, Drop In, feeling that was more casual than going to Suzanne's house. She'd sneaked a look at the class schedule that lay atop a pile of papers at her mother's house, and picked a time, right before closing, that she hoped the store would be empty.

The window display consisted of a beautiful crocheted yellow-and-white crib blanket draped over an old-fashioned white wicker

bassinette. By the wheels lay the most exqui-
site knitted ensemble for a baby Rebecca had
ever seen. She could tell even through the
glass that the yarn was downy soft. Rebecca
stopped, her heart seeming to spasm, as she
stared at the tiny booties, sweater and cap.
What if Gary never did feel he wanted a
child? Could she give up the hope of
someday holding her baby to her breast?

She didn't know. Wanted to believe she'd
never have to find out. Surely, surely, he
could be persuaded that he would make a
great father.

Finally, she closed her eyes, composed
herself and continued through the front door.

Suzanne was ringing up a customer at
the counter. She looked up, her breath
visibly catching.

"Rebecca! Oh! Are you here about—?"

Belatedly, Rebecca realized Suzanne might
think she'd come to tell her about a child available for adoption. "No," she said hastily. "No,
it was Gary I wanted to ask you about."

Suzanne let out a puff of air. "Oh. Well,
let me just finish here." She nodded toward
the door. "Why don't you turn the sign to
closed for me?"

Rebecca did, then wandered through

shelving units that filled the front half of the store, each divided into bins that were filled with an extraordinary selection of yarns. She was fascinated by the textures as much as the colors, by the spiderweb-fine yarns next to the thick, soft ones, the nubby beside the even. She was stroking a skein of alpaca yarn dyed a deep, eggplant purple when Suzanne found her.

"Is something wrong? Did you hear from Gary?"

This was the hard part. She withdrew her hand and turned to face Gary's sister.

"No, it's not that." She hesitated. "I keep thinking about things he said before he left. Um… Did he talk about me at all?"

"He told me you were a nice woman." Suzanne saw from her face that she hadn't helped. "Honestly…he didn't. You know, I had to pry everything about his life out of him. He wasn't big on confiding. Only, that last night, I could tell something was terribly wrong when he got home. He wouldn't talk about it, though."

"Really?" That gave her hope. "Nothing did happen, except he said goodbye. And…he told me he wasn't the guy for me. But the thing is," she took a deep breath, "he is."

Suzanne frowned. "Why would he look

devastated just because he'd tried to let you down?"

"I don't know. We said a civil goodbye."

"He came in and walked through the living room as if I weren't even there, this terrible expression on his face. He shut himself in his room for maybe an hour, then came out to tell me he was leaving in the morning."

"So he hadn't told you. I didn't think so."

"Told me what?" Without waiting for an answer, Suzanne returned to the main point. "I thought…well, that he was leaving because of me. Because of something I said. Only then I decided maybe you'd broken things off with him."

Rebecca shook her head. "I'm in love with him."

"Really?" Suzanne's face lit, then dimmed. "So what's the problem?"

"I wish I was sure. If he doesn't feel the same about me… He never *said* he did…" She took a deep breath and stopped. "But that night, he fixated on the fact that I want a family someday, and told me he didn't know how to be a father. That the only example he'd had was Harold, who used his belt every time he got angry."

"I've never felt violent about anyone in

my life, but I hate that man!" His sister nodded toward a circle of love seats and upholstered chairs in the back that must be where she conducted classes. "Come on, let's sit down."

They chose seats next to each other. Suzanne tucked one foot under her and sat sideways facing Rebecca.

"I know what you mean about hating him," Rebecca confessed. "To think Gary is afraid of being like that...that awful man!"

"He's just not capable of it! Gary is always so soft-spoken and kind, even when I could tell he wanted to bolt. Do you know how much work he did on my house? And that he offered me some additional income?"

Rebecca shook her head.

"I said no. I think he interpreted my refusal to mean that..." She stopped. "I don't know. He just went blank, said he understood, and then we never talked again. Not really. Afterward, I realized he needed me to take that money. As if doing something for me meant a lot to him. Only I don't know why."

"So much about him is closed inside. That's common with abused children, you know. They learn to hide what they're feeling."

Suzanne let out a small cry. "I don't want

to think of him as an abused child! That makes me feel even worse." She tried to smile. "When he was born, Mom said, 'You're the big sister. I'm counting on you to help take care of your little brother.' In the end…"

"You found him. You tried to bring him home again."

"But somehow I failed him again," Suzanne said unhappily.

"I don't think so," Rebecca said with growing certainty. "I think he got scared. Maybe both of us scared him. He wanted something from you when he got here, right? My theory is, he was looking for everything he missed in his childhood, and he did find it. That was stressful enough for him, and then there was me."

Suzanne was nodding. "He fell in love with you. That makes sense! On the one hand he wanted to recapture an attachment to Carrie and me, but you… *You* represent the whole shebang. Wife. Children. *Family.*"

"So he took off," Rebecca finished.

"And I thought maybe he saw my reject-ing his offer of money as a rejection."

"Maybe he did. Or maybe that was just an excuse to retreat." Rebecca made a face. "Or maybe it was just time for him to get back to work, and I was nothing but a diversion while he was here!"

"Do you believe that?"

"I don't want to," Rebecca said honestly. "The chances are I'm going to embarrass myself horribly and get really hurt, but I've decided I need to find out. I need to say 'I love you' and find out what he says in return."

"Are you going down there?"

Rebecca nodded. "Except...I need his address. I hope he gave it to you. I checked directory assistance already, and he's unlisted."

"He did give it to me. In case I needed him. And I do, but not in the way he understood."

"Gary has a whole lot to learn about family."

Suzanne nodded. "Will you tell him that, once I bring a child home, I won't say no again to some financial help from him? That, um, I'm sorry I let pride get in my way?"

"I'll tell him," Rebecca agreed.

"I have his address and phone number in my purse." Suzanne stood. "When are you going?"

"As soon as possible. Tomorrow, if I can get a flight." Rebecca stood, too, then pressed a hand to her stomach. "Oh, Lord! I'm terrified!"

"I hope..." Suzanne didn't even try to find the words. Didn't have to.

They exchanged shaky smiles of complete understanding.

"Me, too," Rebecca said.

LATE THE FOLLOWING AFTERNOON, she flew into Albuquerque, rented a car and drove north on Highway 25, fascinated to realize she was following the Rio Grande.

The landscape was so different than anyplace she'd ever been before, dry and yet not bleak in the way she thought of deserts. She knew she was actually on a plateau that had been carved by erosion to form the mesas and canyons for which the Southwest was famous. Santa Fe was at 7,000 feet above sea level, even though it nestled at the foot of a mountain range that was really the southern end of the Rockies.

The road signs and dots on the map were for places with lovely names, or ones that were historic. La Cienaga. Jemez Pueblo. Los Alamos. And there was a place called Wagon Mound, which reminded her that the famous Santa Fe Trail had come through here.

Dusk was settling when she reached the outskirts of Santa Fe. The mountains were backlit. At first she was disappointed by developments that could have been in any city, but, following the map, she reached the old town of Santa Fe and was glad there was just enough light left to circle a few blocks and see the Palace of the Governors, a long, low adobe building that dated to the early 17th century, and a chapel and a cathedral not far away that emphasized how powerful Catholicism was in the region. There were shops, cafés and galleries everywhere. One sign leaped out at her—Chimayo Coffee Company. From the bag of coffee beans she'd bought at Trader Joe's, she recognized the logo of a stylized bull above the lettering. That might even be Gary's first coffee shop.

When a car honked behind her, she realized she'd stopped to stare. Flustered, she started forward again.

She'd picked out a moderately priced hotel from her guidebook, and now stopped to register. She hoped she wouldn't need the room at all, but she didn't want to arrive at Gary's with suitcase in hand, either. She needed to have a preplanned refuge.

After getting the key, she studied her map and set out again. She was too nervous to be hungry, even though she'd only nibbled on the airplane. Gary might be out this evening—what if he'd taken another woman to dinner? Or he might be just sitting down to eat, or entertaining. Or not home at all. He must travel on business. What if he was gone for three days?

Then she would wait. She'd never been to the Southwest at all, and she might not ever get here again. She'd do tourist things. Drive out to see the ancient ruins at Bandelier National Monument, and go to museums. See a pueblo. She'd told them at work that she might be away as long as a week. Everyone had been really nice, shifting their own schedules to accommodate her appointments. She hadn't told them she might be quitting. Because really, the chances were much, much bigger that she'd be coming home chastened and sad.

She couldn't tell much about his house when she found it, except that the neighborhood was expensive and that it was made of adobe. She couldn't see either his Harley-Davidson or the pickup truck he'd said he owned, but light shone from the tall, narrow windows.

Rebecca parked on the street, then sat unmoving for a long time. She suddenly didn't know if she had the nerve to go knock on his door. "Hey, I wanted to say, well, that I'm madly in love with you," sounded horrifyingly presumptuous. Her reasoning began to seem incredibly flimsy, even fantastical; what the man had said was, *I'm not your guy.* Oh, God. And she'd chased after him anyway. He would hate to find her on his doorstep!

"I can't do this," she whispered. Her stomach roiled and she was in such a panic her breathing had become shallow and fast.

Her hand was shaking so much, when she tried to start the car again, the wheel locked. She bent her head and took a dozen deep, slow breaths.

Calm down. You don't have to go to the door. You can go back to the hotel, wait until tomorrow. But even if you do go knock now, what's the worst that can happen? He says I'm sorry, I'm not interested. You knew that could happen, that it was likely.

She couldn't live with not having tried.

But, oh, this was hard! So much harder than she'd thought it would be.

She jiggled the wheel and unlocked it, took the keys from the ignition and got out. Biting her lip until she tasted blood, Rebecca started up the driveway.

The porch light wasn't on, so she had to go slowly. It looked like there were cactus in his yard. She didn't want to stray. She could just make out the bare branches of a tree at the corner of the house. She didn't know what grew around here. Cottonwood, maybe? She must have read about the settlers using the cottonwood.

As if she cared what kind of tree grew in Gary's yard. But distracting herself helped a little.

The doorstep was recessed in the thick walls, some rough-hewn beams emerging from the adobe to form a sort of arbor overhead. She groped to each side for a doorbell and found one.

For a moment, her fingers refused to obey her order to push the button. Then, in a sort of delayed response, she stabbed it.

She heard nothing. The walls and the carved door were so thick, she didn't even hear the bell within. Or else it was broken, and she'd have to make herself hammer on the door.

A porch light suddenly came on, and she froze, feeling like a deer caught in the headlights. He was going to lift that eyebrow and say, "Rebecca? What are you doing here?"

He was unlikely to believe her if she said, "Oh, gosh, happened to be in Santa Fe and thought I'd drop by." No, she was stuck now.

FEELING IMPATIENT, Gary opened the door. He wasn't in the mood for company. If it was Jagger...

For a moment, he thought she was a desert mirage, the shimmer on hot pavement. He'd thought about nothing but Rebecca, and now he imagined her standing on his doorstep.

Was he going *loco?*

But she didn't fade away. There she stood, purse pressed to her side, wearing slacks and a purple V-neck sweater he didn't remember seeing before. She was so damn beautiful, her mouth lush and tempting, her hair bundled atop her head, her skin creamy and dusted with cinnamon freckles.

"Rebecca?" He looked behind her, as if he'd see... Who knew? Santa Claus? The Easter Bunny? "What are you doing here?"

She winced, and he suddenly realized that she was trying real hard to hide the fact that she was scared to death. She also had to be freezing, with no coat on.

"For God's sake, they're talking about early snow tomorrow! Come in." When she didn't move, he reached out and hauled her inside, shutting the door behind her.

Inside, she shivered. "It is cold out there. I thought you said it was warm here."

"I said it didn't rain incessantly. It's almost winter, and we're in the mountains."

"Oh."

What a pointless topic of conversation! But he was afraid to ask what she'd come to say. Afraid to let himself hope too much.

"Come on in. Let's sit down."

She looked around. "Your place is nice."

Turning and seeing it through her eyes, he realized how bare it was. The living area had a state-of-the-art stereo system, which he valued, a comfortable sofa and chair, a coffee table he could put his feet on, and not much else. He had gradually, as something caught his eye, bought native art. A red, black and white Navaho rug covered the floor in front of the sofa. A tall pot from the Taos Pueblo stood beside the curved adobe fireplace. On the rough-hewn mantel were a couple of Hopi baskets. Another antique Navaho rug hung above the fireplace.

That was it. The starkness of his home pretty much epitomized his life.

"Thanks," he said. "Sit."

She chose the end of the sofa, although she sat school-marm straight, her back not touching the cushions.

Was this the place where he sank to his

knees in front of her and said, *I can't live without you?*

God, he was nervous! Terrified she'd come for some other reason. Had something happened to Suzanne or Carrie? But why would Rebecca be the one to come tell him? And, face it, he wouldn't be the first person anyone would think to inform. He'd barely met them for the first time.

There was blood on her lip. He'd been starting to sit himself, but now he half rose. "You're hurt."

"Hurt?" She stared at him, uncomprehending.

"Your lip…"

"Oh." She touched it. "No, it's nothing. I just, um…"

Voice ragged, Gary said, "Tell me why you're here."

Her gaze touched his, shied away. "Suzanne gave me your address. She said to tell you that, once she has adopted, she wouldn't say no if you made your offer again. She said she could use help."

Rebecca had come to Santa Fe to tell him that his sister had changed her mind about accepting financial help from him?

"That's not why you're here."

"I didn't know how hard this would be."

Hope had been ripping at him with vicious claws. He hadn't known it could be so painful, maybe because it wasn't an emotion he'd felt much before. He'd never trusted it. He'd hoped for too long that Judith would come back for him, but she never had. After that, Gary had pretty much given up on it.

At last, Rebecca looked at him, her eyes huge and dilated, her teeth sinking into her lower lip.

She'd made it bleed, he realized.

So fast the words jammed against each other, she said, "I came to say I fell in love with you. And..." Finally, a pause, a stammer. "And you're wrong. You are the guy for me."

He sat stunned, unable to believe what he'd heard. She loved him? Not just enough to give him a chance once he laid out his case, but so much she'd had to come down here and offer herself?

At his shocked silence, a tide of red climbed her cheeks. "I know you may not feel the same. I guess that's what you tried to tell me. But I wanted to be sure you knew that I truly do believe you're capable of being everything you're afraid you can't be. I also wanted to say that if...if you don't want children, it's okay."

He could tell it wasn't okay; it was her own, desperate bargaining chip.

"I'll go away if you tell me you don't love me. I just...sometimes I thought that maybe you did. That I couldn't be alone in that."

"You weren't alone," he said hoarsely.

"I know my coming here looks really—" She stopped. Her voice dropped to a whisper. "I...I wasn't?"

"God, Rebecca." He wasn't sure he could move, but somehow he did, dropping to his knees on the rug and reaching for her hands. They were icy-cold, but returned his grip as fervently. "I've been in a black hole since I came home. Trying to figure out how to convince you to give me a chance."

Her eyes welled with tears that clung to her lashes. "Why didn't you say?"

"I convinced myself you'd be better off without me. I'm no prize, Rebecca. You know that."

"I don't!" She sounded fierce. "How can you even think that? You're the sexiest man I've ever met, you're smart, you're successful." She waved at the house around them. "You're *rich*."

He shook his head. "That's not what I mean."

"I know it isn't what you mean. But you're wrong about that, too. And I'm not the only one who thinks so. Suzanne said she couldn't believe you were afraid you were like Harold. She said even when she could tell she was overwhelming you, you were always soft-spoken and kind."

"I was pretending. Sometimes I wanted to get away from her, from all of them, so much it was all I could do not to just walk out, get on my bike and ride away."

"I know that." Her grip had gone from desperate to reassuring. "She does, too. She knows that coming to meet her and Carrie was incredibly stressful for you, but you did it anyway." Her eyes searched his. "Why did you, Gary? Was it for their sake? Or yours?"

He wished he could say, "Both." But it would be a lie. He'd felt shamed after Carrie's phone call, but Gary didn't know if he'd have ever acted on that shame. Not if he'd felt his life was rich and full without the family he'd lost so long ago.

"Mine." His voice was scratchy. "I realized one day that not much of anyone in the world gave a damn about me. A friend or two, but they'd get over it if I dropped from sight or died. My marriage failed pretty damn quickly, which didn't surprise me." He moved his shoulders in an awkward shrug. "I thought maybe finding out about my real family would make a difference. I told myself all I wanted to do was meet Carrie and Suzanne, but I think I had some kind of unrealistic belief that they'd enfold me in family and heal me." He was trying to sound mocking and failing. "I kept hanging around, until one day I realized Suzanne must desperately want her house to herself again."

"Gary, you're wrong. I think having you back in her life was the most wonderful thing that had ever happened to her. Remember, I saw her face the day you showed up. She was afraid she'd driven you away when she refused to take money from you. She told me she didn't want you to think that you had to buy a relationship with her."

If he hadn't been holding Rebecca's hands, he'd have rocked back. "Is that what I was trying to do?"

"I don't know."

He squeezed his eyes shut for a moment. "Yeah. Maybe it is. I thought…"

Her voice was a balm. "You didn't have anything else to offer."

"Yeah." God. She knew him too well. He just hoped she wasn't mistaking pity for love.

"Rebecca…" Voice raw, he asked, "You're sure?"

"That I love you?" Her smile was glorious, radiant. Prettier than sunset behind the Sangre de Cristo mountains.

He'd never thought anything could be.

"I've never been more certain of anything in my life," she told him. "Look at me! I came prepared to make a fool of myself."

"Yeah," he said. "You barely beat me."

"What do you mean?"

"I was going to fly up there next week. Rebecca, I've figured out how I can move there." He talked rapidly. "I'd still have to come down here maybe a week a month. And I'll need to be traveling some on business, but I do that anyway. I'm going to work on expanding the sales of our roast, while Jagger handles operations here. I know you love your job, and you want to stay close to your mom. I can't ask you to move down here."

"Isn't it lucky you don't have to, then." Her smile dawned again. "Since I already offered."

"You offered?" She'd stunned him again.

She laughed, but gently. "Gary, I showed

up at your door ready to offer just about anything! You didn't notice?"

"I thought you were a mirage."

"Really? Is that why you scowled at me?"

"That would be why." He cleared his throat. "Since I'm down here on my knees, anyway…will you marry me?"

Roses blossomed in her cheeks and tears started in her eyes again. "Yes. Oh, yes!"

"You're not supposed to cry."

She smiled shakily at him. "Haven't you ever heard of tears of happiness?"

He told the truth. "I've never seen them."

"Oh, Gary!" Rebecca let go of his hands and flung her arms around his neck, all but sliding off the couch. "I love you so much," she whispered, just before their mouths met.

They kissed as if they'd been starving for each other. The need that roared through him was just part of a flash flood of emotions he'd spent a lifetime damming up. Most were unfamiliar to him. He felt as if he were drowning in them, tumbled by rapids until he didn't know up from down. He wasn't sure he cared. If this was what being happy felt like, he'd take it.

He should have been stripping Rebecca of her clothing, but instead he just kept kissing her, touching her, breathing in her scent. He wanted her, that need was as ferocious as ever, but somehow he also felt compelled to take it slower. To be sure they both knew this was about something else.

He rubbed his cheek against hers and realized she was crying. When he lifted his head, he saw she wasn't.

Stunned anew, he reached up and touched his face. *He* was the one crying.

He hadn't even cried when Judith left. He'd waited, and lost hope. But he hadn't cried.

Embarrassed, he scrubbed at his cheeks.

Rebecca's hands came up to frame his face, stopping him. Her voice was full of wonder. "You really do love me."

"Yeah." God, he was snuffling. "I do."

"Will you...will you *say* it?"

The words weren't as hard to get out as he'd thought they would be. "I love you, Rebecca Wilson." He had to say this, too. "I don't know how I'll do at being a dad. But for you, I'm willing. If you'll be patient when I screw up."

"I think," she said, "I won't have to." Her hands stroked his face lovingly. "Why are you crying?"

He couldn't seem to stop. Tears made her

face a blur. "I don't know. *God.*" He blundered to his feet. "I've got to go wash my face."

Rebecca stood, too, right behind him. She laid a hand on his back.

He went still, bowed his head. A spasm of the most astonishing grief struck him. It was the weirdest damn thing, when he was also still bobbing in happiness so intense, it was like a newborn baby must feel breathing for the first time, feeling the air on his skin.

"What is it?" Rebecca asked him.

And then he knew. He was blubbering like that baby, and he knew.

"It's you coming here. Not just loving me, but caring enough to come find me. Except for Suzanne, nobody, ah…" He shuddered. "Nobody has ever bothered before."

"Oh, Gary." Her arms closed around him fiercely. *"Gary."*

He turned, face wet, and wrapped his arms around her in turn, holding her so tightly she should have protested. But she didn't. They clung, as if they'd been separated for years.

Gary laid his cheek against her hair, closed his eyes, and let the emotions have their way. Maybe he *was* being reborn.

They must have stood there, arms locked

around each other, for five minutes. Finally, reluctantly, he loosened his hold and she did the same. He looked down at her and saw that she'd been crying, too. His face probably gave away everything he felt. "Maybe you didn't know you were doing it, but you've given me a gift I won't forget."

"It's funny," she said, shakily, "but you've given me one, too. If you hadn't cried, maybe I wouldn't have been as sure of how you felt. Now...now I believe it's going to be all right. We're going to be happy."

She sounded awed. Maybe she felt that same flash-flood. He guessed she must.

Gary didn't know what he'd ever done to deserve to be loved by this woman, but he hoped it had been something good. Some act of decency that had really meant something to someone.

"I need to make love to you. After I blow my nose." Words he had never expected to say to a woman.

She gave a gurgle of startled laughter. "I want you to make love to me. Except, um, I need to blow my nose, too. And wash my face."

"Well, hell," he said, looping an arm around her shoulder, "I knew there had to be a reason I had the builder put two sinks in my bathroom."

She laughed again. He guessed there were worse ways to start a life together than washing away tears.

* * * *

Don't miss the final instalment of this story.
Kids by Christmas *by Janice Kay Johnson*
is available in December 2007!

MILLS & BOON®
MEDICAL™
Proudly presents

Brides of Penhally Bay

Featuring Dr Nick Tremayne

A pulse-raising collection of emotional, tempting romances and heart-warming stories — devoted doctors, single fathers, Mediterranean heroes, a Sheikh and his guarded heart, royal scandals and miracle babies…

Book One

CHRISTMAS EVE BABY
by Caroline Anderson

Starting 7th December 2007

A COLLECTION TO TREASURE FOREVER!
One book available every month

FREE

2 BOOKS AND A SURPRISE GIFT!

We would like to take this opportunity to thank you for reading this Mills & Boon® book by offering you the chance to take TWO more specially selected titles from the Superromance series absolutely FREE! We're also making this offer to introduce you to the benefits of the Mills & Boon® Reader Service™—

- ★ **FREE home delivery**
- ★ **FREE gifts and competitions**
- ★ **FREE monthly Newsletter**
- ★ **Books available before they're in the shops**
- ★ **Exclusive Reader Service offers**

Accepting these FREE books and gift places you under no obligation to buy; you may cancel at any time, even after receiving your free shipment. Simply complete your details below and return the entire page to the address below. You don't even need a stamp!

YES! Please send me 2 free Superromance books and a surprise gift. I understand that unless you hear from me, I will receive 4 superb new titles every month for just £3.69 each, postage and packing free. I am under no obligation to purchase any books and may cancel my subscription at any time. The free books and gift will be mine to keep in any case.

U7ZEE

Ms/Mrs/Miss/Mr.................................Initials ....
                                                                                    BLOCK CAPITALS PLEASE
Surname ....
Address ....

....

....Postcode ....

Send this whole page to:
The Reader Service, FREEPOST CN81, Croydon, CR9 3WZ